Rose's Run

Rose's Run

DAWN DUMONT

thistledown press

Thistledown Press Ltd.
410 2nd Avenue North
Saskatoon, Saskatchewan, S7K 2C3
www.thistledownpress.com

Library and Archives Canada Cataloguing in Publication

Dumont, Dawn, 1978–, author
Rose's run / Dawn Dumont.
Issued in print and electronic formats.
ISBN 978-1-927068-81-6 (pbk.).—ISBN 978-1-77187-010-8 (html).—
ISBN 978-1-77187-011-5 (pdf)

I. Title.
PS8607.U445R68 2014   C813'.6   C2014-905343-6
C2014-905344-4

Cover artwork by Aaron Paquette
Cover and book design by Jackie Forrie
Printed and bound in Canada

Thistledown Press gratefully acknowledges the financial assistance of the Canada
Council for the Arts, the Saskatchewan Arts Board, and the Government of Canada
through the Canada Book Fund for its publishing program.

The author would like to acknowledge the generous
assistance of the Canada Council for the Arts.

For all my sisters: Patricia, Katherine,
Pamela, Cherysse, and Cissy

DAHLIA INGRAM WAS SIX FEET TWO inches tall with legs that came up to Rose Okanese's bicep, and every inch of those long legs was encased in futuristic-looking silver stretch pants designed to show off every bump and curve — except that Dahlia didn't have any of those. She was a creature of bone and muscle, topped with a mop of blonde curls. Nature had designed Dahlia for one purpose: to run long distances at high speeds with effortless grace, and she, and no one else, was Rose Okanese's competition for the Annual Pesakestew Marathon and Fishing Derby.

In this particular year, Dahlia had already run three marathons, three half marathons, and four 10Ks — and it was only June. This was Rose's second race, in her lifetime. (Fifth if you included races she ran in elementary school.She'd done okay in those — never last, just an innocuous second or third last, depending on whether one or both of the asthmatic Bower twins was in attendance.) She'd never had an athletic performance that resulted in someone taking her aside afterwards like the coach in Rocky and patting her on the shoulder: "Yuh got real talent, kid. But you're still a bum."

Rose had her bumps and curves poured into an orange tank top and a pair of black spandex shorts. The spandex shorts had been $19.99, a Walmart splurge, forced upon her by her sixteen-year-old daughter Sarah, who had added, "There's no law saying you have to be the dorkiest person in the race." Rose kept crossing her legs, subconsciously hoping that it distracted from the size of her thighs.

Probably the best thing she could do to appear smaller was to move away from the human licorice next to her. But the idea of standing alone was more frightening than appearing to be the number ten.

"I'm kind of nervous," she blurted out.

Dahlia continued to stretch her quad muscle, her long leg bent in half like a blonde flamingo.

"I bet you don't get nervous, hey?" Rose continued when there was no reply, as was her way. "This must be like taking a walk in a park or something? Like walking from your bedroom to your kitchen? I bet you'll go for another run this afternoon, right? How long is this run gonna take you, anyway? Three hours? Two and a half? Six?" Rose wished she'd done a little research before the race, like maybe typing into Google, "how long do marathons last if you're not in good shape?"

Dahlia looked at Rose like she had just noticed her for the first time. The Swede's eyes, permanently crinkled at the corners from wind, swept from Rose's full face, already flushed, down to her slightly protruding belly, lower to her knees pointing inwards, all the way down to her purple and white Saucony sneakers.

"Nice shoes," Dahlia said.

Rose beamed. "They were a gift. From my kids."

On cue, Callie yelled: "Mom!" Rose looked over and saw her eight-year-old daughter. "Did you eat?" She held up a bag of cotton candy on the sidelines behind the invisible barrier separating the runners from the people who showed up to watch them and discuss, in between drags on their smokes, why running long distances was hazardous to your health.

"I'm good, honey!" Rose called back. "That's my daughter Callie," she explained to Dahlia. "Do you have any kids?"

Dahlia shook her head. She moved into the runner's stretch and dropped her knee down to the ground in one fluid moment. Rose had never seen a tall woman maneuver her legs like a Romanian gymnast. Of course that didn't mean that the long-limbed couldn't be flexible — only that it looked really weird.

Rose tried to replicate the stretch but her lower back only laughed at her, so she settled for bending forward from the waist in a bouncy motion. "You know ten weeks ago, I hadn't run in twenty years. I sure as hell never thought I'd be here right now, lined up at this race, next to a pro like you. Funny how life throws you into some strange situations, huh? I mean, I know I'm the one who signed up for the race and I'm the one who drove myself here, so when I think about it that way, I'm the one who threw me into this. Still, it's funny . . . "

The race marshal, Charley Big Guns, walked past them to get into position. His top hat was incongruous with his grey, stained sweatpants. He hummed "Chariots of Fire" while he drummed the side of his leg with his starter's pistol.

"I wish they didn't have to use a gun. The gun scares me."

"Cover your ears," Dahlia said.

"That makes sense." Rose looked at the gathering crowd; it was a lot more people than she expected at 8 AM on a Sunday. "Maybe, I should have waited until next year. Can I just pull out? Will anyone get mad? Do you get in trouble for doing that?"

The look on Dahlia's face suggested that the idea had never crossed her mind. She cocked her head as she looked at Rose, trying to figure out exactly why she was here, in this race, standing beside her. Then Dahlia noticed the large Band-Aid on Rose's arm.

"What is that?"

Rose looked down. "Oh that. That was another present, a going away one, thank God."

Dahlia had a question in her eyes. But then the gun went off. Both women remembered where they were and began their race with an awkward sidestep.

One

ROSE NEEDED ONE NUMBER. SHE COULD feel the number bubbling around in the bingo machine, searching for her. It wanted to be there for her, it wanted to jump through the hole, into ol' Charley Big Gun's hand and be announced to the world in his sleepy drawl. She was nervous, and when she was nervous she wanted a smoke, but the band hall had outlawed smoking the month before. But an experienced smoker like Rose could still smell the leftover smoke clinging to the wood and the rafters of the Pesakestew band hall like a desperate ex-lover. She took a deep breath; it helped, but did not sate.

"I'm gonna win," she said to her table companions — her best friend Winter and her hubby (and Rose's cousin) Monty and of course (because they were co-dependent), Rose's youngest daughter Callie. "I got this feeling."

"What's it feel like?" asked Callie. She was in grade two and sat next to Rose with a phonics book ostentatiously propped open in front of her. But Rose wasn't buying it; Callie was too nosy to focus on anything other than adult conversation.

"Like something is welling up inside of me," explained Rose.

"Sounds like gas," Winter suggested. Winter had been Rose's best friend since grade one. They had both been small for their age, and when a burly kindergartener pummelled the two of them in front of the monkey bars, they sobbed in each other's arms afterwards.

"Nothing luckier than a good fart, 'cept for the people around you," Rose joked back.

Winter's husband Monty made an impatient noise to indicate they were disturbing his play.

"Sorry to disturb you at work, Mozart." Winter gave him a gentle nudge. "He needs one number too," Winter told Rose.

"Don't tell her! Now I'm not going to win."

"It's not like it's gonna affect your luck," Winter replied. "Luck isn't even real."

Monty grunted and returned to hunching over his cards.

"Really Auntie?" asked Callie.

"Really really. Just something weak people believe in," Winter replied.

"How come people play bingo then?"

"It's supposed to be fun." Rose dabbed Monty's arm a couple times. He moved it away grumpily.

Rose stared at the bingo caller. Charley sat in his own booth in the centre of the floor. He had a linebacker build and a brush-cut that made his head look like it could be used to clean out a toilet. Rose directed her whispered pleadings to this demigod: "C'mon Charley, I need a new tire. That left back one is so bald it has low self-esteem. Give me an I–25. C'mon Charley, stick your beefy hand in there and pull it out — you can do it."

"Pretty sure he can't hear you," replied Winter. "Old Charley's deaf as a rock."

"I'd pretend to be deaf if I had his job, too," Monty said. "Can you imagine the pressure he's under?"

"B–12," Charley intoned.

"Are you honestly defending a man who sits on his ass and calls out numbers?" Winter asked.

"I'm saying working with the public is stressful."

"He's got his own damned little island," Winter pointed with her lips. Charley was seated on a raised dais in the centre of the floor; the entire hall watched as he raised his white Styrofoam cup up to his Rubenesque lips.

"Oh damn," Rose said, and scratched the underside of her forearm.

"Mom, don't do that. The doctor said it will make it worse," Callie said, and stilled her mother's hand with her own small one.

"Is that your dermatitis?" Winter asked. "I thought the cream was taking care of it."

"Dr. Sheila says it doesn't matter how much cream I put on it if I keep working in the pig barns. I'm allergic to the pigs, and that's that."

"Are you allergic to bacon?" Monty asked.

"I can eat them, I just can't be around them. Or shouldn't be. But the pig barn pays better than anything else, right?"

Winter was a nurse in the local hospital and so could not agree. Monty was a superintendent at a construction site and also did not agree. But for Rose, mother of two girls and married to Gilbert who played in a rock band, the pig barn was the best option and on that — and pretty much only that — she and Gilbert did agree.

Winter knew this as she had full access to the internal memos of Gilbert and Rose's marriage. So instead of responding, Winter offered Rose a Cheezie. Rose munched on the orange finger-shaped snack thoughtfully.

"Can I bum a smoke off you?"

"I've actually been doing pretty good," Winter replied. "Sixty-five days without a cigarette."

"Damn, I was hoping you might have cracked."

"Not this time," Monty said. "We're doing the patch plus we're doing laser therapy."

"Wouldn't smoking just be cheaper?" Rose joked.

Callie exclaimed: "It's not about the money, it's about your health!"

"I'm healthy." Rose fought the urge to clear her throat. There was definitely something in there, scratching away, and a smoke would knock the shit out of it. She took a sip of Coke and the feeling subsided. *Friggin' non-smokers taking over the world,* she thought to herself. You would think you could be safe on the reserve! But no, people had finally figured out that smoking was inextricably linked to the oxygen tanks that elders were dragging behind them nowadays. They were becoming as ubiquitous as missing toes; on that thought, Rose made a mental note to stop putting sugar in her coffee — or at least, not so much.

She had a pack of smokes waiting for her on top of the fridge. The thought of them gave her a secret smile. Winter spotted the smile, sensed the reason for it, and gave her a disapproving look.

"Under the O, sixty-nine," said Charley. "That's always someone's lucky number."

The crowd laughed, as if it was the first time they had ever heard that joke, though statistically they were likely to hear it at least once per night.

Rose snuck a glance at Callie who thankfully did not understand the comment because she was curiously looking at the snortlling bingo patrons.

"How's Gilbert doing?" asked Winter.

"He got home this morning after being on the road for a week. They hit about six towns, I think. Including a gig in Regina. Gilbert said it was a big one." Course he still seemed to be broke, she didn't add. She made a mental note to dig through his pockets, suitcase, and shaving kit before bed; there was a chance he was holding out on her.

"I don't know how he keeps up that schedule and his job at the band office," Winter commented.

"He got fired from the band office," Rose said reluctantly. Probably better for them to hear it from her because they would definitely hear it from someone else.

"I see," said Winter.

Monty grunted, "That fucking idiot, does he — "

"Ahem." Rose looked meaningfully at Callie.

"I heard they found Albert," Winter said, changing the subject. Albert was an elder with two wives. Both women kicked him out regularly and invited him back only when they got jealous of the other woman. Any week he could be found commuting by foot from one house to the other.

"He was missing?" For the past three months, Rose had been working twelve-hour shifts, six days a week at the pig barns, and was always out of the loop. A shame, since she dearly loved gossip.

"For four days. If it was anyone else, people would have noticed quicker, but you know, Edna thought Gladys had him and vice versa. But anyways, they found him hiding in an old barn because he said he saw a — "

Ol' Charley broke in with his deep monotone: "Under the I . . ."

Rose leaned forward, ready to dab her number, and scream bingo louder than anyone had screamed in months.

"Twenty-two," Charley finished.

"Bingo!" screamed four female voices and one male voice.

"There it goes," Winter said.

"Frick," said Rose.

"You would've shared with lots of people anyways, Mom," said Callie as she packed up her book.

"Yeah," said Rose, still looking at her card. "You ever wonder if they check the cards all the way through, like maybe someone can sneak their card in there if they had the right winning number?"

Winter raised an eyebrow. "Are you questioning the professionalism of the Pesakestew bingo hall? These people have received almost ten minutes of training. No, my friend, your fortune will not be made in bingo." She squeezed Rose's shoulder.

Rose crumpled up her card and tossed it in the garbage with a gusto that she did not feel.

Monty went to get cards for him and his wife for the second bingo. Winter wasn't a fan of midnight madness, but she toughed it out for Monty.

"Why don't you keep me company for the next one? My treat," Winter said.

"Nah, she has school tomorrow and we have to pick up Sarah," Rose replied.

"Where is she?"

"I dropped her off at Ronnie's Saturday afternoon. They're studying for their English test."

"Ronnie — that the one with all the rings in her face?"

"Yup."

"And her mom is Jane, the director over at the women's centre?"

Rose nodded.

"Yeah, that woman went to Ottawa for the Women's Wellness conference this weekend," Winter said.

"Sarah never mentioned that." Rose could feel anxiety and irritation clawing up from the pit of her stomach.

"She definitely didn't mention that," echoed Callie.

"Teenagers," Winter said.

"And you want one?" Rose asked.

Winter smiled.

Rose pushed Callie in front of her. "Let's go, Callie. I'm pretty sure your sister's already had more fun than any sixteen-year-old should ever have."

"Wait." Callie tugged on her aunt's arm. "What did he see?"

"Who?"

"Albert."

"Oh, he said he saw a ghost and it chased him!"

"For real?" Callie's eyes were huge.

Winter ruffled Callie's hair. "Silly old bastard was probably half-cut."

∽

Rose and Callie pulled up in front of a rundown but well-lit house. Clearly the inhabitants were under the impression ten lights could do the same work as one. From the car, Rose could hear music pumping. It was a cross between punk and rap music. *Not a good sign*, thought Rose. She beeped the horn. There was no reaction from the house, although a fat tabby glared as he sauntered across the yard.

"Callie, go get her. Their music is probably too loud."

Callie eagerly threw her seatbelt off and rushed out of the car. She ran up the front steps and knocked on the door. Once, twice, three times, no answer. She turned and made the "I don't know" motion with her arms.

Rose turned the car off. "Damned Sarah."

Rose walked up the front steps and opened the door and walked inside with Callie close on her heels. The smell of weed hit Rose's face like a bag full of baseballs. She and Callie both sneezed.

"Go sit in the car," Rose commanded Callie.

Callie hung back a bit, then followed her mother anyway.

Rose sniffed the air again. They had to be making pot stronger than when she was young, because this smoke felt like warm soup moving down her throat. She walked through the living room and glanced into the kitchen; she saw a mess in there: bags of chips, empty pop cans, a beer box on its side. Rose observed that the box was empty. Then she turned and headed for the hallway where some rapper lyrically promised to show a woman the time of her life and then kick her out the next morning.

Rose leaned her ear on the door and heard voices. She listened for the sulky voice of a teenage girl but didn't hear it. She heard a male voice and her pulse rose slightly.

Callie bounced on her toes.

Rose opened the door with a powerful push; it slammed against the wall with a decisive bang, she noted proudly. She surveyed the room with military precision: six teens, averaging from ages fifteen to nineteen, perhaps even early twenties, three males, three females, all with slits for eyes. They stared at her like infants. Rose recognized only two of them: Ronnie, her daughter's best friend, and right next to her, the first fruit of her loins.

"Sarah," Rose snapped.

"Mom?" Sarah sat cross-legged on the floor opposite the door.

"Get up."

Sarah moved as if to get up and then fell backwards. She giggled.

"Holy shit," said Callie, "she's higher than a hot air balloon." It was a phrase that Rose often used when she caught Gilbert in a similar state.

"Get up!" Rose commanded. Sarah struggled on the floor, her long skinny legs stretching in front of her like a fawn. Rose stomped through the centre of the circle, hoping to trample one of the teens' bare feet, and pulled Sarah to standing.

"I don't know where my jacket is," Sarah said, and then giggled. Then one of the other girls started giggling, and then another, and then the boys — one by one, like giggling dominoes. There was probably a time in her life when Rose would have found this entertaining, but that was in the past before she became a mom — when the word fun became forever divorced from risk.

"Wow," said Callie. "So this is what being stoned is like. Cool."

Rose glanced at her younger daughter. Rose wished she knew the right thing to say that would ensure that she never saw Callie in this room. "These drug addicts are frying up their precious brain cells like bacon. And your body doesn't make any more brain cells. Once you burn them, that's it, then you have no more sense than a raccoon," Rose pontificated. Internally, she questioned her own statement: Were raccoons dumb animals or were they actually smart? Because they seemed really good at prying open garbage cans. Maybe it was ducks that were the morons of the animal kingdom?

The "drug addicts" only laughed harder.

Rose leaned forward and grabbed Sarah by the arm. Sarah yelped in pain, though Rose wasn't hurting her. She struggled to break free but Rose was a lot stronger, thanks to years of carrying slippery pigs.

"Hey," protested Ronnie.

"You have a problem?" Rose's voice was sharp enough to cut cold cheese. "Cuz, I sure have a problem with you, and trust me, your mom is gonna be hearing from me!"

Ronnie blinked and looked down at her feet. Rose wondered when Ronnie's mom Jane would be home. She travelled most of the month as the director of the health and healing centre.

"Bye everyone!" Sarah called over her shoulder as Rose frog-marched her down the hallway.

"You just wait, Sarah, your dad is gonna kick your ass. I can't believe you lied to me — did you think I wouldn't find out? How dumb do you think I am?"

Sarah giggled.

"Her eyes look weird." Callie peered close into Sarah's face. "Maybe we should take her to a hospital."

Rose half-pulled, half-carried Sarah down the stairs and shoved her into the car's backseat. Sarah flopped sideways.

"My jacket?" Sarah's voice was muffled by the cloth seats.

"Should I go get it?" Callie asked.

"We're not her goddamn maids. Get in the car." Rose slammed her door closed. Callie jumped in next to her.

"Should we call the police?" Callie asked as she buckled up her seatbelt.

"What would they do?" The sentence was out of Rose's mouth before she could stop it. It sounded so backwards and hopeless, like something Gilbert or one of those meatheads who hung out at the band office would say.

"Isn't it illegal to smoke weed if you're a minor?"

"It's always illegal," Rose said. Unless of course you had a doctor's note, but Rose didn't feel like launching into an explanation of Gilbert's medical claim that he was agoraphobic. Rose never understood how he got away with that. His "phobia" got him weed but didn't prevent him from performing in front of crowds or going to house parties with groupies afterwards.

"Then how come dad — "

"Just stop talking for a bit Callie, my head is friggin' killing me."

Callie said okay without making a sound. She leaned her head on the window and stared into the rear-view mirror, watching the house fade into darkness.

The stars were out. Rose knew that if she was lying on her back, it would be like a scene out of *Star Wars* when the space ship goes into warp speed and the stars rush toward you. It wasn't a scary feeling at all, it made you feel like the universe was within reach.

Rose focused on the road in front of her. Their beat up little Dodge Neon that was nearly as old as Callie moved uncertainly over the potholes and ruts as she drove a little too fast. All she wanted to do was get home, tell Gilbert about his daughter (and yell at him for being a pothead himself for the one millionth time), take a shower, and go to bed for a thousand hours.

Behind her, she heard a movement, and then someone vomiting. A thick cloud of barbecue chips, beer, and bile wafted over the seat.

"That is really gross." Callie turned to look and was rewarded with a head push from her sister. She screeched: "Sarah assaulted me!"

"Just leave her alone, Callie. She's gonna hear about it from her dad and then she's gonna clean it up tomorrow."

Rose pulled into her approach. A grey Honda Civic was parked in front of the house.

"Whozzat?" Rose and Callie asked at the same time.

"One of Dad's friends?" Callie offered as they parked next to the car. A very large, pink, beaded headdress hung from the rear-view mirror.

Sarah's head poked up. "That's Auntie Michelle."

Sarah's breath brought tears to Rose's eyes, so she ducked out of the car quickly. She looked at the jazzy little car parked haphazardly in front of the house. It was only three or four years old, the closest to a new car that Rose had ever seen.

Michelle was her younger cousin by a year, a teacher's aide at a school in the city. Single, no kids — that's how you afforded new cars.

"I saw her at school on Friday," Sarah croaked from the backseat.

"Why is Miss Fancypants out here?" Rose wondered aloud.

"Maybe she brought gifts for us — like an early Christmas!" Callie had never heard a question that she would not attempt to answer.

"It's barely spring, stup — " Sarah's voice broke in the middle of her diss as a wave of nausea hit her.

Rose's heart sank as she walked toward the house. Michelle never came around if things were going well. She must have lost her job in the city (again) and now would want to stay for a month or two until she got another one. She was good company — agreeable and a damn fine gossip — but hard to get rid of once her charm and money had run out. *Another thing*, Rose thought to herself, *another goddamn thing.*

Callie ran up the stairs ahead, yelling, "Auntie Michelle!" at the top of her lungs.

Sarah stopped ahead of Rose on the stairs and scrunched up her face like she smelled a bad fart. Then she bent herself over the railing and dry-heaved. Rose put a gentle hand on her thin back. "I'm not finished with you."

Sarah waved her off.

Rose opened the screen door and sighed. She had tidied up before she left and now there were empty beer bottles on the coffee table and an ashtray full of ashes so high that they had spilled over the side. Rose inhaled the smell of warm beer and B.O. — Gilbert was such a charmer.

Callie claimed the couch with the remote control in one hand and a Popsicle in the other.

"Where's your aunt?"

"She's not in the kitchen or the bathroom or the backyard or the linen closet. I gave up." She bit into her Popsicle.

Rose deposited the beer bottles in the kitchen sink and then walked down the hallway toward the bedrooms.

"Michelle?" She glanced into Callie's bedroom. Nothing. She walked past Sarah's bedroom and opened the door — no bags, no slyly smiling younger cousin. The door to Rose's bedroom was closed.

No.

Rose knew that on the other side of the door she was going to see something that was going to change her life. Not because Gilbert had never fooled around before, of course he had, he was a *rock star*. But with family, in her house? Rose put her hand on the knob and thought for a second. Was it necessary to know? She could grab a towel from the closet and head for the shower and be under it while one of them opened the door and checked to see if the coast was clear. Michelle would sneak out without being seen, and then say, "Wow, I was out like a light." Yes, and then they and Rose could pretend that everything was okay until everything was okay. Fake it until you make it, right?

It was amazing how many secrets you could keep even in a tiny house.

Rose was already turning away from the door when she felt a pressure on her back, like a handprint, propelling her forward. If you asked her if it was courage or curiosity that made her open the door, her answer would have been neither. It was momentum, pure and simple.

Gilbert was standing in front of the window, wearing his boxer shorts, those stupid raggedy Budweiser ones. A woman's butt was disappearing out the window. Rose rushed for the window and missed an ankle by a fingernail. Gilbert grabbed her arm.

"Don't hurt her."

Rose slapped him with her other hand. She caught more jaw than cheek so there was no satisfying thwack but there was no time to make it right. She looked out the window. She saw Michelle's hair flaring behind her as she ran around the corner.

Rose was in a flat-out run by the time she hit the hallway. Callie called out "Mom?" as Rose sprinted through the living room. Then Rose ran out the front door, slid around Sarah still on the steps, jumped over all the steps and hit the ground without falling forward — *that was surprising*, she thought to herself — then she barrelled toward Michelle's car. Michelle was already in the driver's seat. Rose threw the passenger door open and lunged through it as Michelle dove out the driver's side. Rose pulled the keys out of the ignition and threw them far into the long grass that Gilbert was too lazy to mow.

"Jesus, Rose, let's talk about this!" Michelle's eyes were big with fear as they met Rose's over the top of the car.

"Sure. But first I want to punch you in the face." Rose slid across the car's hood. (Maybe not slid so much as scooted her butt across as the metal protested.)

Michelle ran to the back of the car. "I'm sorry! I'm sorry!" she repeated.

"Stay still!" Rose yelled, running to meet her. Michelle turned on a dime and kept the car between them.

"Mom!" Callie was on the front steps, her hands in front of her mouth like Munch's *Scream*. Rose could always count on Callie to rise to each dramatic occasion.

"Go. Inside. Callie." Rose was out of breath.

"Please talk to me, Rose. I'm your cousin. I love you." Michelle wasn't the least bit winded.

"Stay still!" Rose demanded. But it came out, "Shtay shtill."

"You're very angry, I understand that, but we're cousins! Remember when I gave you those cute little white leather boots?"

"They were too small!"

Rose lunged at Michelle and caught a wrist. In a move that suggested Michelle remembered her Tae Kwon Do moves from elementary school, she twisted her wrist and slid out of Rose's grasp and then put another corner of the car between them.

"I'm sorry!"

"Stop moving," Rose rasped.

Michelle yelled over her shoulder. "This isn't fair, Rose — you know I have anemia!"

Rose lunged at Michelle and caught her by the back of her leather coat. Soft buttery leather, the kind of expensive

24

shit Rose had never owned in her whole damn life. Michelle twisted out of her grasp and made it around to the other side of the car.

"What's happening?" Callie screeched. She was now at the bottom of the steps. Sarah put a hand on her shoulder to keep her from running into the fray.

"Mom caught Michelle in bed with Dad," Sarah said flatly.

"It wasn't like that!" Michelle looked at the girls: "Sarah, I love you and your sister very much."

Rose gave the slide across the hood another try. She had better luck this time and made it all the way across. She swung her legs to the ground and grabbed a handful of brown hair. Michelle's head snapped back.

"You're going to break her neck!" Callie yelled.

Michelle threw her head forward like a recalcitrant pony, leaving Rose with strands of hair woven between her fingers. Michelle screamed in pain. Rose flicked the hair off her fingers.

"You're scaring your girls, Rose! Stop this," Michelle urged.

"Bitch!" Rose lunged at Michelle and missed. Rose's feet slipped on the gravel and she fell on the ground; little stones stabbed into her palms and knees. "Aw fuck."

She heard the sound of Michelle's footsteps on the approach.

"Are you okay?" Callie ran to Rose's side.

Rose pushed her away and took off after her prey. Michelle wasn't that fast. Sure, she was skinny, but she had no muscle tone and she sat on her ass all day flashing cards in kid's faces. *I can catch her*, Rose thought, *I can do this. I have God on my side*. Well, maybe not God but at least one avenging angel. There's probably even a patron saint of married women who have to kick a home-wrecker's ass.

Michelle looked behind her and saw Rose coming. She ran faster. Rose reached deep within herself and found another gear. The distance began to narrow. Michelle glanced back again, saw Rose gaining, and then she really began to run.

Before she could adjust her pace, Rose's lungs reached up and put a death grip on her throat. Rose disobeyed the command. She pumped her arms faster and tricked her legs into thinking they were supposed to be moving faster, too. She tried to ignore the fact that her knees were already swollen and achy.

"Run, you fat bitch," she scolded herself, and for once, her self listened. Her feet dug divots in the dirt as she rounded the corner to the main road. She reached the place where the girls' dog had gotten hit by a car a few years before and realized that this was the furthest she had run in years.

Then her body just up and quit. Her lungs shut off oxygen supply. A cramp clenched the left side of her body. Her legs teetered, then tottered until Rose collapsed to her knees in slow motion. Like I'm praying, she thought, but the only thing I'd be praying for would be for that bitch to get hit by a car. She shifted back onto her bum and sat cross-legged in the gravel and wheezed until oxygen was able to reach her brain. She wished that she had a smoke. "I would give my right tit for one," Rose rasped. She looked up at the stars, they had never seemed so far away.

Did this really just happen? She thought. *Did I just chase my cousin down the road in hopes of grabbing her by the hair and punching her in the face like a couple of guests on the Jerry Springer show?* Rose felt for every woman she'd ever seen go punch-crazy on that show.

Rose had only been in one fight in her adult life. It was with some cow in a dive bar in the city. That fight had been over Gilbert, too. The chick had been staring at Gilbert through the show, crushing on him and his too-tight Wranglers. She'd even gotten on stage and kissed him.

Rose wasn't going to do anything about it because she wasn't the type to scrap in a dive bar (not to mention, the woman had at least sixty pounds on her and was hanging out with a bunch of bikers). But the choice was taken from her when the woman came up to her after the show and sucker-punched Rose in the face , right in the kisser (the next day, her lips looked like they'd been stung by two wasps.)

Rose had fought back, more trying to get away than anything else. She got one punch in. She still remembered the satisfying thwack as her fist connected with the biker chick's cheek and how her fat head had drifted to the right. The woman returned the favour with a few powerful jabs to Rose's face. Eventually the bouncers got bored of watching and pulled them apart.

Gilbert, of course, did nothing.

She heard the car start up and looked toward the house. Maybe Sarah was sneaking off? Rose wouldn't put it past her to use this moment to justify heading back to her friends' party. Rose really hoped not because she didn't have the strength to play bad cop. Damn Sarah, why was she on such a collision course with failure? She was failing classes, barely talked to Rose anymore, and was always fighting with her sister. And now, she was boozing it up and doing God knows what drugs.

Didn't she want something better with her life? The car pulled out of the yard and turned toward her. She blocked the road with her body. It slowed — Rose could see Gilbert's big square head behind the wheel.

"Where the fuck are you going?" Her voice was a hoarse siren in the black night, but the windows were rolled up and Steve Earle was blaring from the stereo.

Gilbert waved for her to move out of the way.

Rose marched toward the car like a warrior marching to her destiny. On top of everything, he wasn't taking the goddamned car. Gilbert beeped the horn. Rose gave him the finger and kept walking. She was so angry that she was sure she could stop the car if he came toward her. There was no way to find out, Gilbert drove the car off the road into the ditch and tore around her.

"Coward!" Rose threw a stone at the car. It was pointless but she admired the quality of her aim and the way her arm moved through the air like she threw stones at cars every day. Rose threw her head back to scream away the injustice of this world, they would be able to hear it in Vancouver as they stirred their lattes and wondered if a plane had gone down. But screaming was too much to ask from her sore throat and her scream was nothing more than a sore swallow followed by a coughing fit.

"Mom?"

Rose's shut her mouth and turned around. She saw Callie perched on her bike, weaving her way toward her.

"Dad stole the car."

"Yeah."

"I wonder if he smelled the puke yet."

Rose shrugged.

"I thought you left, too." Callie searched her mother's face for evidence of something.

"Where would I go?"

"I don't know what's happening."

Rose watched the car's lights move down the road. The red lights came on and Rose figured he'd reached Michelle at last. Then the car moved on until it turned left at the four-way stop, which meant they were probably heading into town to the bar. Michelle would wash off her crocodile tears and then reapply her makeup. Then over beers, they'd regale the bar with the story of Rose going ape-shit, and, everyone would laugh and laugh.

"Let them laugh," Rose muttered.

"Who's laughing?"

"Nobody." Rose dragged her nails through the gravel. It felt wet and cold and cut into her nail beds but she enjoyed the marks, like a bear sharpening its claws before a kill.

"What are you doing?" Callie sounded like she'd rather not ask the question.

"I'm going to bed. I got work and you got school," Rose said finally.

Rose tested her legs. Her left knee felt stiff and swollen. She put some weight on it. "Owwwwwwww . . . " Now she was a coyote.

"You okay?"

"Yup, just need a little help."

Rose held out her hand and Callie pulled her to standing.

Rose limped toward the direction of the house. Callie walked her bike next to her.

"You sure can run fast, Mom."

"Not fast enough, apparently."

"She had a head start, so that doesn't count. Next time you'll beat her for sure."

In more ways than one, Rose promised herself.

Two

THE RIDE HOME FROM MIDNIGHT MADNESS was quiet. Monty hadn't won and was still grumpy. He gripped the wheel and swore at all the slow drivers making the drive home seem like a funeral procession.

"You have a gas pedal!" He yelled at the car in front of them. Monty was following so close that they could read the hand scrawled message, "Wash me" across the trunk.

"They're old ladies," Winter reminded him, then turned off her hearing when he launched into another tirade.

Winter's mind was on a thousand different things. She felt bloated, which made her wonder if it was a symptom of pregnancy or if it was her period, so should she bother mentioning it to Monty? He'd get his hopes up and she'd get her hopes up and then if nothing happened — again — they'd both have shitty weeks. Winter wasn't up to feeling that emptiness. Not unhappy but not able to be happy either. Since they'd started having their fertility problems (or "challenges," as the doctor wanted them to call it) Winter could not remember experiencing a single moment of joy. Sometimes she drank extra caffeine just to feel a jolt of something.

Having kids seemed so damned easy for everyone on this stupid reserve, except for them. *It's like we're being punished for being successful*, she thought for the thousandth time, and then pulled the unkind thought back.

Winter was used to the looks of pity from the women on the reserve. The way babies got an extra grateful hug from their mommies when they saw Winter looking in their direction. Like how people stand up straight when they see a person crippled over with osteoporosis.

Even tonight at bingo, she saw a teenage girl with a big belly give her a sad look. Don't pity me, you little bitch, Winter felt like saying, pity your kid who will forever be hearing "no" from you because you're too broke to afford anything.

Before everyone found out that she and Monty were trying to conceive, everyone used to think that they didn't like kids. People just called them selfish then. That was better.

"How the hell does Lorna win twice in one night? Does she have a horseshoe shoved up her ass?" Monty mumbled.

"You talking to me?"

"I know you don't care."

"How's the new site?" Monty was developing a subdivision outside of the city. It was the biggest project he'd ever handled.

"S'okay. Guys are adjusting. Had to fire those two Bigknife kids. Showed up half-cut. And then some of the guys were grumbling about Indian this and Indian that so I had to tell them off."

"Ellie'll be mad."

"Yeah, well, I should be mad at her. She told me her grandkids were ready to work. I doubt either of them had ever handled a hammer before. Why don't people think?"

"What did you think of Gilbert losing his job?"

Monty grunted. "That fucking idiot."

"She's gonna leave him one of these days."

"More like he'll leave her. Did I tell you I saw a kid in the city looked just like Callie? The stuff Rose doesn't know."

"Rose knows more than she thinks she does."

They parked their car in the garage and Monty made sure it was locked behind them. They had a couple of break-ins the year before and they were extra cautious now. It turned out to be some kids from a few houses away — too young to press charges. They had gotten a dog a month later, a handsome German shepherd who was smart as a whip and scary-looking as hell. He kept the house safe while they were on vacation. But then someone stole the dog. Monty was still pissed about that. Every time they drove across the reserve he kept his eyes peeled for it in someone's yard.

"It was like someone stealing my wife," he told people after it happened.

Winter hadn't been pleased to be on equal footing with a canine that drooled all the time, licked his own balls, and peed in the corner of the garage.

Winter turned on the kitchen light. There was food every-where. "Monty!"

"What?" he yelled from the garage.

"What's with this mess?"

Winter could hear him bounding up the steps. "I was gonna clean it up."

"Look at this cheese!" she waved the container in his face. "Why didn't you throw it in the fridge after you were finished?"

"I wasn't thinking," Monty said. "Tiger was on."

Winter rolled her eyes. Monty's addiction to bingo was only surpassed by his addiction to golf.

"It would have only taken five seconds. And now it's probably ruined." Winter took a whiff of rancid soft cheese, and then she emptied her guts all over the floor, her pant legs, her shoes, and Monty's bare feet.

"What the hell?" Monty said.

Winter pushed him out of the way. She headed toward the bathroom where she stood over the toilet and waited for more to come.

"Winter?"

She didn't look up from the bowl. Her stomach felt like it had a lot of complaints. "What did I eat?" was the running commentary in her brain as she felt the acid travelling up her throat.

When she was done (and showered and tooth-brushed and gargled), she padded into the living room in her pajamas. Monty had the TV tuned into Tiger teeing up a shot. He looked up at her as she walked in.

"Hey," Monty said. "I cleaned up your puke."

"Thanks."

"Flu?"

Winter shook her head. "I got the flu shot."

She sat down next to him and like a couple on a first date, they thought about things to say but didn't say them.

Three

ROSE WOKE TO THE SOUND OF a large vehicle driving away. "The bus," she thought to herself. Then she rolled over and saw Callie sleeping next to her. "Crap."

Then the memory of the night before hit her like a train. Rose bounced up and then immediately fell backwards as every muscle in her thighs locked down on her.

Rose stared at the ceiling. She held her hands up in front of her; fortunately, she could move them easily enough. These gravel-stained hands were all she had to get them out of this mess. But which mess, exactly? Getting left by a bad man, being betrayed by her cousin, kid missing school because she was up late watching her parents' drama, sleeping in and missing work again, or . . . ?

"Sarah." Rose's feet found their way to the side of the bed. She stood up and a strangled scream escaped her mouth. She glanced at Callie; she was undisturbed. Rose reached for her emergency smokes hidden under the mattress, but couldn't bend far enough to get them.

"Omigod, omigod," she said breathlessly and slowly eased herself to standing. Her legs hurt everywhere: calves, thighs, butt, even her back was sending out bolts of pain.

Coffee would help. Didn't it deaden nerves or something? Rose slid her legs forward. "You can do this, you can do this," she whispered to herself as she clung to the wall.

She made it to Sarah's room. The door was open, the bed was messy and Sarah was gone. "Okay," Rose assured herself. "Not necessarily a bad thing."

Rose continued to inch down the hallway. "At this pace, I should be at work by midnight."

Rose looked around the kitchen; there was a box of cereal on the table. Wherever Sarah had gone, at least she'd eaten first.

Rose looked in the direction of the coffeemaker, but it was empty. "She does drugs but she won't drink coffee . . . " Rose filled the machine and stood next to it while it percolated. Winter was always telling her that meditation was something everyone should do — "it's all about turning off your brain and focusing on one thing only" — and Rose figured that hovering over the coffee maker every morning was her version of it.

With her first sip of coffee in her, Rose decided to tackle the first item on her to-do list. She picked up the phone and carefully eased herself into a chair.

"Hello, Green Acres!" said a voice dripping with fake enthusiasm. That was Susie, the owner of the pig farm. Susie could carry a one hundred pound pig like a baby. Rose was pretty scared of her.

"Hey Susie, it's Rose."

Susie sighed. "Why aren't you at work, Rose? It's goddamn eight o'clock."

"My car is — well, I don't have it. My husband ran off with it."

"I see. And when are you getting it back?"

"My husband or my car?" Rose faked a laugh and then regretted it when the effort sent a bit of snot flying out her noise.

"Rose, missing work isn't funny."

"No, it sure isn't." Rose sensed the lecture chugging down the train tracks. It did suck being thirty-four and getting talked down to by a twenty-eight-year-old single woman who had never had to stay up all night with a sick kid and who had inherited her business from her dad. But that was the working world.

"Not only does this show a lack of respect for me, my business, our customers, and the pigs, it shows a lack of respect for yourself. Do you see that?"

"See what?" Susie had lost her around the first respect.

"Just answer me: do you respect yourself?"

Rose took a sip of coffee and reflected on that. Do I respect myself? Was that the same as liking oneself? Because Rose wasn't sure if she did. And couldn't you respect someone even if you didn't like him or her? Rose remembered that from that theatre play about the salesman who died — what was it called again? *Dead Salesmen Only Wear Plaid?* Was respect like trusting someone? Like if I owned a really expensive car like a Maserati, would I trust me to borrow it? Rose was still thinking about the answer when Susie started again.

"The bottom line is that I need people that I and my pigs can rely on. Do you think you are that person?"

What, am I in charge of firing myself now? Why couldn't bosses just fire you and forget about all this "you brought this on yourself" stuff? But then Rose remembered the little person sleeping in the bedroom and took a deep breath: "Susie I promise you that I will be on time for the rest of the month and the rest of the year. This will never happen again. It's one of those one-off totally unique circumstance things. You know how it is, Susie. Everyone has bad luck sometimes and this happens to be my turn. It won't happen again."

"How are you going to ensure that?"

Rose looked out the window at the green Corolla sitting in her driveway. "I have access to another car, my cousin's. She and I traded for it." There you go Rose, you sound responsible and sane.

"Then why aren't you at work right now?"

"Because the keys are missing. Sort of. I mean I know where they are, I just have to find them." Now slightly less responsible and sane.

"I see." But Susie did not see. She was confused, and when Susie got confused, she got mad, and when Susie got mad, pigs went flying.

"I promise I will be there tomorrow," Rose said. Then, sensing the anger building on the other side of the phone lines, she decided to go all the way, "Please don't fire me Susie, I need this job. Please don't do this. Please." That last "please" felt like overkill, but subtlety was something only people with employment insurance could afford.

"Rose." Susie said her name with a finality that Rose had heard before — when she worked at the gas station, at that family restaurant in town, at that meat packing place and that ill-fated weekend as a phone psychic. (At that last job, getting fired was the only thing Rose had correctly predicted.)

After she hung up, Rose took a sip of her coffee. It was cold and bitter. Rose added more sugar hoping to take the taste of begging out of her mouth. "That did not go well," she assured the kitchen cupboards.

Next she dialled the school. She gave the secretary a convoluted story about a forgotten homework assignment and asked for Sarah. While on hold, she cleaned the counters, surveyed the fridge, and made a grocery list. She was filling the sink with water for the dishes when Sarah got on the phone.

"What?"

"I wanted to know where you were."

Sarah snapped her gum. "I'm here. Obviously."

"Okay, see you at home later and don't — "

Sarah hung up.

"Lovely child." Rose forgot about the dishes and poured herself another cup of coffee.

Mentally, Rose reorganized her to-do list. Applying for welfare was moved to the top. No wait, first she had to find the keys to Michelle's car. Rose visualized herself crawling through the deep grass on her oh-so-tender knees and took a deep breath and called, "Callie-baby, time to get up!"

❧

"You didn't throw very far Mom, they were pretty close."

"Lucky for us."

Rose pulled out of the yard and headed in the direction of the band office.

"So is this our car now?" Callie tried out the automatic window buttons.

"Technically, no. Morally, yes." An eye for an eye and a car for an old dirty bastard.

"So was Auntie Michelle having an affair with Dad, like Sarah said?"

"What do you think an affair is?" Rose asked.

"When two people who are married or one of them is married, I think, and then they do stuff to one another and then they have a baby?"

"I hope they don't do that," Rose said mildly.

"I hate Dad."

"What goes on between your dad and me has nothing to do with you."

"Sarah hates him too."

"Did she tell you that?"

"Yes."

"Does she hate me too?"

Callie paused for a second as she chose the right words. "Sometimes she is very mad at you and she calls you bad names like — "

"I don't need to hear them."

"No problemo." Callie leaned back in her seat and put her feet on the dashboard.

"Okay, so what went on last night is our business, nobody needs to know about it. You got that?"

"Yup."

"All right then, we're gonna go into the band office, I'm gonna get a cheque and then we're going for groceries, got it?"

"What happens if someone asks me why I'm not in school?"

"Can you pretend a sore throat?"

"Like this?" croaked Callie.

"Perfect."

They high-fived.

"Nothing can stop us now!" Callie cheered.

∾

They got stopped as they turned onto the main road. Rose tapped her fingers impatiently on the steering wheel as she waited for the cop — officially known as Sergeant Nolan Martin, unofficially known as Officer Tubbs — to get out of his car. Rose had known him all her life. In nursery school, he was a skinny kid. By elementary, he was husky. By the time he reached high school, he was obese. He'd filled out a lot since then. He was huffing by the time he reached her window.

"Well, well, if it ain't a whole lot of Rosie."

He'd been saying this since they were teens and she hadn't laughed yet.

"License and registration?" His nose was sweating from where his aviators sat.

Rose reached for her purse and pulled out her license. "Callie, check the glove compartment."

"Where you going?"

"Band Office. Lost my job."

"Nice car. When'd you get it?"

"It's actually my cousin's."

"Michelle the hottie?" Nolan seemed to sweat a little more.

"Yes." Rose's teeth were so tightly gritted together, soup couldn't get through them.

"There's nothing in there, Mom," Callie said.

"She probably has the stuff with her," Rose explained and tapped the steering wheel impatiently.

Nolan went to the back of the car to look at the plates. Then he came back to the window.

"You wanna get out of the car?"

Rose complied but took her time doing it. Nolan brought her around to the back and pointed at the plates.

"Is this car registered?"

Rose shrugged. "I assume."

"Plates say January."

Rose peered closer. "Oh. Maybe they mean January of next year."

"Why would your cousin let you drive her car if it's unregistered?"

"To be perfectly honest, she's a bit of a bitch."

"This is serious."

"I didn't know the car was unregistered."

"Tell you want, I'll let it go if you, y'know, cook me a nice dinner and provide some after dinner entertain — "

"We're cousins and I have a husband."

"Cousins, smuzins. My mom said we're third at best." Nolan leaned against the car. "So when you gonna dump that man of yours and go out with me?"

"We're second cousins at least. Look we even have the same gap in our teeth."

"So you've been staring at my mouth?" He grabbed her arm and pulled her toward him. Rose wriggled away from him.

"You are nuts." She stomped back to the driver's side.

"I was kidding!" Nolan called.

Rose climbed into the car and slammed the door.

"You get a ticket?" Callie asked.

"No, he's not that kind of cop."

∾

From looking at the cars in the band office, Rose surmised that it was going to be packed as hell in there. Normally she would turn around and drive home but the idea of sitting on her couch, in that house, after they had . . . made her shudder. Javex, she thought, lots of Javex. But first, money.

Gilbert was a bad man. Winter had told her that bad men will do bad things and that they will never stop. Just when you think they've done something so awful that you don't think you will ever survive, then they will top themselves. "But I didn't listen!" Rose blurted out.

"What?"

"Just talking to myself," Rose said. Callie had a look on her face that suggested she was storing this moment away for a future therapy appointment.

A young guy, Evan, leaned against the band office doorway smoking and checking his phone. Evan was nineteen and used to play some pretty good hockey. Now he worked part time in construction and got girls pregnant.

Rose limped up the walkway with Callie behind her.

"Hey Rose," Evan opened the door for her. "You fall or something?"

"No, just getting out of shape. How's your mom and dad doing?" Rose asked.

"Getting old," he laughed. As she passed, Evan checked out Rose's tits. Rose was shocked and somewhat flattered. Still, she gave him a pious, I-know-your-parents look, as she sidled past him through the double doors into the band office.

The band office opened into a large common room that was sometimes called the "waiting area" or the "lobby" but was most fittingly the "card room." The doorways to the offices of the chief and counsellors, band nurse, and welfare administrator were located off the card room like spokes on a wheel. There was a short hallway that led to a couple of large storage rooms that the band used as smaller meeting rooms, the bathrooms, and the back exit that was always propped open in the hopes that fresh air would suck the smoke out.

A cloud of cigarette smoke hung in the air. It fought the smell of coffee for dominance. There was a raucous game of cards in the waiting room. That was not a good sign; people had come early and dug in their heels. Rose went to the receptionist desk. Kaylee Adams had been the band secretary for three years; she was also one of the councillor's daughters and a mean drunk if you looked at her the wrong way on a Saturday night.

"Morning Kaylee."

"Hey Rose." Kaylee didn't look up from her Facebook.

"Is that a new tattoo?" Rose pointed at the delicate dragon that wound its way around Kaylee's neck and down onto her chest. Its tail dipped into her cleavage.

"Yeah, my boyfriend bought it for me."

"It's very pretty."

"Yeah, I was thinking about getting a portrait of Tupac, but everyone does that. So what's up?"

"I have to get some welfare. Lost my job this morning."

"Oh, shitty. Well, Liz is really behind today. Can you come back tomorrow?" Kaylee's eyes went back to her computer. "Fuck me, some bitch just liked my boyfriend's picture."

Rose made appropriate noises of disgust at the offending bitch. Then she waited until Kaylee finished typing an ass-kicking message to the Facebook ho. "I was hoping maybe you could sneak me in? We need groceries and I have to take Callie to the doctor."

Callie coughed loudly.

"Oh shitty." Kaylee glanced around the band office. People laughed loudly as others yelled their jokes across the tables.

"I can't make it obvious, okay?"

Rose nodded. "Thanks, Kaylee."

Callie coughed again, for good measure.

Rose grabbed a Styrofoam cup from the stack and poured herself a coffee and mixed in some sugar and whitener. She took her time — no sense rushing in the band office. Callie followed her lead and filled a cup with water and added in some sugar and whitener.

They turned around and looked at everyone. Rose nodded at a few smiling faces who looked up from their cards.

"Are we going to play cards?" Callie asked.

"Nah, they're probably playing for smokes and I don't have any with me. Just gonna say hi."

"How come there's so many people here?

Rose shrugged.

Every seat at the poker table was taken. There were the regulars, the elders: Albert Akapew, Lorna Adams, and Gladys Stonewoman. And a few young drop-ins, Jason Bull (Jason Six) and Will Akapew, who were always between jobs and jail at any given moment.

Albert, the man with two wives, was holding court at the moment. "It was her. I swear on my grandfather's grave, she was standing right in front of me."

"Whatever, you old stud, you were hitting on her." Will took a drag of his smoke and blew a huge smoke ring.

"She smelled worse than a dance party at an old folk's home." Albert looked frustrated.

"Oh c'mon, Albert, you've done worse, admit it." Jason Six had the permanent sleepy eyes of a stoner.

Gladys gently placed two cards on the table. "What did she want?"

"She wanted to kill me."

"Wouldn't be the first woman," commented Lorna. She and Gladys shared a chuckle.

"That's when I started running and goddamnit, every time I turned, there she was over and over again, finally I just barreled right through her."

"You ran through a ghost?" Callie's eyes were huge.

"Worse feeling ever. Like having the cold hands of death wrap themselves around you— "

"Albert!" Rose covered Callie's ears.

"I nearly passed out, but I told myself, 'C'mon Albert, you gotta run or this woman is gonna murder you.' But I felt like I'd had the life sucked out of me . . . like when you go on a ten-day drunk and forget to eat . . . but when you're scared your body can do some crazy things. My legs kept moving like I wasn't even running them — then I saw the old barn and I knew I'd be safe . . . "

"Why?" Rose and Callie asked at the same time.

"Because that barn is off the — " someone kicked him under the table and Albert winced. Rose looked at the two old ladies, they were glaring at Albert.

He took a step back, out of kicking distance and continued, "So then when I got to the old barn, I slept for a whole day. Best sleep I ever had." Albert sat down; his energy sucked out of him once more.

"Oh you're so full of shit." Jason Six had a grumpy look on his face; none of his cards were coming this morning.

"You're too old for that nonsense. Stay home and look after your grandchildren," said Lorna.

"I didn't make this up!" Albert roared. He rose unsteadily to his feet and pulled up his shirt; there were red dots across his torso. To Rose, they looked like tiny bite-marks.

The table went silent.

"Looks like someone took a roll with a hooker with measles. Some guys pay extra for that." Will guffawed at his own joke and looked for approval from the others; nobody else was laughing.

Gladys peered at Albert over her cards. "Looks like a rash."

Albert hit the table with his hand. "You know what it is! It's the bad medicine of the Dream — "

"Control yourself," Gladys hissed. Rose had never seen the gentle Gladys so worked up; there was a touch of red in her pale soft cheeks.

There was an unusual lull in the band office as the elders exchanged looks. Across the room, even Kaylee noticed the difference in energy and looked up from her Facebook chat.

Albert looked around him as if remembering where he was. He picked up his cards, mumbling to himself, "I know the old story."

"How's that garden coming along?" Gladys asked Lorna in a loud voice. Lorna took the cue and launched into a long explanation about the importance of getting the seeds in the ground early.

"What old story?" Callie asked.

Rose placed her hands on Callie's shoulder. "Let's go sit down."

As they turned away, Will whooped: "Read 'em and weep!"

Everyone was distracted as they abused him for having a flush and winning the entire pot.

Rose made her way to the couch where Annabelle Bull sat with an infant on her lap. Annabelle was about twenty-five, pretty, and always had a neck full of hickeys. She always had smokes too.

"Hey Annie-belle, how's Mariah doing?"

"Getting fat. Can you hold her for a sec?" Annabelle passed the baby to Rose and then lit up a smoke. "You want one?"

"God, yes."

"Saw you at the bingo last night."

"Yeah, didn't win shit all."

"My sis won the jackpot with six other people. She got a hundred. I borrowed twenty," Annabelle laughed. She handed Rose a lit smoke. Rose shifted the baby to her left arm and grabbed the smoke with her right.

"You seeing Liz today?" Rose asked.

"Yeah, I got to get some moving funds. I'm heading back to the city."

"Going to school?"

"I wish. Nah, I want to get away from Jason Six, he's driving me crazy." She pointed with her lips at the card table.

"Is he paying child support?"

"No, and he says he won't until we get back together. He says until then he's going to set all of his paycheques on fire."

"I guess that's sort've romantic."

"But I can't take him back, not after I caught him with my cousin Marlene, which is so gross because she's totally old — she's almost thirty!"

Callie gasped.

"Holee, I shouldn't be talking like that in front of your kid. Sorry Callie, this is big people talk."

"No, my mom just got ashes on your baby." Callie pointed at the baby's face.

Rose looked down. Ash peppered the baby's face. Rose daintily blew it off.

Annabelle laughed. "At least she's not allergic."

"I used to do it to Callie all the time."

"Mom, I'm calling children's services!"

Annabelle and Rose shared a head thrown back laugh. It drew a few comments like, "What are you two witches up to?" and "Who's the lucky guy getting cut up?" and so on.

"Why's it so busy today?" Rose asked.

Annabelle smiled. "The new chief, Taylor Gordon."

"Oh, right. He's starting today."

"Oh yeah. And he is a tasty piece of meat. Glad I wore my Juicy sweat pants."

Rose looked down at her dull grey T-shirt that had once been midnight black and then lower to her acid-washed jeans. She was pretty sure that other than in her closet, the only other place you could still find acid-washed jeans was in a few eastern European countries.

This was not how she wanted to look the first time she saw Taylor Gordon face to face.

She'd heard Taylor speak a few weeks ago at the band nomination meeting. She'd stood at the doorway of the hall, with one foot in and one out. He stood at the front of the room lined up with the other nominees looking like a racehorse in a herd of caribou.

Honestly, Taylor didn't even need to speak. Everyone was already sick of the old Chief, Thomas "The Bull" Bull. The Bull had been caught with his hooves in the till too many times. Three audits in two years, people were ready to butcher him.

Taylor was athletic and college-educated, but people tried not to hold that against him. As he walked to the podium on nomination day, Rose prayed that he wouldn't drop a bunch of big words or big ideas like "political sovereignty" and "the battle for full recognition of our treaty rights" that built up everyone's hopes but just kept the lawyers busy buying second homes. The reserve had learned the hard way that any fight with the government only got them a killer legal bill. But Taylor didn't say any of that. He played it cool and said things like, "youth" and "culture" and "elders." He was a smart one, that one. Rose left the nominations right after he spoke, not wanting to run into him. She didn't want to find out if he remembered her or not.

"You know he doesn't have a wife," Annabelle said. "Course, he's pretty young."

"He's thirty-five."

"Really? Doesn't look it."

"Same age as my mom!" Callie crowed.

"I'm thirty-four." Rose corrected her.

"Yeah, but your birthday is only two months away."

"Callie." Rose put a warning in her voice.

"Did you know him in school?" Annabelle asked.

"He only went to the rez school for a few years, then his parents moved to the city."

"Was he your schoolyard BF?" Annabelle joked, then laughed heartily. Callie also laughed.

He was, Rose wanted to say. But somehow she figured that would make her look more like a loser than less.

"I'm sure he's got a long list of ladies. Probably into white girls, too," Rose said unkindly.

"I dunno, I heard he was running around with a Gambler girl in the city. She was a Roughrider's cheerleader."

"Jesus." Rose tucked in her gut.

"Probably got fake tits."

"What are those?" Callie looked very curious.

"Hey! Stop listening," Rose said. "Go play outside."

"But I'm sick."

"Go play over there, then." Rose pointed with her lips in the direction of the bulletin board.

"Callie sure is getting tall," Annabelle commented as they watched her sullenly cross the band office.

"Yeah. Like her dad, I guess."

"How's he doing?"

Rose made a face.

"Things not going well?"

"Oh, it's simply wonderful," Rose cooed. "Today he brought me a bouquet of roses and recited poetry to me while he gave me a massage."

Annabelle snorted coffee through her nose. "Not good, then?"

"The worst."

"Oh, you guys will work it out. You always do. How long you been together, like fifteen years?"

"Seventeen."

"Holy shit, that's longer than anyone I know. I don't know how you guys do it."

"I don't know why."

"Cuz he's got a big one!" Annabelle poked her in the ribs.

Rose rolled her eyes. It was a bad sign when people spoke confidently of your husband's dick size. Of course, Gilbert had a habit of pulling it out at parties when he got drunk and once at a community barbecue when he was participating in a pissing contest (literally).

Liz's office door opened and a smiling woman with a baby exited. Then Liz emerged. Liz's girth nearly filled the entire doorway. Her white Afro of curls stood out on her head like an orphan Annie wig. She was a mom to eight, a grandmother to dozens, and a great-grandmother to at least ten. Despite her big family — or maybe because of — Liz worked constantly. She'd been a counsellor for years, then chief for one disastrous term, then she had sort of fallen into the social services administrator job and stayed there forever. She'd looked tired since the early 1990s. Liz nodded at Kaylee across the band office, who then bellowed, "Annabelle!"

Annabelle hastily stamped out her smoke and then gathered up her purse, jean jacket, and baby seat in one smooth movement.

"Such a pretty girl." Rose put Mariah in her car seat and dusted the last of the ashes off her pudgy face. "Do you mind if I get another smoke?"

Annabelle opened her pack and tossed one at Rose before she hurried to Liz's open door.

Rose took a drag of her second to last smoke. She thought about joining the card table but figured someone might bring up the night before, so she kept to herself. People generally liked her and Gilbert, but a good fight kept people laughing for weeks. The teasing would go on for years.

At least her and Gilbert weren't beating each other up. He had a temper but he was never home long enough to get worked up over anything. When he was home, he was either stoned or working on his car. It was generally agreed by everyone that Gilbert and Rose were a good couple as long as they weren't together.

Then he slept with her cousin, in her bed. Rose accidentally bit down on the inside of her cheek. She pressed her tongue against the wound.

The door to the chief's office opened up. Rose examined their faces to deduce how the first Chief and Council meeting had gone.

The four councillors were the first ones out: two were old guys in their late fifties and brothers to the old Chief, Neville and Jason Bull (Jason Four). They stomped through the door with their large heads bent low as if they saw something they wanted to charge. But Tisha and Jason Akapew (Jason Five), two cousins in their thirties (Tisha and Rose had actually been in the same grade), had a bounce in their step and a freshness in their smiles that suggested a changing of the guard had occurred.

Tisha looked professional in a conservative pantsuit. Rose didn't like her. Mostly because Tisha acted like everyone but her was an idiot even though she only had a one-year business certificate that it took her three years to get. Also, Rose didn't like the how Tisha flared her nostrils all the time; it made her look like a tiny dragon.

Then Taylor exited the office and Rose exhaled so hard she nearly blew out her smoke. He walked with his head up, confident and optimistic, a few men cheered as he passed them. There were quite a few wolf whistles too. Everybody loved the new chief — this week, anyway. He high-fived the hands offered to him, fist-pumped some others, and ruffled the hair of a child standing near the card table. Then he strolled over to the coffee maker and poured himself a rancid cup of coffee like he'd been there his whole life.

Rose ate him up with her eyes. His upper body was firm and muscular, and his butt was as perky as a Christian at a church picnic.

Rose tried to find a fault. He dressed in the predictable Native politician uniform: a golf shirt and a pair of dockers. But instead of having a big belly that cast a shadow over his casual black sneakers, Taylor's was pancake-flat. Crepe would probably be a better comparison, Rose told herself, and made a mental note to learn how to make those things someday.

Rose pushed herself deeper in the couch and wished for an invisibility machine (and liposuction and a winning lottery ticket and fake boobs and, of course, a dozen cartons of smokes).

Taylor chatted behind her with Tisha. Rose heard words like "earmark" and "funding" and "applications" and "deadlines." Tisha spoke fast and used her smart voice — bossy with a faint British accent. Taylor sounded like himself: confident, calm, and smooth.

As they walked closer, Rose sank deeper into the couch, willing herself to be one with the couch, to blend into its beige slipcovers, spotted with cigarette burns.

"Rose?"

Rose's eyes went up to the ceiling and she gave a silent, sarcastic prayer of thanks to her maker. "Oh Creator . . . many thanks for making my life so wonderful, particularly this moment when I have to turn around and make conversation with someone I would rather not see for the rest of my life, yes, thank you for that."

It wasn't that Rose didn't like Taylor. She did. But she didn't want to know that there were men like Taylor out there who worked out, ate well, and didn't smell like skunk weed. She didn't want to know men actually existed who took showers without being nagged and who didn't think fine dining could happen in a Hooters.

"Rose?"

Rose took a deep breath and sat up a little straighter. She turned around and swished her long brown hair like a super-model. "Hi, Chief." A few hairs got caught in her mouth and she self-consciously pulled them away but kept her super-model smile bright.

"How's it going?" Taylor made his way over to the couch and sat on the arm next to her.

Too close, too close, too close! Her brain screamed and a wave of desire like Rose had not felt in a thousand years crashed down on her. She felt her lungs flatten and made a sound halfway between a gasp and a whinny.

"What?" Taylor looked confused.

"Okay. Things are going okay." Rose's voice came out like a throaty growl.

"How's Gilbert's band doing? He still has a band, right?"

"He sure does." Gilbert wasn't one to grow up and shelve boyhood dreams for adult responsibilities, that's for sure. "Uh, you know, he's getting a lot of gigs and touring and selling T-shirts and, y'know, rocker stuff."

"I was in a band for a few years. But I didn't have Gilbert's voice. That guy has a great voice."

"Sure does." Rose couldn't remember the last time she'd heard Gilbert sing. She was more familiar with how his farts sounded.

"What are you up to these days?"

"She works in the pig barns." Tisha moved to stand next to Taylor. The witch had an innocent expression on her face.

"Actually, I don't work there anymore. I've moved on." Rose congratulated herself on her word choice. "Moving on" sounded so much better than "got canned".

"Plus, who wants to smell like a pig barn?" Tisha laughed. Her nostrils flared extra wide when she did.

"You got that right," Rose said good-naturedly while she imagined shoving her pig-stained boots into Tisha's gap-toothed mouth.

"I'm glad to hear things are going well." Taylor smiled, and Rose wondered if anyone else could see that halo around his head.

"Yup, I'm pretty lucky." Rose pulled out her successful smile that she usually saved for Christmas recitals while standing around with other proud parents whose kids had managed to memorize "Silent Night".

The door to Liz's office opened and Annabelle scurried out with her baby.

"Rose!" bellowed Kaylee.

Rose's successful smile faded slightly.

"You're being paged by Liz," Tisha said. "Liz is the welfare administrator," Tisha explained to Taylor, as if he didn't already know.

"Well . . . " Rose mentally filed through a few different lies: "It's Rose Bull being paged," or "I'm applying for a job," or "I'm here to report a welfare fraud."

"Rose Okanese!" yelled Kaylee, and Rose decided that there wasn't any time to waste on a lie.

Rose jerked to her feet, remembered her tired legs and tottered backwards, spilling some coffee on her shirt. Taylor caught her arm, which made her blood pressure skyrocket. *Oh dear God, are you trying to kill me?* Rose thought.

"You okay?" Taylor asked.

"My legs." Rose fluttered her hand in their direction. "I went running yesterday."

"I know exactly what you're feeling," Taylor said. "That's always how I am when I'm getting back into running."

"Yes, getting back into it."

"You run?" asked Tisha, staring pointedly at Rose's tummy undulating under her T-shirt.

"Sure do." Rose made an exaggerated show of running in slow motion to Liz's office (and away from Taylor). Her efforts won her big laughs from the card tables and one half-hearted wolf whistle.

Callie joined her at Liz's door.

"In or out?" Rose asked.

"In."

Rose ushered Callie inside and shut the door behind them.

Liz sat at her big desk with a file open in front of her. Her office was scented equally with vanilla perfume and cigarette smoke. It was a welcoming smell, like walking into a freshly baked loaf of bread. Without looking up, Liz gestured for Rose and Callie to sit down. Callie bounced into a chair and Rose gingerly set herself down into the seat. Liz took a deep drag from her smoke and blew it out slowly.

"May I?" Rose pointed her lips toward Liz's open package of smokes.

"That's what they're for."

Rose grabbed a smoke and lit it with fumbling fingers. She took a quick drag. "So, how's the grandkids?"

"Fat, bossy, and wild," Liz answered. "So much energy, they make me feel old."

"Oh, go on, you're not old."

"I'm old." Liz's tone said the topic was closed.

"Yup, kids, they're a handful. I remember when this one was toddling around, those were some wild days, barely got any sleep — had dark circles bigger than black holes because

Callie could cry for five hours straight if she was in the mood."

Callie leaned forward; she loved hearing about herself.

"She's big now," Liz said. "Gonna be a tall girl."

Callie's grin approached Jack-Nicholson-in-*The Shining* exuberance.

"Yup," Rose replied.

"How's the other one? Your little beauty?"

"She's in school. High school. Doing alright." As far as I know, Rose growled to herself.

"I hear good things about her. She's real responsible."

"She sure is. Never have to worry about her," Rose lied.

"And how's Gilbert?"

Now the good stuff skids to a stop, Rose thought. "Well" — now, how to put this exactly? Rose had to be sad, but not despondent, scared but hopeful — "he's run off with that cunt Michelle."

"Ahhhh . . . " Liz made a note in the file.

"And I couldn't get to work this morning cuz he took the car and so I lost my job at the pig barn."

"Ahhhh . . . " More notes.

"And my last cheque from the pig barn won't come for at least a couple of weeks and Gilbert left me with nothing. As usual." She uttered the last part with a long sigh. Rose was always surprised at how much disappointment was stored in her lungs.

Liz looked up from her notes at the calendar beside her desk. "A couple of weeks, huh?"

Rose nodded. "And I have to get groceries — "

"And my science project," Callie added, leaning forward to make sure Liz wrote that down.

"Hush," Rose said.

Liz made another note. Then she read over the notes. Finally she looked up at Rose. "How many times have you and Gilbert broken up over the past few years?"

"Lots."

"He ever hit you?"

"No." Shook me a few times, threw a shoe at me once, and locked me out of the house during a blizzard, but Rose figured that was normal husband and wife stuff.

"You ever think of divorcing him?"

"Of course," answered Callie.

Rose looked at her in surprise. Callie looked at Rose, "You always say that. 'I'm gonna divorce his lazy ass and get a real man.'"

"I don't say that. Not always."

Liz sat back in her chair and looked at the calendar again. It was a picture of a kitten sleeping on a big dog's head. "I've been doing this job for twenty-six years. Almost as long as you've been alive, Rose, and you wanna know something?"

Not that I have a choice, thought Rose, as she settled deeper into the chair and took a drag of her smoke. On the reserve, money always came with lectures, which was why Rose tried never to rely on the band office for anything. Besides, Rose already knew what Liz was going to say. She's heard it hundreds of times from Winter, from Sarah, from credit collection agencies, from cops, and even from Gilbert himself.

"A guy like Gilbert will never change. Ever. And the longer you stay with him, the lower he's gonna drag you," Liz said.

Rose nodded. "Yeah I know, I know." And she did know, but knowing didn't make life any damn easier.

"I knew your mother, Callista," People always drew out every syllable of her name, "and this . . . is not what she would have wanted for you."

Rose blinked quickly and nodded.

"The hardest part is already done, he's gone. Now you just have to keep the door closed." Liz looked at the calendar again. "Cuz, I would hate to give you a cheque and then find out that he's back and the two of you are in the exact same situation. That would make me the third idiot in the equation, y'know?"

Rose nodded.

"So the question is: are you gonna keep him out?"

"She can't. He's got a key," explained Callie. "And one time, he climbed into the house through a basement window but he fell down cuz he was drunk."

Liz laughed. "He's lucky he didn't break his fool neck."

Rose glared at Callie and sent her a reminder look about "our business." Callie caught the look and sat back, somewhat chastened but also pleased to have made an adult laugh.

"He's out, Liz. This time it's different. Rock bottom — that's what drunks say, right? We're there."

Liz stared at her. Rose felt her cheeks burning so she kept talking to fill the silence, "My life doesn't look the best right now. I know that. But it's gonna change. I have a plan."

"What's your plan?"

"Just, y'know, do better and get a better job and, y'know, live better, eat better, work out, run." Rose could feel sweat pooling in her pits.

"Run?"

"Yeah, I used to be a runner."

"When?" asked Callie and Liz, simultaneously.

"When I was younger. Much younger."

"I didn't know that about you," Liz said. "I know your dad ran and your grandfather, but you . . . "

"It's in the genes."

"You run in jeans?" Callie looked skeptical.

"You're running now?" Liz asked.

"Went for my first run last night. That's why I'm so stiff today." Rose cracked a knee to back up her point.

"That's good. That's really good to hear," Liz said. She took a drag on her smoke. Rose leaned forward, then sat back. She wanted to borrow another smoke but knew it would affect the credibility of her running story.

Liz stared at Rose as she exhaled. Rose was wilting under her gaze but kept up a brave front. "I can see things changing for you. I see you getting stronger."

She stabbed out her smoke and pulled open a screechy desk drawer. She plopped an oversized, leather-bound cheque book on the desk. It fell on the desk like a long distance swimmer hitting soft white sand.

"Yup, I really love running," Rose said as she watched Liz make out the cheque.

Four

SARAH TOOK A DRAG OF THE joint and passed it to the teenage girl with a blue-black Mohawk and three nose rings, one of which was a large spike. Sarah was looking forward to the moment when her best friend Ronnie got sick of the goth look because she hated looking at all that nose jewelry. *How did she scratch her nose when it got itchy? What happened when she had a cold?*

"My mom is pissed," Sarah said. "I got a bad feeling this time."

Ronnie fluttered her fingers in a gesture that said Sarah's concerns were irrelevant. "We can't worry about stuff like moms and their bullshit. We have a mission." She blew a smoke ring.

Sarah hated it when Ronnie started her mission talk. She just wanted a place to hang out where she didn't have to babysit or listen to her parents fight. Ronnie's place had been perfect until she'd started all this spiritual shit.

"We totally did something this weekend. Could you feel it?"

"I threw up in my dad's car. I felt that."

"I mean before the party. Y'know, during the ceremony."

The "ceremony," yeah right, thought Sarah. They'd dug a bunch of rocks off a mound and then lit two candles. Ronnie had said it was a grave; to Sarah it looked like an abandoned anthill.

"Did you find out whose grave that was?" Sarah asked.

"My mom didn't know. She thinks maybe it was a pet's grave. But who the fuck buries their animals on the rez?"

"I buried my dog Turtle."

"That grave was like, really old." Ronnie dropped her voice to a whisper. "I think I know whose grave it was."

Sarah waited for Ronnie to finish her big moment.

"Hey, sluts!" Sarah looked over and saw the Ewchuk cousins, Jonah and Brendan, in the parking lot. The blond one was Jonah, the dark haired one was Brendan, or vice versa. Sarah had known them since elementary school and still got them mixed up. "They looked!" They laughed and high-fived. Sarah gave them the finger.

"Assholes," Sarah said, making sure they could read her lips.

"Racist pricks."

"Probably more sexism in this case, but yes, pricks. But let's get back to what you were saying." Sarah had always suspected that Ronnie had a case of undiagnosed ADD, or maybe it was all the weed she smoked — either way, she had to be directed.

Ronnie composed herself, sat up straight, pulled her collar up a bit to hide her hickeys. "The Dream Woman."

"Who?"

Ronnie was clearly disappointed that Sarah didn't recognize the name. "She was a famous healer!"

Sarah shrugged.

"Some people called her the Old Woman cuz she was old as dirt. Your mom never told you about her?"

"Me and my mom do not have long talks about old dead people."

"What about your dad?"

Sarah made a face.

"Well, me and my mom talk about stuff like that."

When she's around, thought Sarah peevishly.

"And anyway, the woman was this powerful person who could cure anything, like epilepsy and cancer and rabies. But when she died she took all her knowledge with her. All those old folks did. It's like they didn't trust our parents' generation."

"That's fair. I don't trust them, either. Bunch of fuck ups." Sarah lit a smoke and took a drag.

"But see, we're the seventh generation and we are the ones who are supposed to have the knowledge."

"And do what with it?" Sarah had been hearing about the seventh generation prophecy since she was a kid and still wasn't convinced she wanted to be a part of it. She imagined it involved wearing a tie-dyed dress and reading people's medicine wheels in a dank storefront next to a rundown Chinese restaurant. Or worse, it would somehow involve camping. Sarah shuddered.

"Help people, duh." Ronnie leaned into Sarah's face and flicked her hands emphatically in front of her. Her big breasts heaved forwards and nearly fell out of her shirt. Sarah wondered if the spirits should trust sacred teachings with someone who refused to wear a bra.

"You ever hear of doctors? Medicine? It's the twenty-first century, Ronnie, we have science."

"But it isn't worth shit!" Ronnie's eyes watered. Too late, Sarah remembered. Ronnie's dad Gary had died the summer before. Pancreatic cancer. He went lightning fast.

Ronnie sat back and flicked black nail polish off her nail.

"What do you think this Dream Woman would want us to know?" Sarah asked finally.

"I dunno. But something, definitely. You saw the candles."

The candles had flickered and gone out after Ronnie had finished her prayer.

"Could have been the wind."

"Could have." Ronnie had the same look in her eyes that Sarah got watching *The Lion King* after the daddy lion got killed.

"Wanna ditch class and go get some soft serve?" Sarah asked. Ronnie's eyes lit up. Even goths loved ice cream.

Five

"THREE HUNDRED AND SIXTY DOLLARS AND no cents." Callie held the cheque out in front of her with both hands as if appraising it under the fluorescent lights.

"It isn't a lot."

"I definitely did not say that."

Rose pushed a tiny cart in front of her and Callie walked beside her in the Ingram Family Grocery and Toiletry store (the name was bigger than the store). Rose preferred to shop at the big IGA in the valley, but Ingram's was the closest to the reserve.

"Don't be a smartass." Rose grabbed a box of no-name cornflakes and stuck it in the cart.

Callie fanned the cheque in front of her face. "How long till you can get another job?"

"Maybe the pig farm will take me back in a few days." Rose scratched her arm.

"Don't scratch," Callie said reflexively. "Maybe you could go back to school. Like finish that teaching course you were taking."

"That sounds like a good idea."

"Then why don't you?"

"Excuse me? What's with the tone?"

"I just . . . don't like you working at doing stuff you hate."

"I didn't hate it." The pigs were actually nice, smart, and playful. The teeth were scary but Rose had never been bitten. She cuddled the piglets when the other workers weren't looking. She even named a couple of them — Gilbert and Genghis — and when slaughtering time came, she hid them in a backroom. Standing in that room, while she heard the pigs being loaded up, Rose had never felt so brave or so stupid. When Suzy noticed the extra-large pigs, Rose told her that she believed they were a different breed that had spontaneously appeared in the herd. Her lie hadn't worked very long. Special breed or no, pigs were only good for one thing. Rose hadn't eaten pork or watched the movie, *Babe*, since.

Callie went on, "Cuz you were always so grumpy and then your rash kept getting worse and when you came home you smelled . . . not good."

Rose laughed. "Now that is an understatement."

"And you know what else?"

"What? You hated the way my overalls looked?"

"You never listened to me. Like I would tell you a story and you would nod but then I'd tell you again and you wouldn't remember that I told you."

"You shouldn't test people like that, that's not nice." Rose wasn't surprised. Winter had pointed it out a few times, comparing Rose to a zombie. But it was either stumbling through life half-awake, or welfare.

"There is more stuff you can do, right?" Callie had a desperate look in her eye.

"I can't get into the teaching course right now. I have to wait until fall, that's four months away."

"When do you think Auntie Michelle's gonna come get her car?'

"Probably will sneak over tonight."

"You gonna beat her up?"

"Nah." The anger had faded. Rose tried to place herself back in the room, watching her cousin's ass disappear through the window, seeing Gilbert stand there with that confused look on his bloated but still handsome face. Confused, because for some reason, he never ever thought he would get caught. Confused because pretending not to be aware was how he got away with so much.

"How do your legs feel?'

"Sore."

"Remember when you used to coach my soccer team?"

"Yeah, little cuties all running after the ball, scoring on your own goalkeeper. God, that was funny."

"You were kind of skinny back then."

"Well, I kind of thank you for that compliment."

"And you could run fast too, I remembered."

Rose made a mental note to explain tenses to Callie again. As soon as she refreshed her own memory of them.

"Probably seemed fast to you because you were six."

Callie pulled a piece of paper out of her pocket and unfolded it. She flattened it with her hand.

"What's that?" Rose glanced at the paper. She saw the words Pesakestew across the top and a cartoon picture of a road-runner wearing a feather. The feather seemed sort of redundant.

"It's for the marathon; you know, the one my grandpa won."

"Is that here already?"

"It's in two months. Or eight weeks. Or sixty days." Callie said.

"Thank you Rainman." Rose took the paper. "My dad used to drag me to that all the time. Even after he stopped running. Do you know how boring watching a marathon is?"

"It says the first prize is a brand new car, a Toyota Yaris, and one thousand dollars."

Rose whistled. "Wouldn't that be nice? Well I guess Dahlia Ingram will enjoy that." Rose handed the paper back to Callie.

"Who's she?"

"She's Mr. Ingram's daughter. She's won the marathon for, well, I don't even know, she just always wins. They ought to rename the marathon after her. She even beats the men who enter."

"Why don't you enter it?"

Rose laughed. "Yeah, right. Do I look like I can run fifty miles?" She pointed at her tummy hanging over her waistband and grabbed a handful of it for good measure.

"It's only twenty-six miles."

"Only twenty-six!" Rose hooted. "You really are my funny daughter."

Callie smiled for a second, happy to be better than Sarah at something.

Rose stood in front of the ice cream freezer. Weren't people supposed to eat ice cream when they broke up with their boyfriend? And Gilbert was her husband, so shouldn't she be allowed to eat even more ice cream?

"We can't afford it," Callie said, and pulled on her mom's sleeve.

Rose looked at Callie in shock. "A kid who doesn't want ice cream? What kind of freak are you?"

"We have to be practical. Ice cream is nothing but empty calories and we have to be frigid with money."

"Frugal."

Rose pushed the cart to the front. Mr. Ingram stood there staring out the window.

"Hello, Hans." Rose stacked her groceries in front of him. "Watcha looking at?"

"Tyler Horton at the drug store is staring out his window and I'm trying to figure out what he's looking at."

"Oh, maybe there's" — Rose was at a loss — "a bird walking down the street?"

"Could be, but why would Tyler care? Maybe he's thinking of shooting it. I wouldn't put it past him — that miserable English bastard! Go back to England and your stupid queen!" Hans made a fist at the window.

He turned back to Rose and noticed Callie. "Why's the little one not in school?"

"Sore throat."

Callie coughed for good measure.

"Oh there's lots of that going around. Try some honey with lemon in it. Always worked for my girl."

"Oh right, Dahlia. She getting ready for the big marathon?"

"Of course, she's always training for one race or another. Did you know there's a big race in Japan? A marathon — on those tiny little islands. I asked her if they have to travel by boat from island to island but she tells me they run around and around a single island."

"I think it feels bigger the longer you're there," Rose said.

"Like being inside a classroom," Callie offered, and then coughed.

"I suppose. I wish she would stay home for a while, but she's got to run every race she sees."

"She'll be home soon, Hans."

"September is not soon."

"What about the Pesakestew marathon?" asked Callie.

"Oh she doesn't have time for that one, she'll be running in Antarctica — no, that can't be right — Armenia? Does Armenia still exist? God knows what those communists are up to over there."

"I don't think they're communists anymore."

"They aren't? Socialists?"

Rose shrugged.

"Well, it's somewhere. She's sponsored, you know. Heineken."

"My dad drinks that!" said Callie.

"Must be nice to get paid to do something you love," Rose said.

"That reminds me, can you ask Susie to double my bacon order next month?"

"I don't — yes, I'll tell her," Rose said.

"But you don't work there," corrected Callie.

"What happened? Were you fired?" asked Hans.

"Um . . . yes."

"Why?"

"Layoffs," Rose said.

"Goddamn corporations, shipping all our jobs overseas, handing them over to foreigners," said Hans, forgetting that he was a Swedish man talking to a First Nations woman.

"I'll find something else."

"Where?"

"I'm sure someone's hiring."

"I haven't heard that. In fact, I heard that the bar had to let their waitress go and now the bartender, Ralph, is running it himself. Not a good idea, of course, he's such a drunk — and the Lee family at the gas station let go of that Korean girl that was working for them, so it's just the couple now. Can you drive a combine?"

"Maybe."

"The big farms will be hiring combine drivers, but that's in the fall."

"I'll practice all summer, then," Rose said. "Thank you for your help."

"I just want to keep people off the damned welfare. It's a horrible thing, makes people lazy like goddamned sheep. So how will you be paying?"

Callie placed the welfare cheque on the counter. Rose gave Hans a crooked smile.

∾

Rose parked in front of Lowell High School and stared at the big green doors. A couple of students stood outside puffing on smokes. *Lucky little bastards*, she thought. *Bet they don't even buy their own smokes.*

"Why are we here?" asked Callie.

Rose checked her watch. "It's almost three; I'm going to pick up your sister."

"Oh, she'll love that," said Callie.

"Ha ha. You coming in?"

"I'm sick, remember? No, I'll lie down in the backseat and take a nap."

"Fair enough."

∾

Rose walked through the corridors. She dragged her hand along the lockers. Sarah had biology as the last class of the day, which was in Mr. Walker's room at the end of the hall.

Rose peeked in the window and searched through the students. There was Sarah at the back of the classroom. Staring out the window. So beautiful. Rose wasn't one of those mothers who assumed her child was gorgeous just because she pushed it out of her vagina. Sarah had been turning heads since she was an infant. Rose had even become bored by the compliments, "Yes, thank you," "Takes after her mother, thank you," or, "No she's never modelled, but maybe someday."

Sarah wasn't dumb, either. She'd always done well in school, yet she drifted through life with her head hanging down and her feet dragging like an extra in a zombie movie. It made Rose want to scream sometimes, "You are amazing! You are so lucky!"

Rose had worn braces in high school, had large cyst pimples on her cheeks and wore the same pair of jeans every day. She didn't even know that people didn't do that until a girl in her class had asked, "Is that like the only pair of jeans that you own?" Rose had skipped school the next day. Her only goal during high school was to graduate, go to university, and never come back. Then Gilbert appeared and Sarah happened and things got complicated. From university acceptance to a pig barn: the Rose Okanese story.

The bell rang, or more like buzzed. Students closed their books and dipped beside their desk to slip them into their book bags. Sarah took her time. A teenage boy bumped Sarah deliberately and gave her a grin, which she ignored. "Good job," whispered Rose, "you make them work for it."

The students piled out and laughingly strolled past Rose, not even noticing her by the doorway. Sarah was the last student out the door.

"Sarah."

Sarah started, then glared at Rose. "What are you doing here?"

"Picking you up." Rose turned on her heel. The teenagers were making her nervous; she suddenly felt very aware of the large man's jacket she was wearing and also the fact that she had worn it to work in the pig barn. Don't sweat, she told herself, don't sweat.

"You don't trust me?" hissed Sarah behind her.

"Now that is the understatement of the year." Rose waved to a couple of teachers she recognized in what she hoped was a confident, carefree manner as she weaved around the students filling the hallways.

"You really make me sick, you know that," Sarah whispered.

"No, boozing and drugging it up makes you sick," Rose hissed back.

"I'm not going to do it again!"

"Said the spider to the fly . . . "

"What the fuck does that mean?"

"It means . . . that you're luring me in and that you're tempting me with your dead flies and . . . I forget what it means but goddamn it, there's no law saying I'm supposed to believe you." Rose felt her blood pressure climbing into the rafters. How did this kid make her so angry, so fast?

They reached the front doors and Rose nearly dropped to her knees in relief. They had made it through the school with no major embarrassments. She glanced at Sarah, she was pouting.

"I came to get you because I don't want you slipping off. And I hope you appreciate the fact that I didn't try to embarrass you," Rose said.

Sarah unwrapped some gum and put it in her mouth.

"We're going to go home, make dinner, and have a long talk about your life and what I expect from you," said Rose. She admired her strong, confident tone — she was nailing this mother thing today.

"Yeah, because you have your life all figured out," mumbled Sarah under her breath.

Rose wished there was a way to backhand someone under your breath.

She wiped her brow. She was already tired and she hadn't even begun to harangue Sarah. Rose stopped suddenly. The car was gone. Had Callie moved the car? When did Callie learn to drive?

"Over here," Callie yelled from the opposite sidewalk.

Rose looked over. Callie stood there surrounded by their bags of groceries.

Rose ran across the street. "What happened?"

"Auntie Michelle walked up to the car and told me to get out. So I did. And then she was going to drive away and I said,

'What about our groceries?' So she took them out and left me here."

"That fucking . . . fucking . . . " Rose searched for a word.

"Bitch?" offered Sarah.

"Cunt!" said Rose at a higher volume than she intended. A group of teenage boys hooted.

"I'm sorry, Mom," said Callie. "Should I have stayed in the car?"

"You did the right thing. I mean, she's your aunt, you didn't know she was a total fucking whorish bitch that deserves to get punched in the face with a pitchfork."

A few teenagers clapped. Sarah's homeroom teacher was opening her car door and turned to give Rose a horrified look.

"Mom, cool it," Sarah said.

"I'm sorry Mom. I should have called her a bitch for you," said Callie, her eyes teary.

"Don't worry, you'll get another chance, I'm sure," replied Rose.

"How are we getting home?" asked Callie.

Rose looked in the direction of the schoolyard where the school buses were lining up. "Pick up some groceries, we're taking the bus."

Callie picked up a bag of potatoes and tottered away. Rose grabbed four bags and nodded at Sarah, "Well, grab the rest."

Sarah glanced at the school and the crowd gathered there, smoking cigarettes and laughing.

"Thanks for not embarrassing me," Sarah said as she stooped to pick up the remainder of the grocery bags.

༄

Rose set the plates on the table and called the girls for supper. Callie ran up to the table and sat down.

"Go eat in the living room."

"Why?"

"I want to talk to your sister," said Rose.

"Oh . . . well shouldn't I be involved? I mean, I'm also a part of this family. And I am also not impressed with her behaviour."

"Don't be a pest."

Callie laughed. "I just wanted to say that I am not impressed. 'I'm not impressed.'" She laughed and grabbed her plate and walked into the living room.

Rose sat down and began to eat. She needed nourishment for the battle ahead. Though why was it a battle? Why was talking to Sarah something that demanded all her energy? Because it was Sarah. And she couldn't fuck this up like she had fucked up everything else.

Sarah sauntered into the kitchen. She grabbed herself a glass of water and leaned against the counter.

"Can you sit down?"

"No."

"Are you going to eat?"

"I'm not hungry."

"You need to eat. You need food to survive."

"Hamburger Helper is food?" Sarah raised an eyebrow.

"I'm sorry that I don't have any foie gross for you to feast upon."

"Do you even know what foie gross is?"

"It's butter. A special French butter." Rose said. Sarah looked at her sideways but Rose could tell she didn't know, either.

Rose smiled despite her annoyance and then pushed her smile away. "No more drugs," she said, launching into her speech at the midpoint — why did she always do that? — "No more drugs, no more parties, no more sneaking off, no more nights with friends, period."

"So just nothing, ever?"

"Until I can trust you again. You really fucked up, Sarah."

"Why do you always have to be so dramatic?"

"Because you don't think!"

"I think!"

"Not about the big stuff! Like what you're putting inside of your head! It doesn't get any bigger than that!"

"Dad does drugs!"

"He also screws your aunt! Are you gonna do that, too!"

From the other room, Callie snickered.

"Stop listening, you brat!" yelled Sarah.

"Don't yell at her," said Rose.

"Your favourite."

"Compared to you? Yes, she is my favourite. Because she doesn't scare the shit out of me, for one thing," said Rose.

Sarah sipped her water. "So I'm just a prisoner now, I never get to go anywhere or do anything?"

"Get your grades up, help out at home, and then we'll talk. But I catch you doing drugs again and it'll be a lot worse."

"How could it be worse?"

Rose honestly didn't know. Send her to live with her father? Rose didn't even know where he was. Call the police? Rose had never seen that work yet. Military school? This is Canada, there probably are no military schools — maybe a peacekeeping school? But Rose didn't want to send Sarah away. Please let this work, she prayed to the gods of parenting, because I have nothing else. "Oh, it'll be worse, trust me. Now, sit down and eat."

"I'm not hungry," Sarah said. She held her arms close to her and her small shoulders rounded as she walked down the hallway, turned into her room, and closed the door behind her.

It did not escape Rose's notice that she had just laid down the law to Sarah and she had defied her at her first opportunity, but she had no more energy to fight and shovelled a forkful of processed food into her mouth instead.

"Can I come back to the kitchen now?" asked Callie.

"Sure."

Callie set her plate down, in Sarah's regular spot. Kids never missed a chance to piss each other off, Rose observed.

"She got what she deserved," Callie said.

"Mind your own business."

Callie chewed on her food for a few seconds and then swallowed. "So what am I going to do my science project on this year?"

"Your teacher didn't give you a topic?"

"The topic is science."

"When is it due?"

"In a month, it's like fifty percent of my mark."

"What!"

"I know. Mrs. O'Watch is on drugs or something."

Science had never been Rose's best subject. She didn't care how things worked, she just wanted them to work. "How about worms? You can cut them in half and show them wriggling in two different directions?"

Callie looked at Rose as if she were a worm. "Cutting up worms? You actually did that?"

"Not for a science project, just for fun . . . and curiosity. And they do survive."

"Yeah, but what kind of a life do you have with only half your body?"

"I don't think worms have exciting lives to begin with. So now it's only half as exciting," said Rose.

Callie put her fork down and looked into Rose's eyes. "How are we going to survive without a car? How are we gonna get groceries? How are we gonna go to get mail? Or what if we have an emergency? Or what if I want to stay late for soccer?"

Rose looked down at her plate. Good questions, all of them. "I'm going to call Winter."

"Okay, that sounds like an idea," said Callie. "It's a start."

"You're starting to annoy me, Callie."

Callie put a forkful of hamburger into her mouth. "What about a volcano?" she asked.

"Overdone. Maybe if you put some ants on it and then they can get run over by the lava."

"Mom, we're not allowed to kill things. But a regular volcano will get me at least a B."

"Good point, but expensive."

"Maybe there's a way to make a real volcano out of stuff around the house?"

The two of them glanced around the kitchen.

"Maybe you'll get a job right away," Callie offered.

"Maybe."

∿

Winter stopped by after work, still wearing her scrubs. Callie ran and threw her arms around Winter's waist as soon as she walked into the door.

"Why didn't you call me last night?" Winter asked, dragging Callie behind her.

"It was too late. Callie, get off your aunt."

Callie made an indistinct reply from behind Winter's back. Rose sometimes worried that people thought she never gave Callie attention from the way she acted when people came to visit.

"It's never too late when it comes to you and the girls. I've told you that a hundred times. Where's Sarah?"

"She's in her bedroom."

Winter pried Callie's hands off of her and then headed down the hallway and knocked on Sarah's door.

Rose went to the coffee-maker and poured two cups of coffee. Rose would rather Winter not get involved when it came to Sarah, but there was no stopping her. Working at the hospital, Winter had seen what happened to kids doing drugs too many times.

Winter emerged from Sarah's room. "Teenagers," she said with disgust.

Rose grunted.

"How are you getting to work tomorrow?" Winter asked.

"Susie fired me. So that's one less thing to worry about."

"That bitch."

"I can see it from her point of view. I'm constant drama. I'm late all the time, I have to leave early, I take time off for doctor's appointments for Callie . . . even in a good week, I'm trouble."

Winter sighed. "Is that what I have to look forward to?"

Rose turned and studied her friend; Winter was trying hard to restrain her grin and then it broke free: "I'm pregnant."

Rose whooped and threw her arms around Winter.

Callie ran into the room, "What's wrong?"

"Winter's pregnant! I'm going to be an auntie."

"Oh, that's nice." Callie attempted enthusiasm. "Really nice." At least one kid announced their mom's pregnancy on Callie's school bus per week.

It's a big deal! Rose wanted to say but couldn't. Winter's years of waiting and crying phone calls to Rose at 4 AM were too private, too recent, and too sad for eight-year-old ears.

"Your uncle Monty and I have wanted children for a long time," Winter explained.

"Why?"

"Because people love kids."

Callie looked unconvinced, but asked, "So, what are you going to name it? Can you name him Justin?" Callie had papered her wall with Bieber's posters.

"I don't know the sex yet."

"You could call it Biebera if it's a girl. I just made that up." Callie grinned at her own joke.

Sarah was in the kitchen suddenly. She moved so silently, Rose never knew where the hell she was. "Congrats," she said, and squeezed Winter's shoulder. That was Sarah's version of affection.

"Don't you get any ideas," Winter teased. "I don't want you even thinking about kids until after you've graduated from law school."

"Why would I want any? I already half raised this brat."

"Hey!" Callie and Rose said in unison.

"What's that supposed to mean?" Rose asked.

"Yeah, I raised myself," Callie said.

"No, I raised you," Rose replied. "Do you honestly think that you did more work than I did?"

"I babysit a lot is what I mean," Sarah said.

"I never go anywhere. And your dad is always home if I'm not."

Sarah stared hard at her. "Remember it how you want, then."

"But I'm remembering it right," Rose said. "I am," she added to Winter defensively.

"We haven't told our parents yet, so don't say anything for a while, okay?" Winter said. "We're taking his out to dinner this weekend and we want to surprise them."

Rose said. "They're gonna piss themselves. Finally a grandchild for them to spoil!"

"Nobody spoils me," Callie pointed out.

"It's not always about you, pisshead," Sarah replied.

A push-fight commenced; Rose was forced to intercede.

∾

Winter and Rose sat on the front steps; Winter cradled a cup of chamomile in her hands while Rose sipped a coffee that she would regret at bedtime.

"Did you talk to him yet?"

"No."

"Do you know where he is?"

Rose sucked some coffee off her front teeth. "They're probably at his brother's house on the west end. Chuck's girlfriend left him last year and so he's got that big house to himself. It's *the* party house, I hear."

She took a cigarette out of her pack and lit it.

"I wish you wouldn't."

"Oh sorry." Rose stamped the smoke's head into the steps and then put it in her pocket. She felt the tip of it where it was still warm. "I don't know what I would say to him even if he did call."

"You know how I feel." Winter's hatred of Gilbert had never wavered. It was as reliable as the tides.

"It's going to be hard without him."

"Without him? When was he ever here? And when he is here, he's stoned out of his head. Sarah can't stand him and he just makes a mess out of the house."

"Did she say that?" asked Rose.

"You have to start communicating with her better. In two years, she'll be gone and you'll never see her," Winter warned.

"Promise?"

"Rose."

"Girls are not easy. You better hope for a boy."

Winter smiled and then looked out at the empty yard. "You're better off without him."

"Yeah, I know."

"But would you take him back if he asked?"

Rose thought about Gilbert, his smile, his big shoulders, the way he drove a car with one hand and the other arm out the window, his hand playing with the wind. She thought about seeing him underneath the hood of the car, making miraculous repairs to a vehicle that was more dead than alive.

She thought about waking up at night and then hearing him snore and falling back to sleep.

"You're taking too long to answer," observed Winter.

"You don't know how it is, Winter. It's next to impossible to raise these girls without another cheque or without someone to help me out. You'll see."

"He doesn't give a shit about you or the kids," Winter said quietly.

"He's my husband," Rose said.

"Only on paper."

Rose picked up her smoke and brought to her lips and then remembered and stopped herself.

"Here's something — why don't you call him and ask for child support?" Winter asked. "If he says yes, then you know he cares about you and the girls but if he makes excuses then you know he's the same old selfish bastard he's always been and then you can pay me five dollars to kick him in the balls or I'll pay you, whatever you prefer."

"He isn't working regularly," Rose said.

"He always has money for pot and booze, doesn't he?"

Rose nodded reluctantly. "That's sort of how it goes when you're an addict," she joked.

"I can ask him for you," Winter said. "Nothing would make me happier than telling that piece of shit off."

"Wow, I hope Monty never pisses you off."

Winter gave Rose a look that said she was not impressed with the comparison.

"So what about a job?"

Rose shrugged. "Not much I can do without a car."

"True," Winter said. "Unless you work at the band office."

"I don't want to work there."

"Rose. A job's a job."

"Yeah but, Taylor works there now. "

"So?"

"He's . . . he's really fucking cute and I can't be myself around him, you should see how I sweat. I would have to take constant cold showers to get through the day. I can't be around him. I don't know if I can be around normal people at all actually. I miss the pigs."

"You're an idiot."

"I know."

"I hear they need a new supervisor for the daycare program."

"I'm not qualified." Of course, kids couldn't be much harder than pigs.

"You got a year of a teaching degree. Better you than some brainless idiot with no experience who got the job just cuz of whose daughter she is."

"Yeah."

"Well?"

"I'm going to apply! God, quit being so pushy for once in your life."

Winter smiled. "I want my baby to have the best godmother." She stroked her belly with her hand. Rose groaned inwardly. Winter was going to be one of those pregnant women who pawed their stomachs, bought an entire maternity wardrobe, and fretted over her baby name until the second she gave birth. Rose had alternated between two pairs of sweats and two hockey jerseys, picked the baby's name the second she saw their bawling red face, and charged a dollar to touch her stomach.

Winter sighed happily. "I can't believe I have a person growing inside of my body. I feel so grateful, so wonderfully grateful."

Rose rolled her eyes. "Wait till the hemorrhoids start, then it won't be so goddamn magical."

Six

Drayden
David
Delaney
Mackenzie
Dustin
. . . these were Winter's top choices for a boy's name.
Halle
Asia
Chloe
Danika
Brittany
Ashley
. . . those were her top choices for a girl. She went over
the pros and cons of each name as she scrubbed her kitchen
counters. Would it be okay for their kid to have more than
four names or would people think that was pretentious?

Monty had made some noise about Jack for a boy and
Cindy for a girl but Winter had already eliminated him from
the baby-naming process.

"You get to choose when you can give birth to something
the size of a watermelon," she told him. He complained that it
was unfair and she promised him choice of second name but
only if it wasn't stupid, like Tiger or Maximus.

Ten years she'd waited for this moment and now it was here. She felt like she should be on *Oprah* telling everyone, "Dreams really do come true, you just have to have faith!" with a big shit-eating grin on her face.

No matter who she told, nobody understood, like really understood, what was happening: she, Winter Yuzicappi-Okanese, was going to have a baby!

Out here pregnant females were ubiquitous. People had babies even when they hadn't planned for them and then they'd announce, "Yup, just got knocked up again," as if they were announcing that a new mole had appeared on their arm instead of the world's most miraculous occurrence.

In a few months maybe she'd be like them — blasé about her big belly and wide, flat feet. But Winter didn't think so. Even if she never mentioned it to anyone, she'd know. She'd know what she'd gone through, what *they* had gone through. It wasn't only her that would stand in the bathroom and weep with the fan on.

People must know how happy she was. She felt light on her feet and a smile had been sneaking onto her face the whole day. She got cut off in traffic, one of the orderlies ran over her foot with a gurney, and the chicken salad sandwich she had for lunch was mushy, but none of it mattered.

She had a tiny being inside her that would be hers forever. A little bit of Monty, a little bit of her, maybe even the grandparents would show up here and there. Having a baby was real magic.

She went over the doctor's appointment in her mind again. She had called Monty before she saw him. "I'm going in now," she had reported to him.

"Call me as soon as you know something," he'd replied. "As soon as you know."

"Of course. Okay, I'm going now. Bye." She hadn't bothered telling him that she'd already done three over the counter tests and littered a public washroom with three positive sticks. (He would have been a little annoyed about the wasted money. The tests were twenty bucks a pop. And yet he spent over two hundred bucks on a pair of golf shoes!)

"What do you think?" she'd asked Dr. Brighten after telling him about the indigestion the night before.

"Food poisoning?"

"My breasts feel tender."

"That could be your period too."

"Don't I look different?" Winter had asked.

"Are you asking me if you 'look' pregnant?"

"I guess so."

Dr. Brighten looked her up and down. "Actually . . . "

"What?"

"You do have a certain — "

"Glow?"

"Don't get your hopes up, Winter. I don't want to see you going up and down like this. It's important to be patient and cautious."

Winter had nodded dutifully, but it was too late. Her heart was already slamming in her chest.

Dr. Brighten had given Winter a quick exam and sent her to the lab for blood work. Winter had chatted happily to Ingrid, who took her blood, and then stood waiting at the counter to hear the result. Ingrid returned a few minutes later with a big smile on her face.

"So it's for sure?" Winter had asked.

Ingrid nodded.

Winter took out her cellphone and pressed redial.

"What?" Monty sounded breathless.

"Yes."

"Holy shit."

"Yeah."

"Holy shit." Monty took a deep breath and then yelled off the phone, "I'm having a kid!"

Winter heard some cheering on the other end. She'd rather he hadn't announced the contents of her uterus to a bunch of hungover construction workers, but hearing him say it made it even more real.

"So I'm pregnant."

"Wow."

She'd turned to face the wall. On it was a poster showing what happened when you quit smoking. It took seven years but somehow the body managed to bounce back. There was light at the end of the tunnel after all.

"What do you want for dinner tonight?" she'd asked, grabbing at something to hold onto.

"I'll grab some takeout. What do you want?"

They had decided on Boston Pizza, and then Winter got off the phone. She took the elevator back to her floor. Normally she'd have felt guilty for having spent two hours on a doctor's appointment. But she didn't care if they fired her. Not that day.

Winter hummed as she finished cleaning the counter. She made a mental note to buy organic cleansers the next time she was in the city.

Then she turned on the dishwasher and went to turn out the kitchen light. She noticed Monty's cellphone lying on the counter. The battery light was blinking so she picked it up to go plug it into the charger. It drove him crazy when his cellphone died at work; he said it was because he needed to have a phone if there was an emergency on the job site but Winter figured it was because he was addicted to Tetris.

Winter scrolled through his text messages to make sure that he hadn't texted any of his family. He told her he wouldn't but he was notorious for getting carried away in the moment. Winter wanted to do this right, not that usual helter-skelter way his family carried on. Pregnancies announced at funerals, serious illnesses announced at baby showers and the like. His family had the bad timing of Jehovah's Witnesses.

She saw a dozen messages from herself and then a woman's name caught her eye, "Aislyn." She clicked on it. There were quite a few messages from Aislyn. Winter didn't remember Monty mentioning an Aislyn before. A new secretary? She read a few messages and her heart started beating faster. "U r hawt," Aislyn wrote. "U are to," Monty wrote back.

"It's 'too,' idiot," Winter said. She read further. There was more awkward flirting and atrocious spelling.

Winter flung his phone across the room and it hit the dining room wall. It wasn't loud at all, which surprised her.

"Monty!"

Winter remembered that he was in the garage. She shoved her feet into her slippers and banged through the door.

He stood in front of his truck motor, his hand on his hip, another hand holding a screwdriver. In the background, she could hear Derek Miller howling through his sound system.

"Who's Aislyn?" she said to his back.

Monty's spine did some crazy things. First he slouched like he expected a shoe to the back of the head, then he straightened as if reminding himself that he had to play it cool. But he most definitely did not turn around.

"She's the flag girl at work." He laid on a heavy layer of casual.

"Really? A flag girl? Isn't that just fucking great?"

Monty nodded to the hood of his truck.

"You sleep with her?"

He turned slowly. He was white with dots of hot pink on his cheeks. He shook his head. Then, he said, "No." Then, "Absolutely not." Then, "What?"

"You talk like that to all your co-workers? You send 'I want to fuck you' texts to Randy?"

Monty half-smiled. "No, cuz he'd probably take it seriously."

"What the fuck, Monty?"

He stared down at his feet.

"Are you in love with her?"

Monty scoffed. "Of course not. It's nothing. It's just a buncha texts . . . "

"Then what is this? Explain it to me." Before I hit you in the face with a wrench, she wanted to add, but restrained herself. No sense in letting him get prepared. Where did he keep the wrenches again? God, why was this garage always a mess when she explicitly told him to keep it organized?

"Okay. Well, Aislyn is a flirty girl and — "

"So it's her fault? You're blaming the fucking kid?" Nothing made Winter more angry than seeing the young girl get all the blame by some old fart with piggy thoughts.

"I'm trying to explain, Winter."

"Can you? Can you really explain? We've been married for fifteen years. Fifteen fucking years and you're flirting with some little ho? How old is she?"

"I dunno."

"Oh fuck you, you know."

"I got carried away. But it was just a distraction. A stupid game."

"A game," Winter said quietly.

Monty opened his mouth but decided that silence would serve him best. He nodded grimly.

Winter picked up the tool closest to her hand (it was a hammer) and flung it. It hit the passenger window and a deep crack appeared.

"The fuck, Winter!"

"I was aiming for your head."

Monty swallowed.

Winter turned on her feet and walked inside the house. She wanted a glass of wine but obviously that wouldn't do. She put her hand over her tummy.

She poured herself a glass of milk and forced herself to drink it.

∾

That night, Winter had a dream. She was walking through a playground. There were children playing all around her, making those chattering sounds that are equal parts laughter and yelling. She knew that her child was there: a little girl with black hair like Monty and curly like hers. She saw a spare swing and sat on it. She kept an eye out for her daughter but she could only catch glimpses of her disappearing behind the other children.

Winter leaned back in the swing and pumped her legs. She had always loved swinging.

She heard footsteps and expected to see Rose standing there. Rose showed up in her dreams a lot; she intruded upon her waking hours, so why not the sleeping ones, too? But it wasn't her. Winter looked up and her eyes met the face of an older woman. Well, not older, just plain ol' old. Lines had set decisively in her face and no Oil of Olay or extreme plastic surgery could ever restore smoothness. But where most elders got smaller and frail as they aged, this woman glistened with power and strength. She sat down on the swing next to Winter. Winter's nerve endings told her to run but her mother's conditioning forced her to stay put. She's just an old lady, she told herself, who happens to have wicked bicep muscles. Maybe she's on hormone replacement therapy and they gave her too much testosterone. Winter waited for the woman to speak.

They sat like that for a while and Winter felt herself grow stronger, as if she'd taken a hit of caffeine. The longer she sat on the swing, the stronger she felt. Like if she tried, she could crack a rebar over her knee.

When she woke up, Monty had already left for work. "Good thing," thought Winter. She poured herself some cereal and milk and felt her dream strength drain out of her as she stared at the empty chair across from her.

She reached for the phone and dialled Rose's home number. Or, her only number. Rose was the only person Winter knew who didn't have a cellphone. It was on a long list of things that she could not have while she stayed married to Gilbert and his horrible credit. Winter sighed and held the phone to her ear. It rang and rang and Winter held the phone to her ear long after the sound began to annoy her.

Seven

"SQUEEZE OVER, CALLIE," ROSE SAID.

"Mom, you can get your own seat, there's lots," Callie complained.

"They're for the students," Rose said. Not for people who couldn't afford cars and so had to catch a ride on the school bus.

Callie groaned but moved over in the narrow black seat. It seemed to Rose that these seats were a whole lot bigger when she was kid. Now her butt was hanging over. She glanced behind her. Sarah sat in the last seat, her head on the window and her white ear buds proclaiming her disconnect from the world.

"You comfortable there, Mrs. Rose?" asked Jimmy, looking at her in his giant rear-view mirror. A young-looking forty, Jimmy had been driving bus since he was eighteen years old. Everyone thought he was crazy to take on such a lame job when he was so young but now he owned four buses, had multiple bus routes on the go, and kept half his family employed. Despite his success, Jimmy was still the same kind, gentle person he had always been. (Except, of course, when the wild Indians got out of control on the bus — then you could count on Jimmy to set them straight.)

I should have married someone like him, Rose thought. She and the other girls used to make fun of his big chubby cheeks; they called him Jimmy Chubbs (they weren't the most original group of girls ever assembled), now every one of their husbands was fatter than him.

"Yeah, I'm okay," Rose replied. "I appreciate you picking me up."

"I can't take you all the way to the band office but I can drop you off pretty close," Jimmy explained. "You're lucky it's warm out."

"I am the luckiest person I know." Rose laughed. Jimmy looked at her curiously in the mirror but made no reply.

What would luck mean to someone like him? she wondered. Someone who made simple choices and then carried them out? Not like Gilbert, who had "Nashville or Bust" tattooed on his arm.

Not that dreaming simply was a recipe for success. Her own dreams hadn't been complex or ambitious: kids, a happy marriage, and a career as a teacher. She got the kids right but the rest went to hell and Rose wasn't sure what she'd done wrong.

Callie tapped her on the shoulder.

"You gonna apply for your job back at the pig farm?" asked Callie.

"I hope it won't come to that," Rose replied. "I'm aiming a bit higher this time."

"Like a singer?" Rose made a mental note to cut down on Callie's TV viewing of *American Idol* and Bieber videos.

"I'm applying for a job at the band office," Rose whispered.

"Why are you whispering?" whispered Callie.

"Probably a lot of people want that job, that's all," Rose said. "There aren't a lot to go around."

"The Chief should invent more, then."

"I'm sure he's gonna try to, but it isn't as easy as that. You gotta have something for people to do."

"How about oil? Oil makes people rich."

"Oil doesn't grow here."

"Why not? Oil comes from dinosaurs. Dinosaurs lived everywhere, including here."

"They did?" Rose asked. "Well if any oil companies start up, I'll apply for those first."

Callie frowned. "You say that a lot, you know. Like if someone starts something, then you'll join. But you never want to start anything yourself."

"You know, Callie, there is a limit to the amount of advice I will take from a second grader."

"I'm almost in third."

The bus slowed to a stop.

"Mrs. Rose, here's your stop," Jimmy called.

Rose stood up and made her way to the front. "Thanks, Jimmy," she said.

"Good luck. Not that you need any more!" He laughed.

Rose echoed his laugh and stepped off. She watched as the bus drove away and turned down the road to the band office. Her legs were still sore but a good kilometre walk should get rid of that.

❧

Rose stopped outside the band office, she tried the door. It was locked. She looked in the window, the lights were out.

She caught a glimpse of herself; all wild hair and a sweaty face. She smoothed down her hair and wiped the sweat from her forehead. A shiny black car pulled into the parking lot. She inwardly cheered.

Then she noticed who was inside the car. Taylor was on the phone and waved at her.

Rose straightened. Don't be embarrassed, she told herself, don't be weird.

"It's not open yet?" Taylor stood on the side of his car, leaning over it. "I guess the secretary isn't a fan of punctuality."

"Who is?"

Taylor gave her an annoyed look. "I am."

"I'm joking. Kaylee is highly unprofessional and should be whipped with the business end of an extension cord."

"Better." Taylor waved her over. "You should wait in your car, it's a bit nippy out here."

"Nah, I'm fine outside," Rose replied.

Taylor looked around the parking lot. "Where is your car?"

"I walked."

"Your car break down?" Taylor asked.

"I felt like walking." *Why are you lying?* Rose's brain yelled at her.

"Huh. Well, get inside, I don't want you to get cold."

Rose opened the passenger side. Her knees cracked as she sat down. "Cold out here," she said loudly, to cover up the sound.

"So you seeing Liz again?"

"I'm here to apply for the daycare position."

"That's good cuz Liz was a no-show yesterday afternoon."

"Really?"

"It was bad. There were people freaking out wanting to see her. I called her cellphone, her home phone, her kids — nobody knew where she went."

"That isn't like Liz."

"That's what everyone was saying. But then I checked her computer and saw all these emails from Costa Rica."

"What did they say?"

"I'm not sure. They were in Spanish. Do you read Spanish?"

Rose shook her head.

"Anyway, I think maybe Liz took off to Costa Rica."

"That's nuts."

"I don't know. Her family is pretty big and she was complaining about her kids wanting this and that and Kaylee said that her ex-husband was banned from the band office."

"Right, because he keyed her car because she didn't pay for his lawyer when he got sued for keying someone's car." It was well-known gossip from a few years ago.

"Well, maybe she got sick of it all and decided to make a break for it."

"Maybe. But that is fucked up. Liz *is* the band office," Rose said. Then she remembered who she was talking to, "I mean, she's been here longer than any one of us."

"I know. Nobody has earned a break more than her, but it makes things very hard for me. Y'know, new council and all and now I've got to find a new social administrator asap."

"Be careful who you put in there. You can't put a Bull in there cuz they'll blackmail all the other families. And you can't put an Akapew in there cuz they'll just screw over the Bulls. Gotta choose someone else. Maybe an Adams or a Horse. Course, most of the Horses live off-reserve. And people don't like that. Makes them feel judged. You don't want to go too young either. Or too educated. You don't want people to feel like someone is talking down to them."

"Jesus. Who's left?"

"There'll be someone. Course, you don't have a lot of time to look around. Welfare day is on Friday, so hire someone right away or else your council is gonna be buried. Did you ask Kaylee? She knows the job inside and out."

"I believe her exact words were, 'Fuck that shit.'"

Rose smiled. "Sucks that you had to face this in your first week."

"I'll figure it out. So, I heard about you and Gilbert. Must be hard."

"Yes, we're having some marital problems, but we'll probably work it out," Rose said.

"Someone told me he was making out with Michelle in the Lowell bar."

Rose felt like she'd been gut punched. This was probably reflected on her face.

"Sorry, I thought you knew."

"No, I knew. But I thought . . . Well, the thing is, I didn't think. I put it out of my mind. Like, I'm not even sure where he's staying. Course, that's probably a good thing cuz then I won't be tempted to go over there with a sawed-off shotgun in the middle of the night."

"He's not worth it."

"Plus I don't even know how to saw off a shotgun. Or why you'd use a sawed-off one instead of a regular one."

"It's so you can tuck it into a coat."

"Oh, I never understood that."

"You must be pretty angry at him — at them."

It was hard to stay angry sitting in a warm car next to a man that smelled of Polo cologne. And what was this leather? Soft and brown, Rose felt like licking it. She kept her scaly elbows away from it, afraid they would scrape it. While she'd been driving a car with fabric seat covers that smelled of gas, dust, and McDonald's fries, the rest of the world had discovered leather. What else had she missed?

"I am mad, but what can I do? I don't want him back but he is my husband and it's embarrassing."

"Do you really care what people think?"

"No. Maybe a bit. I have kids and I don't want them getting their feelings hurt."

"It's better to know. That way you don't keep hoping."

"We had some good times. He was there for me when my mom passed. Not that that was one of the good times, but you know."

"I understood what you meant."

"And Michelle, the cunt — well, she's a grass is greener person; even as a kid she was never happy with anything she had. She could have the prettiest, most expensive doll, and she'd still steal mine. But I dunno, maybe they'll be happy together, I mean as happy as a cunt and an asshole can be . . . "

Stop talking, Rose. "But you know, I've moved on."

"You're handling it better than I would."

"Have you ever been married?"

"Almost. But then I caught her cheating on me."

What kind of a crazy bitch cheats on a man as fine as him? Jesus, they were making women dumber all the time. "I'm sorry to hear that . . . " Rose paused to leave some space for Taylor to fill with details.

He didn't.

"How's the running going?" he asked.

"The what?"

"Your training?"

This was probably the best time to come clean. He'd be the only witness to the knowledge that Rose was a lying lazy shit who only had enough energy in the evenings to walk from the couch to the cupboard for more chips.

Instead she heard this coming out of her mouth: "It's okay. I don't do it every day though."

"You shouldn't, you'll do yourself more bad than good."

"Yeah, that's what I thought." Rose liked how his brow furrowed when he gave advice.

"So the big race is coming up pretty fast."

Rose had no idea what he was talking about. Race? Was that an election? Oh right, the tribal council elections. Was Taylor already planning on leaving the band for the big leagues? Rose's heart sunk. Of course, there was no chance the reserve would keep a guy like this for long.

"So you're running?" she asked.

"I've been thinking about it. But I'm not sure about my knees. I'm not sure I can rely on them."

"Well, I'm sure people will understand if you're not one hundred percent." Was that a joke about ass-kissing?

"Yeah, but I hate it when I can't do my best."

"Isn't running mostly about getting people to like you?"

"What are you talking about? I'm talking about the marathon that you're training for."

"Oh right. That's what I was talking about, too. The marathon." Rose cringed as another chance to come clean slipped by.

"Running's tough on the old bod, that's for sure."

"Especially yours," she joked.

"I'm not that old yet, Rose. We're the same age, remember?"

"Excuse me? I'm six months younger."

"Oh really, a whole six months?"

"That's half a year, old man."

"I had such a crush on you," Taylor looked at her sideways.

"You did?" Rose felt a gush of stress sweat under her arms.

"You and pretty much all of the grade two class. My mom called me the elementary school Romeo. I handed out valentines to every single girl, and little chocolate kisses. I can't believe my parents didn't stop me from making a fool of myself."

"That's a little wussy. But adorable." Rose remembered seven-year-old Taylor. He'd been skinny with long black hair always done up neatly in two braids. "I liked your braids."

"Yup, they were just like yours."

Rose took a deep breath. "To be honest, I had a crush on you, too."

"Liar. You used to torture me."

Rose laughed. "I did not."

"You told me to lick the monkey bars on one of the coldest days of the year because it would taste like a Popsicle — "

"That was a scientific experiment! — "

" — then when I got it stuck, you asked me if I liked you. And you kept saying, 'Taylor, if you don't tell me that you like me, my feelings will be hurt'." He said the last part in a sing-song six-year-old girl voice.

"Wow. That's a little sociopathic."

"I can't believe I tried to answer. Ripped half my tongue off. I learned a valuable lesson about girls that day — never tell them how you really feel," he laughed.

"You should be thanking me for that," Rose replied. "So, did the skin grow back?"

"Most of it. I still have a dent here in the middle." Taylor stuck out his tongue and pointed to it. Rose noted a small dip and also two rows of beautiful white teeth. How could the inside of someone's mouth be sexy?

"Maybe that's the part of the tongue that tastes sour milk, so I actually helped you out."

"That would also mean that I drink sour milk all the time," Taylor observed. "It's getting cold in here."

Taylor started the car and fussed with the heater a bit. Rose watched the muscles on his forearm bulge and her eyes moved up his arm to where his bicep and triceps muscles strained under his shirt. Rose felt another surge of sweat. If they stayed in this car any longer, she would die of dehydration.

"It's funny how you forget all the bad stuff you do to other people and then remember all the bad stuff that people do to you and carry it around like an ugly purse," she blabbed.

"You don't strike me as that type," Taylor replied. "You seem like someone who takes life by the horns. Dumping your husband and training for a marathon. And you have kids too. Three, right?"

"Only two that I know of. Two girls — a sixteen-year-old and an eight-year-old."

"I hear it's always good to have them in pairs. So they can look out for each other."

"If either of them knew how to hire Russian assassins, I'd only have one child."

"I always wanted siblings. I'm surprised your parents didn't have more."

"Rez families are big families. My parents tried but they got nothing — "

"Well, you."

"Yes, their pride and joy. I guess it was kind of a blessing they couldn't have more cuz my mom died so young."

Taylor looked at her. "Sorry, I forgot about that."

Rose shrugged. Even people on the reserve forgot sometimes. Out here, it was fathers that came and went; mothers were rooted to their families like trees.

She looked out the passenger window. There were bright, puffy balls of pollen floating in the wind. "I wasn't a kid, I was sixteen. And I wasn't alone. My dad did his best. Monty was always like a big brother to me and I guess Winter is like my sister. And there was Gilbert." She sighed, "So it all worked out."

"Are Monty and Winter running the marathon too?"

Rose snorted. "Not in this lifetime."

"So you're doing it on your own then? That's even more impressive."

Okay, time to put this lie to bed. Rose took a deep breath, "Well I'm not . . . "

"Finally!" Taylor slapped his hand on the steering wheel.

A shiny red Cavalier pulled up beside them and honked its horn. Kaylee waved graciously from her front seat.

"Looks like we're open for business." Taylor glanced at his watch. "And it's only 9:25," he added dryly.

"That's why we call it Indian-time," Rose said. "See, nobody else was fool enough to show up this early."

"How can you expect a band office to be efficient if we don't open on time?"

"We don't. That's why we call it a band office." Rose gave him a playful punch and then lunged out of the car, her bravado quickly turning to abject fear.

∾

Rose clutched her purse on her lap and faced the firing squad in front of her. *Gum, I wish I had gum,* she thought. That Nicorette stuff. Or Juicy Fruit. Or something plastic to chew on — a pen cap would hit the spot.

She had submitted her resume to Kaylee who had passed it onto Taylor. She was about to head out the door for her five kilometre trek home when Kaylee told her to sit down for a bit.

Rose had joined the card players and listened as they theorized as to the approximate location of Liz's Costa Rican condo and whether or not she had an island lover.

Then Kaylee had tapped her on the shoulder and told her to head over to the boardroom. That's when she saw the assembled people, "You sure they meant me?" she asked Kaylee in a panicked voice.

Kaylee bumped her with a hip and sent her stumbling into the room.

She glanced at the four people assembled in front of her — Tisha, Jason Four, Jason Five, and Neville. Did all of the councillors have to attend? Seemed like a waste of their time. It was only a daycare job.

"Good to see you all." Her voice was as weak as kitten.

"We're not started yet," Tisha growled, without looking up from her Blackberry.

"Oh. Maybe you should have a starter pistol or something," Rose joked. Nobody laughed. The Bull boys were busy tapping on their smart phones. Tisha pulled her cousin Jason close to whisper back and forth over some document in front of them.

Rose studied the faces in front of her. Two Bulls and two Akapews. There was an equal number of both families on the reserve and probably quite a few of them applying for the same job as her. Not only did she lack the advantage of nepotism, she'd never been hired for any full time job on the reserve (she had been the interim community gardener and the interim janitor before she was replaced by people who knew how to play politics better than her). She didn't have a chance in hell. She had a better chance of tearing Brad Pitt away from Angelina Jolie than getting a full time job on the reserve.

Taylor entered in a rush. His energy filled up the whole room. Everyone sat up straighter.

"Sorry 'bout that, Indian Affairs wouldn't get off the phone. Good news, though, looks like the playground funding is untangled."

Tisha clapped her hands like a trained monkey. The other men nodded and smiled through gritted teeth. Good news, but it meant that Taylor's week-old administration had already surpassed the previous council.

"That's cool that you're already making things happen," Rose said, just to drive the point home.

Taylor waved his hand as if to say, "It's nothing," and sat down across from her.

"So the job of the daycare coordinator is filled," he said.

"Oh." Rose fought for control of her face; her smile was sliding down into her neck and she fought to keep it at chin level. "That's good. Really nice for whoever got that job. But uh . . . why am I here then?"

"As you know, Liz is gone and we need the position filled immediately," Taylor said.

"And you need someone to clean her office?"

Taylor laughed. "You have a crazy sense of humour."

"Wait, am I interviewing for Liz's job?" Rose searched the faces of the councillors but they were as stoic as the bronze eagles sitting in the trophy case behind them.

"You're one person out of *many* that we're considering," said Tisha. "Obviously it's a great job and we're not going to give it to just anyone."

"Oh, for sure." Rose was mentally calculating her wages per month minus her new car payment minus a set of new school clothes for the girls.

"So, do you have any experience in administration?" asked Taylor.

No. That was the most accurate answer. But Rose's momma didn't raise no fool. "I have some experience working in administration, yes."

"Can you elaborate?" asked Tisha.

"I — uh . . . administered for the pig farm."

"Pigs require a lot of administration?" sneered Tisha.

"Well, there's paperwork — invoices, inventory, order forms — actually there's a lot. I mean, that wasn't my official job there. But sometimes my boss would get called away, like for her emergency tonsillectomy because she swallowed a loonie and then there was that time she went to Florida and didn't get back for three weeks cuz she fell in love with this Cuban bodybuilder — " Dumb, Rose.

"And so during these incidents, I was expected to step up and fill in for her. Otherwise people couldn't, y'know, get their pork."

The male councillors laughed at the word pork.

"Sounds like experience to me," said Taylor leaning back in his chair.

"How are you gonna handle it when people accuse you of favouring your family members?" asked Neville.

"Family? I don't really have a lot of family on the reserve. I mean there's my dad but he's got a pension from the mill and there's my cousin Michelle — the cunt — but the only thing she'd be getting from me is a punch in the throat. I don't really know who I'd be accused of favouring."

Neville nodded.

"Sounds good to me," Taylor said.

"But Taylor, this is . . . we should really be discussing this further, posting the job — I mean, how will this look?" Tisha's brow was furrowed as she struggled to keep the anger out of her voice. Rose got the feeling Tisha had already promised the job to a family member and she didn't envy her having to deliver the bad news.

"Liz left this week, we get someone to start tomorrow, I think that it'll look like the chief and council don't waste any time." The other councillors nodded. Rose nodded.

"But, Rose is just a. . . " Tisha began.

She wanted to say "a loser"; Rose could tell. But she couldn't, and it was killing her. Rose grinned.

"Rose is university educated and has experience. That's what I see," Taylor said. "I don't understand your reservations."

The male councillors snickered at the word reservations.

"Of course," Tisha replied.

"Let's vote on it!" Taylor raised his arm, the other three men did the same. After a brief hesitation, Tisha flicked her wrist upwards. Taylor grinned at Rose. "So, when can you start?"

"This afternoon?"

Taylor laughed. "I like that eagerness! But you can have a day to get ready."

He looked so sure of himself that Rose started to feel confident herself. *Maybe I can do this job,* she thought.

"By the way, everyone, Rose is running the marathon in June. I mean, what a role model!"

Neville laughed out loud. "What? Are you crazy Rose?"

"Just a bit," Rose replied.

"People die running those things," Tisha observed.

Taylor frowned at Tisha. "That's not very encouraging."

Tisha tried to remember what encouragement looked like and forced an expression of somewhat hopefulness on her face. "Well, I just don't see Rose as the running type. Can people walk the marathon?" she asked Rose.

"I guess so, but that'd be a damned long walk. I'd probably die of boredom."

"What kind of training program are you on?" Taylor asked.

"I'm doing . . . y'know . . . training runs and . . . um . . . wind sprints . . . and uh . . . eating healthy, that kind of thing. It's a system. I don't want to bore you with the details. I'm pumped though, really pumped." To stop herself from babbling on, Rose stood suddenly and held her hand out to the councillors.

Tisha's handshake was weak and her teeth nearly broke as she squeezed out, "Congrats."

Taylor held out his hand to Rose, "Congratulations, social services administrator."

"So that's it?" Rose shook his hand and looked around the room half expecting someone to start laughing and say, "Just kidding!"

"That's it," said Taylor.

Wow, thought Rose, *even the pig barn made me go through three interviews.*

The rest of the afternoon was a blur. There were HR forms to fill out, dirty jokes from Kaylee to laugh at it, "congrats" to receive from the gang playing cards in the lobby, and glares from Tisha to ignore. Before Rose knew, it was four and the office was packing up. It was time to mooch a ride off someone. But the ton of coffee Rose had was weighing on her so she rushed to the bathroom one more time. When she returned to the lobby, everyone was gone.

She stuck her head in a few offices, hoping to see a hardworking soul who left at five after four. But there was no one. "Hellllooooo," she called, and the sound echoed like she was a ghost. She went to the front door, typed in the security code, "password," and then pushed open the big heavy doors. She had a nice long walk home and it wasn't going to get any shorter standing here staring out the window.

༼

"I don't know what to wear." Rose sat heavily on her bed; the springs protested with a slow moan. "I mean, what outfit says, 'hey loser, gimme some freakin' child support'?"

"Wear this." Winter pulled a low cut T-shirt out of Rose's dresser.

Rose made a face. "Too slutty. Plus it makes my gut fat show."

"Put it on." The T-shirt flew across the room onto Rose's lap.

Rose took off her "interview" blouse, the only one she had with a collar and no stains. She squeezed into the T-shirt. She hadn't worn it since before Callie was born.

A one-inch thick roll of belly peeked out from beneath the T-shirt. Rose shoved it under the T-shirt and it rolled back out. She looked up at Winter, annoyed.

"Put a jacket on, nobody will even notice your rolls."

"They'd have to be blind to miss them — " Rose began as a blue torpedo flew into her face. She held it up in front of her. "A jean jacket? You know I'm wearing jeans. Everyone will say I'm wearing a Native tux."

"Put it on."

Rose struggled to button up the jacket. She had bought it nearly a decade ago. It had been a halcyon period in which she had lost all of her pregnancy weight from Sarah (it took her eight years) and she had been working as the community gardener (which of course meant that she had to do all the work at the community garden). During those five weeks, she'd gotten down to her lowest weight ever. She bought a tight jean jacket and went out to celebrate with Gilbert; a few weeks later, she found out she was pregnant with Callie and the jacket was banished to the back of the closet.

Winter surveyed her. "You still have great tits. How did your kids not suck you dry? I heard that's like, a thing."

Winter had been researching motherhood since she was a teenager. She had folders even. If Rose let her, she would have photographed and made detailed descriptions of symptoms for every single month of her pregnancy with Callie. Rose felt that nine months with Sarah was more than enough.

"They were dainty eaters." Rose rolled onto her back and stared up at the ceiling. It was dirty. She rolled onto her side. "This is pointless. I don't need to go, I have a job now, I don't need Gilbert. Plus, he hates being bothered when he's performing."

"Yes he's quite the artistic genius. Must take a lot of concentration to sing about a piece of ass and doing tequila shots every night."

"Tequila Pussy hit number two on the Saskatchewan charts for three days," replied Rose.

Callie sang from the hallway: "Tequila flows so thick and juicy makes me want to lick that — "

"Callie!" Rose yelled and then found herself out of breath. "I'm having trouble breathing." She undid a button of her jean jacket.

"Rose! Focus! You can't walk to work every single day! What if it rains? What if it's cold?"

"Someone always comes around," Rose mumbled. Though of course she had walked all the way home today. She'd never seen the rez roads so desolate. She shivered.

"You need a car, Michelle and Gilbert have two and that's not fair. Plus he should pay child support — they are his kids! Fuck."

Rose smiled. When Winter swore, it never sounded right. Her F-bombs sat at the end of sentences like guard dogs without teeth.

"Yeah, we're his kids," said Callie. She had slunk into the bedroom during the exchange and was now perched on the edge of the bed.

"I like walking." Rose stood up and her knees cracked.

"That's not the point! I don't want something bad happening to you because that selfish bastard wouldn't help you out. I'm sick of men getting away with everything!" Winter's chest heaved.

"Calm down Mommy, your baby will be born with colic," Rose said.

"That's an old wives' tale."

Rose twisted the bedspread in her hands. "Michelle's gonna look great and I'm going to look like a piece of shit. Everybody will say, 'Well, that's why he left her, she's a big fat cow'."

"Fat is a bad word," Callie intoned.

Winter tapped Rose on the head, and not gently. "You're going."

Sarah looked in, "Going where?"

"To the bar of course!" Callie proclaimed.

"It's not an 'of course,'" Rose corrected her.

"Why are you dressed like that?" Sarah looked pointedly at her mom's cleavage.

Rose shrugged. "I dunno. To fit in?"

"Because she looks damn good," Winter replied.

"I look nuts."

"Enjoy your curves because you're going to lose them once you get back into running shape."

"What? How did you hear about that?" Rose had studiously avoided mentioning the race to Winter in case she tried to weasel out of it. Winter's integrity had forced her to do many things in the past: paying parking tickets, apologizing for running over someone's dog, and then apologizing for trying to pass off a similar-looking dog as the dead one.

"People were talking about it at the hospital. Everyone is really . . . What's a word that means proud, incredulous, and amused — all at the same time?" Winter snickered.

"I don't want people talking about me."

"Don't be Native then." Winter said flatly. "Okay, ready to go?"

"I guess I'm babysitting again." Sarah's tone suggested that she was exasperated to be occupying the moral high ground yet again.

"Oh right, can you babysit your sister?" Rose wished cleavage worked on teenage daughters.

"I don't need a babysitter! I'm nine years old for God's sake!" Callie protested.

"Don't yell, Callie. And you're eight. So, is that okay, Sarah?"

"As if it matters," Sarah pointed out. "You're already going!"

"If it makes you feel any better, I'm not expecting to have any fun. This is purely a business decision."

"Oh yeah?" Sarah looked suspicious.

"I'm going to get the car from your dad and ask for —

"Demand!" Winter's expression was set to extreme assertiveness.

" — child support, if he's okay with that."

Winter let out an exasperated sigh.

"Fuck him. I don't want anything from that asshole." Sarah slammed the door. A second later, they heard her bedroom door slam behind her.

"I could come with you, Mom," Callie said, "I could sit in the car and read comics."

"Yes, that would look great for the new welfare adminis-trator. 'Is that your kid in the parking lot?' 'Oh yes it is, Officer,'" remarked Rose. "I'd be the first social services administrator who had their kid taken away by social services."

"I just realized this: You, Rose, are a person of power," Winter mused.

"Yes I am," Rose said as she dusted a heavy serving of blush between her boobs.

∾

Lowell's Hotel Bar and Chinese and Canadian Food Restaurant was run by a Greek couple, Adonis and Sandra Papadakis. They'd taken over from the other owners, two brothers who had picked up and left just before the police raided them for selling crystal meth.

Adonis and Sandra were Lowell's first Greeks and more importantly, its first swingers, and they took their position seriously. They leered at everyone who entered their establishment and extended frequent invitations to the upper floors where all kinds of swinger stuff went on.

For the first few months after the Papadakis couple arrived, it was big gossip about who walked up those stairs, but now nobody really cared. Lowell's swingers were old news.

The bar was packed as it always was on a Saturday night. Lowell Bar was the perfect choice for those wanting to get a little drunk and be a little glamorous but not be all full of yourself while doing it.

Rose and Winter wound their way through the crowd. Rose noticed a large mural of Greek ruins over the bar. "That's new."

"Looks like they're trying to class up the old dump," Winter said.

"Nah they just put it up to cover the bullet holes," said Kaylee, who was perched on a bar stool next to them.

"Who shot at who?"

"You know that young white cop who had the pretty wife with the big lips?"

"Corporal Emory?" Rose had bet Winter twenty-five bucks that the lips weren't real, but neither of them had the guts to ask her.

"Yeah, well, he brought his gun in here one night and saw Adonis talking to his wife and well, you know, shit happens."

"Did he get fired from the force?" asked Rose.

"Nobody reported it. Besides, she was just trying to get back at him cuz he went upstairs with Sandra. You know, games." Kaylee finished her beer in one long swallow.

Adonis stepped in front of Winter and Rose, "Ladies, what can I get you? Beer, wine, or a bite of my spanakopita?"

Adonis was old, fat, and bald, but that in no way impeded his confidence. Also, his moves seemed to be working. Rose had heard his name being giggled over in the band office more times than she could count.

"One Budweiser and one cranberry juice," said Winter. "And your spanky can stay in your pants."

"You don't know what you're missing," declared Adonis as he twisted the beer open. His tone conveyed sincere pity for them.

With practiced ease, Winter and Rose leaned back against the bar. They were in the sweet spot. The stage was directly ahead. It looked ready to go even though there was no one on the stage yet. They could see every table around them, five or six people packed at every one of them. They could even see the bouncers standing by the exits, their Popeye arms folded in front of them.

"Band do a set yet?" Rose asked Kaylee.

"Nah, and I hope they don't. Fucking Gilbert and Runaways suck shit if you ask me. No offense Rose."

"None taken," Rose said. "We broke up, you know."

"Yeah, I heard that. Plus I saw your cousin, Michelle — "

"The cunt."

"Yeah, she was sitting on his lap. I gave her a look but she pretended like she didn't see me, dumb twat. You gonna kick her ass or what?"

Rose shook her head. "Not my style."

Winter's laugh suggested she didn't think Rose had a style.

"I'd kick the bitch's head in, but that's me." Kaylee finished her beer. "Adonis get your sweet fat ass over here!"

Winter looked longingly at Rose's beer. "I wish I could have a drink."

"Only eight months to go."

"Seven."

"How's Monty, still out of his mind over the baby?" asked Rose.

"I haven't talked to him much lately," Winter replied.

"He busy with work or something?"

Winter put her hand on Rose's arm. "Over there," she said, and pointed.

Rose's gaze followed Winter's finger down its length, then it jumped across the crowd. It flew passed a few middle-aged couples, more nosy than out to have a good time. Then it veered around a couple of teenage girls who'd snuck in and soared over three old dudes checking out the teenage girls while sucking in their bellies. It danced over two rubbies a few years away from full-blown cirrhosis to a table left of the stage, where Gilbert held court with his band.

Michelle sat next to him. She wore a red shirt and matching flower in her hair. That was something Michelle would do — wear a stupid flower as if she was hanging out in a swanky nightclub instead of a bar in the middle of nowhere-fuck Saskatchewan. Despite what Rose had said to Kaylee about being over it, Rose felt her fighting juices well up. She didn't even know she had them!

Like an identical twin, Winter didn't even need to ask if Rose was ready, she just started moving. Rose put her shoulders back and followed. She could feel her biceps filling with blood, getting ready to dole out a well-deserved beating.

Rose could see the back of Gilbert's big square head through the crowd. Winter reached him first.

"Hey, stupid." Winter planted herself in front of him. Gilbert sat up straight.

"Oh, hi Winter . . . oh, you brought . . . hi Rose." Gilbert glanced around, looking for exits and such. Seeing that none were close, he grabbed his beer around the neck, took a sip and smiled.

"Give Rose your car," Winter demanded.

Gilbert laughed. "Not gonna happen. It's my car, not hers. I gave her the kids and the house, fair is fair."

"No, dumbass, fair is child support — but I doubt you can support yourself on what Gilbert and Losers make in a year," Winter said.

Gilbert's band members looked grumpy but said nothing.

"Why doesn't Rose speak for herself?" asked Michelle. Perhaps it was a shadow from the stupid flower in her hair, but Rose thought she saw the hint of a smirk on Michelle's face. Whatever it was, it pushed Rose over the edge.

Rose lunged at Michelle, knocking her off her perch. They both hit the floor with a thud. The crowd parted with practiced ease.

"Fight!" someone called out helpfully.

"Help!" screamed Michelle from underneath Rose's bulk.

Michelle could yell all she wanted. There wasn't anyone who would stick up for her. The general code for female bar fights was that men stayed out of it. The way the men figured it, it was always better to have two women at each other's throats than at theirs. Plus two women scrapping meant there was always a chance for random boob flashes. (There had been the legendary Bra Scrap of 1993 in which two women had fought in the parking lot for fifteen minutes in nothing more than a lacy black number and a heavy-duty white maternity bra. That night was still reminisced about on cold prairie nights.)

As for the women in the crowd, a woman who stole another woman's man deserved no mercy. The only women who might step in to help you were your own relatives, and since Michelle had stolen her own cousin's man — well, she was shit out of luck.

Rose wrestled Michelle's arms to the ground and put her knees on top of them. Michelle bucked like a wild horse but she was already half-cut and much smaller than Rose.

"Get. Off. Me. You. Fat. Cow!" hissed Michelle.

Rose slapped her in the face.

"Hey now, get off of her," said Gilbert. "It's not even fair." He half-heartedly reached for Rose's arm and Winter slapped his hand away.

"Gilbert!" screamed Michelle. "Gilbert!"

"Hit her again!" yelled Kaylee, who had found her way to the front of the crowd.

Rose stared down at her cousin. Michelle avoided her eyes and kept looking at Gilbert.

She and Michelle used to be more girlfriends than cousins. When they were teenagers they used to walk around the city fair together, flirting with the carnies and sharing cardboard containers of fries.

"Why are you such a bitch?" she asked Michelle.

Michelle's eyes welled up. "You're hurting me!"

"Don't you care about your nieces?"

"I love them!" Michelle wailed. Then she began crying for real, with hiccupping tears and everything.

Rose let go of Michelle's hands and stood up. She held out her hand to Gilbert. "Car keys."

"Fuck you," Gilbert said. "It's my car."

"I need the car to get to work, Gilbert. So that I can feed your kids."

"How do I even know they're my kids?" Gilbert said belligerently.

Rose's mouth fell open and she froze, so Winter slapped him for her.

"Bitch," Gilbert growled, so Winter slapped him again. Her hand went back, she seemed to be on some kind of roll, but he grabbed it and jumped to his feet.

Rose inserted herself between them. "Don't, she's pregnant."

Gilbert dropped his hands. "Sorry . . . uh . . . congratulations to you and Monty."

"What's going on here?" a deep voice asked. Rose turned and looked into the light brown eyes of Lloyd Okanese. They were soft eyes, but they always made her feel small.

"Hi Dad," Rose said.

Gilbert sat down and busied himself with his beer.

"You and your fella break up again?" asked Lloyd.

"Yeah, and he ran off with Michelle and he took the damn car!" yelled Winter.

"I'm old, not deaf," said Lloyd. He looked at Gilbert. "This true?"

"Lloyd, I got a show in fifteen minutes, I don't have time for this," Gilbert said.

"I guess you have to make time," Lloyd said. "Give her the keys."

"How the hell am I gonna get to gigs?"

"You got five band members, you'll figure something out. The keys."

Gilbert was at least four inches taller and twenty years younger than Lloyd, but he still refused to stand up. With his broad shoulders and formidable belly, Lloyd had a powerful look about him.

Gilbert threw the keys on the table. Winter grabbed them fast as a mongoose and laughed in Gilbert's face. "Thanks fuck face!" she yelled. Then she whooped a few times. Her enthusiasm was infectious and a few people high-fived her.

Rose stared at Gilbert, who was pouting now. She looked at Michelle, who was halfway across the bar repairing her red flower.

Rose looked down at her hands, which were red from Michelle's lipstick. She wiped them on her jeans.

Rose bumped into Lloyd as she walked away from the table. "Why are you here anyways?" she asked. "I thought being in a place like this went against your beliefs."

"I had a feeling I should be here," Lloyd said. He looked down at her with a curious look on his face. "When did you get so fat?" he asked.

Rose glared at him. "What kind of question is that? Besides, I'm not the only one who lost their girlish figure." She stared pointedly at his pregnant belly.

"I was surprised," he looked away from her and then said to the wall, "You gonna be okay, then?"

"Yeah," Rose replied, and then in an effort to rescue both of them from their mutually created awkward moment, headed toward Winter.

Rose was unable to put her thoughts into order. Things were happening a bit too fast: husband, no husband, job, no job, then job; car, no car, then car. Why couldn't things slow down a bit?

A hand tapped her on the shoulder, Rose looked up into Taylor's handsome face. She made a sound that was halfway between a grunt and hello.

"Can I talk to you outside?" he asked.

∽

Taylor was wearing a black polo shirt and jeans that fit exactly the way jeans are supposed to fit. When Rose's eyes finally made it to his face, she noted that he did not look happy.

"Do you know how this makes me look? You were my choice."

"I know. Sorry."

"Stop hanging your head, I'm not your dad."

Rose picked her head up slightly but avoided his eyes.

"I don't like this whole timid rez thing you're doing."

Rose laughed despite herself. "Is that what I'm doing?"

"Yes, you're making me feel like a bully!"

"Sorry, it's just that lots of times people won't believe you're sorry unless you look sorry."

"I guess. But don't do that with me, okay?" He rubbed the back of his neck. "So that was Michelle?"

"Yeah."

"She looks pretty good for someone who just got sat on."

Rose made a face at him.

"But of course she's a horrible person and that makes her really ugly. Gross even," he amended.

"That's better."

"So is this done or do you think you ladies will be throwing down again? Wait, is this normal for you?"

Rose shook her head. She stared at the corner of the bar. It was dull red brick, chipped away by time, drunken brawls, and drivers that ought to have had their keys taken away. Rose sighed.

"What's that sigh?"

"I never had a job before where it mattered what I did."

"I didn't mean to make you feel bad."

"Yes you did!"

Taylor grinned. "Well, maybe a little bit. I might have freaked out." Taylor looked embarrassed. "I didn't expect to see you rolling around like you were in a women's prison."

"I didn't even think I was mad at her. I mean, she helped me get rid of a total loser — I should be thanking her." Rose remembered the scared look on Michelle's face. "It felt like hitting a bad child that didn't understand."

"I don't want to be in a position where I have to choose between protecting the band office and protecting my friend."

The word reverberated around her head and then flew out her mouth: "Friend?"

"Aren't we?"

Rose tore at the label of her beer. "I want to be your friend," she said finally. "But I don't understand why you'd want to be mine."

"To be honest, you're the only person who isn't related to a family that's out to get me," he laughed.

"Can I ask you a question?" asked Rose.

"No, I don't dye my hair. Well, maybe a little frosting," he added with a smile.

"Why are you here?"

Taylor shrugged, "What the hell else am I gonna do on a Saturday night?"

"No I mean why are you back on the rez?"

"I could ask you how come you never left."

"I did leave. For six months. Now answer my question."

"Six months? What happened there?"

"My question first."

"I always knew I was coming back. I'm not a city guy, no matter how hard my parents tried. Plus, I got tired of reading about our reserve in the news. Figured I could do better," he said. "Of course, now I'm realizing it's a helluva lot hard harder than I thought." He stuck his hands into his pockets. This made the muscles in his arms bulge like a carpenter on HGTV. Rose had a desire to run across the space between them and launch herself into his arms. She'd always wanted to try that but the fear that the guy would take a step backwards instead of catching her stopped that madness.

The back door to the bar opened and Winter peeked out: "Rose?"

"Yup."

Winter spotted Taylor. "Oh, hi Chief! Didn't see you there."

"Hello, Winter. I heard the news. Congratulations!"

"Thanks."

"I'll be there in a second," Rose said.

"Be where? I'm not in any hurry," Winter said.

"Don't you have work tomorrow?"

"Nope." Winter was lying.

"I believe you are mistaken."

"You're definitely wrong. Stay where you are and continue talking." Winter closed the door behind her.

Rose rolled her eyes. "We have to go."

"Why aren't you sticking around?" asked Taylor.

"I don't know if you noticed, but it's my ex-husband's band playing and he's sleeping with my cousin, and maybe I'm crazy, but I can't handle that much happiness in one night," Rose said dryly.

"Have a good night then. And be good."

"Ha! All I want to do is curl up on my couch with my girls and watch TLC for the rest of the year," she said and finished off her beer. "Beware of the Greeks."

"Bearing gifts?" asked Taylor.

"More like baring a big dick."

"What?"

"You've been warned." Rose tried to look sexy as she headed up the stairs to the bar.

Eight

ROSE WOKE UP WITH A GOOD feeling. What was it? Was it the feel of her baby girl curled up beside her? Was it the heat through the window that said it was going to be a warm day? Nah, it was knowing that there was a car in her driveway and that for once, she had gotten the best of Gilbert. "Yes," Rose said and stretched long and hard. About five seconds into the stretch, her right calf seized up and she stared at the ceiling in agony, holding her breath and staying rigid until it ebbed away.

"Time for coffee," Rose limped into the kitchen, noting that limping into the kitchen seemed to be a way of life these days.

Sarah sat there eating cereal with a math textbook open in front of her.

"Wow. You're up early."

"Where else would I be? I went to sleep at 9 PM, unlike every other person on this fucking reserve," replied Sarah.

"Any coffee?" asked Rose.

Sarah nodded curtly.

"Oh good, thanks," Rose said and limped to the counter to pour her coffee. As she mixed in the cream and sugar she thought about a few thousand things she could say to Sarah — thank you for being here, thank you for listening to me, I'm sorry, I wish I was your age again because your skin looks amazing, I love you, your dad is awful, I hope I haven't screwed you up in any permanent way because all I've ever wanted is the best for you, I wish I knew how to be the kind of mother you need, please, please don't leave me . . .

Rose settled for "Good coffee."

Sarah turned a page of her math book.

Rose limped back to the table and sat down.

"How's math class?"

"It's algebra," corrected Sarah.

"Oh, right. I forgot all about algebra. I used to like it, though, all those quadratic equations. I heard Lisa Loeb used to do quadratic equations to relax."

"Who?"

"Lisa Loeb. A singer. She sang some song about . . . people and changing the world?" Rose was at a loss. "She wore cool glasses, y'know, as cool as glasses can be." Rose added. Sarah was looking at her like she had a penis growing out of her head. This was the longest conversation they'd had in a long time. "Hey, did you notice the car outside?"

"Is he back too?" Sarah's eyes went from cold to accusing in 2.5 seconds.

"No," said Rose. "And he isn't coming back."

"Really?"

"Really."

Sarah shrugged her shoulders as if to say I'll believe that when I see it.

"Looks like our luck is changing," Rose said.

"It's not luck that's the problem," Sarah mumbled.

"Something wrong?"

"I'm trying to concentrate so I can get good grades so I can get into university and the fuck away from this reserve and its collective low expectations," Sarah explained.

"That's nice." Rose stirred more sugar into her coffee though it didn't need it. Then she took a long sip, put it down and stood up.

"Okay," she said.

"Okay what?"

"I'm ready for my run."

Sarah didn't even bother looking up. "Right."

Rose didn't answer. She was already in the closet, rummaging through the shoebox looking for her sneakers. There they were at the bottom, the laces grey with dirt. She knocked them together and dried mud fell off. She noticed a hole in the netting of the left one, shrugged and laced them up.

"If I'm not back in an hour, call an ambulance," she said as she walked out the door.

Sarah stared at her.

∾

Running was hard, Rose decided three steps into her run. In theory it was as simple as putting one foot in front of the other, slightly faster than a fast walk but in practice it was this horrible jiggling mess of limbs and flesh. And, her neck hurt. Why?

Rose felt a churning in her stomach, like the morning sickness she used to get with the girls, and if it hadn't been nearly a year since the last time she had sex with Gilbert then she would've suspected that she was pregnant.

"People do this," she grunted under her breath. "This is not a big deal." Her lungs sucked back air in mighty gulps. She kept her legs moving and remembered to hold her arms loose but firm. "Pump your arms to go faster," she whispered. Her arms pumped and her legs obeyed.

Rose was surprised. There was life in these old bones yet. She came upon the four-way stop that no one ever used as a four-way stop, preferring to motor through and hope for the best. Rose silently acknowledged that it was the farthest she'd run since she was twelve years old. And she kept running.

Rose's dad had taken her running as a kid. Rose would jog alongside him and think nothing of it because it was something she had done since she was small. On those runs she and her dad were silent, moving down the grid road, kicking up gold dust behind them.

Then after twenty minutes, they'd turn onto a path into the crops that led right to the big bush. There, horse trails wove in and out of the woods. This was Rose's favourite part. She could have run that trail blindfolded. The soft ground cradled your feet and it felt like, yes this was something you were supposed to be doing with your limbs, and she would pick up speed. Her dad would respond to her speed and move a step faster and faster until the two of them were running so fast that stopping would hurt. There was no distance counted, only time. Sometimes they ran for an hour, sometimes for two, once for four hours straight.

When they returned to their yard, her mom would be sitting on the front steps in her green and white housecoat. She would hold her tea, her legs folded in front of her, laughing at something the puppies were doing at her feet. Her dad would run past the house to cool down in the backyard but Rose would stop right in front of her mom and smile at her through the sweat dripping into her eyes and the heaving of her breath. Then, she'd take a sip of her mom's sweet tea.

Back then Rose didn't have to follow the rules — drink lots of water, stretch, etc. Her body was exactly formed for moving, fast or slow, it didn't matter.

Rose would sit on the steps next to her mom waiting for Lloyd to make his way back to them. Then they'd go somewhere — to town, to the beach, out to the big community garden — didn't matter really where. That was how their days went.

Rose stopped at the end of her memory like an invisible cord had yanked her backwards. She pivoted on her feet and looked back toward her house. It was far off. She couldn't even make out the front door. "Gotta be at least a mile," she said to herself and turned around. She smiled to herself. Maybe this was going to be easier than she thought.

It got much harder on the way back. Her throat hurt and her left knee ached like it had a cavity in it. "A little farther," she said. Her left shoulder popped and Rose stopped to rub it. "What the hell?" she said. Where were all these aches and pains coming from?

Her right hip began to sting like someone stuck a knife in it. Rose slowed to a jog and her body still complained. So she turned it into a fast a walk and still it nagged. She turned around and looked down the road, hoping for a car to hitch a ride with — there was none. How was she going to do this? This was only one mile and she couldn't do that? The marathon was in less than three months! There was no way she could do this.

"I can't do this!" Rose huffed and remembered her sore throat and regretted it immediately. She needed water so bad she would pay a million dollars for a scoop of muddy pond water, but the grid road was bone dry. The house was still at least half a mile away. It would take a long time to walk it so Rose started to jog again; her body jangled like a set of keys.

"This sucks," she said, "Oh my fucking god this sucks." But she didn't stop.

The house was getting closer. To a bystander, it would not appear that she was running at all, it would look like more like a shambling walk. Fortunately, Rose had reached that point where she did not care what she looked like anymore. "I'm gonna make it," she mouthed, because sound took too much energy.

It was then that she heard a voice call out to her, "Rose." Rose recognized the voice immediately — it was her mom. She looked around her as if expecting to see Callista standing beside the road, as if there had been some giant mistake, the doctor was wrong, the cancer was cured and that she had been in hiding all this time.

Rose stopped short and her knees protested with a jolt of pain. "Mom?" She heard the wind, a dog barking a few miles away, and the distant sound of cars.

Rose kicked her legs out a bit and pulled up her foot for a hamstring stretch. It was nothing. A daydream. But, thought Rose, she'd never had a daydream with a voice in it. And a real voice, as real as if her mother had been sitting across from her at the kitchen table.

"Enough procrastinating," she told herself and resumed her jog. Things were still jiggling but it was the homestretch and everything seemed easier. Then, as suddenly as before, "Rose."

Rose stopped. "What? Who is that?" Her voice was low and gravelly. She looked around her. There was no one, and Rose could see for miles and miles — this was Saskatchewan, after all.

Rose was a little freaked and began to walk fast in the direction of home. Fast walking transitioned into a jog that kept picking up speed until she was racing down her approach. The house was growing in front of her and in less than a minute she'd be on the stairs, then inside the house.

"Rose, the hair," her mother's voice said into her ear. A little louder than polite conversation, as though she wanted to be sure that Rose damn well heard it.

Rose didn't want to look but had to. She turned her head and saw a shape standing on the gravel road behind her. She found another gear and kept going. She hit the stairs at her fastest speed and ran up them two at a time. Then she threw open the door, leapt over the doorway, and landed in the living room.

"Callie! Sarah!" she called. "Where are you?"

"Right here," said Callie. She sat cross-legged in front of the TV, a foot away from Rose's kneecap, with a bowl of cereal in front of her.

Rose jumped what felt like a metre in the air (but was probably a couple of centimetres). "Holy shit, you scared me," said Rose. She put her hand on her chest where it was still rapidly beating.

"What happened?"

"I heard a ghost."

Sarah walked into the living room with her arms crossed, "What are you yelling about?"

"Mom saw a ghost."

"No, I heard a ghost." Rose's throat hurt. She got up and went to the kitchen. She turned on the faucet. She grabbed a cup but her hands were shaking so much she dropped it in the sink. She stuck her head under the faucet and lapped.

"Gross, Mom," Sarah said.

"How did you know it was a ghost?" asked Callie. "Was it spooky?"

Rose turned off the faucet and wiped her chin with a tea towel. Her hands were still shaking. "It was my mom."

"Cool!" Callie bounced up and down. "Did she ask about me?"

"That's sick." Sarah headed back to her bedroom.

"I'm not joking, I heard my mom. I'm not making this up!" Rose shouted around the corner.

Sarah's bedroom door slammed in response.

Callie waved her hand to dismiss Sarah's dramatic gesture. "So what did ghost grandma say?"

"She said, 'the hair.'"

"The hair? Whose hair? Your hair?"

"I don't know."

"That's weird mom."

"Maybe she meant to say beware."

"What does beware mean?"

"It means watch out, bad stuff is coming."

Callie opened the fridge and took out the orange juice. "That's probably it then."

"Why would you say that?"

Callie poured the OJ into her cup, some of it slopping over the sides. "If I was a ghost, I'd only talk to people when I had something important to say."

Rose stared at Callie.

"C'mon, Mom, let's go watch *SpongeBob*. Then you won't be scared." Callie took her mom's hand and led her into the living room.

∾

Rose snapped the water out of a damp blouse and held it up to the clothesline. She grabbed a pin from her mouth and clipped it. Then added another. She pulled the line closer to her and picked another top out of the basket.

Callie sat on the back steps eating a Popsicle. "Your face is still red," she said.

Rose walked up to the front steps and held her hand out for the Popsicle. For a second Callie looked as if she might be cheap but then handed the Popsicle over.

"You do realize it's like only ten degrees today?" asked Callie, "and you are wearing shorts?"

Rose looked down and shrugged. She'd been thinking about the voice all afternoon as she did the laundry. It might have been a hallucination, but Rose had never had one of those before, not even in the depths of drugged out labour, not even that time she smoked that strange weed with Gilbert when she was eighteen years old. Everyone else at the party had claimed to be seeing things but all Rose saw was Gilbert's hand on some slut's leg.

"So I was thinking about my science project, and I think I've got a good one."

Rose had placed a couple of clothespins in her mouth and so nodded for Callie to continue.

"I'm going to take onions and then cut them in half and see if it makes me cry."

If Rose had a dream of being the mother of a famous scientist, that remark dashed the dream forever.

"I took your idea of cutting up stuff — because I think cutting stuff with a knife is a good experiment — but I picked food instead of animals. Because I like animals," Callie explained.

Rose removed her clothespins and stuck them to her shirt, and then plunged in, "It's not an experiment if it's already proven. And it's proven already that onions make people teary-eyed."

"Oh," said Callie, "well, how about tomatoes then?'

"That is . . . an experiment . . . I think."

"I could do potatoes and celery and apples — wait, do you think I should stay with vegetables? I should stay with veggies."

"Do we have any veggies?"

"Some old potatoes and a can of corn."

Rose mentally castigated herself for her poor grocery-buying ways as she balanced her empty basket on the edge of a finger and walked up the stairs.

Callie followed her into the house, reciting more vegetables for experimentation.

Figuring it was about time to rustle up some supper, Rose opened the fridge. There wasn't much to rustle. The phone rang and Callie grabbed it immediately.

"Hello Callie speaking. . . yes she's here. She's in the fridge. I don't know what she's doing. She went running this morning and guess what?"

Rose grabbed the phone out of Callie's hands. "Hello?"

"Hey, Speedy." It was Winter.

"What's up?"

"What are you doing for dinner tonight?"

"Pork chops for the girls, Kraft dinner for me." Susie had given Rose a lifetime's supply of chops and whenever grocery money ran short, Rose went back to them.

Callie gagged behind Rose. Pork had long ago lost its charm for her girls.

"Why does your voice sound like that?" asked Winter.

"Running. Hurts. Throat."

"Oh, okay. Do you think you and the girls can make it?"

"Hell yes."

Callie looked questioningly at Rose. Rose mouthed the words, "Winter's cooking." Callie clapped her hands together excitedly. Winter was known as the best cook in all of Treaty Four.

"See you at six and drink some warm tea for your throat."

Rose put the phone down. Callie looked out the window and smiled, "I knew this was gonna be a good day."

"It smells like puke in here," said Sarah climbing into the front seat.

"Yes, that's your puke."

"Dad didn't clean it! Like any of it." Callie poked her head over the back seat with her fingers holding her nose shut.

"That surprises you? The man hasn't cleaned anything in the entire time I've known him."

"He takes showers sometimes," Callie piped in.

"I stand corrected."

"It's not fair that I have to sit in the back with Sarah's puke," Callie added.

"Shut it, pisshead."

"She's right," Rose said, "you'll clean it when we get home." Rose gave Sarah her "I mean it" face which could also double as her "don't you dare take that parking spot" face in a pinch.

Rose turned the key. The car refused to turn over. "Ah, fuck," Rose said. Callie "tsked" from the back seat.

Gilbert's legendary recalcitrant car was up to its old tricks — he called it Trixie for this very reason. Rose pulled the lever for the hood.

Rose lifted the hood and touched one of the battery cables with her hand. "I know you don't like me," Rose said to the car, "but you could try to be civil for the sake of the girls. They are his girls, by the way, no matter what he told you."

She tightened it with her hand and then tightened the other one. "There you go," she said, "you wanted to be appreciated, right? I can understand that. I'm a woman, too."

Rose yelled, "Try it now Sarah."

The car turned over.

"Thank you." Rose patted the side of the battery.

Monty and Winter's place was high up on a hill. It was called "Monty's Mansion" by most people on the reserve, with a high degree of envy. It wasn't a mansion really, it was a sprawling ranch house that Monty had designed and built himself. It had a large deck that stretched from the front to the back of the house where Rose and her kids had spent many happy weekends. It was surrounded by well-kept lawns that Rose knew Monty battled every summer for — the surrounding Saskatchewan foliage was always trying to insinuate its cheeky self into their yard.

Callie ran in first, throwing the door open and calling, "We're here!" at the top of her lungs.

"I should get around to teaching her some manners." Rose had a stack of baby books in her hand and garbage bag of baby clothes in the other. She handed Sarah a bassinet. Sarah took it without comment.

"But then again, it's not like we go to a lot of fancy places." Rose looked at Sarah. "Would you like to go to fancy places?"

Sarah laughed. "Like where? Red Lobster?"

"I don't even know the proper shoes to wear to Red Lobster."

Sarah groaned at her mom's attempt at humour.

"I've only been there twice," Rose mused. "Once with Winter and Monty after you were born and once with my mom and dad. Mom thought it was too expensive and refused to order anything other than an appetizer and water. Dad was so mad at her." Rose smiled at the memory. "I really did hear her voice."

"She's not like some kind of spooky ghost."

"I would never say that . . . I mean, it was scary. I'm not the kind of person who hears things."

"You know hearing things is a sign of schizophrenia."

Rose decided not to tell her about the shape she'd seen.

"You look like her you know," Rose said.

"You've told me."

Rose put her hand on Sarah's shoulder and Sarah let it stay for a second, then she moved ahead and Rose's hand slipped off.

Prickly princess, Rose thought to herself, and for the one millionth time wished that Sarah was four years old again, with a gap-toothed smile and an addiction to holding hands with her Mommy.

∾

Rose joined Winter in the kitchen. Winter was chopping some onions and some other vegetables that Rose didn't recognize and efficiently transferring them from the cutting board to a sizzling wok. It was an organized cacophony of sounds and smells that immediately intimidated Rose.

"Do you need some help?" Rose asked, as this was the polite thing to do.

"You can open the wine."

Rose rummaged through the cutlery drawer for the wine opener. She liked coming to Winter's where everything had a place and was in its place. At home, if she wanted a glass of wine she had to use a butter knife to push the cork to the bottom of the bottle. This always resulted in splash, which is why Rose always drank wine wearing her red T-shirt.

"Thanks for inviting us. The girls were so excited they didn't eat all afternoon."

Winter gave her an incredulous look. "That's a lot of pressure on me."

"Well you better deliver. None of this lame three course meal stuff, I won't settle for anything less than a six course meal."

"Ha."

Rose cocked her head and studied Winter. Her face was pale. "Are you feeling okay?"

Winter glanced at the living room where Monty was failing to convince the girls that Wii Golf was as fun as Guitar Hero.

"I have something to tell you." Winter's chopping speeded up. "We were going to announce it during dinner but . . . that seems stupid now. Of course that was Monty's idea, I was the one who was like, bad news and food don't go together-"

"Now, you're freaking me out," Rose said. "Just say it."

Winter stopped chopping and wiped her hands on her apron.

Rose put up her hand. "Wait." She sat down on a stool on the side of the counter and took a gulp of wine. "Okay, now."

"Monty and I are splitting up."

"What? No. No way."

Winter nodded.

"But you guys are . . ." Rose gestured at the beautiful kitchen, the gas stove, the cooking implements, the glass of wine — "perfect."

"I'm not. I'm pushy and demanding and cold, apparently."

"Oh really?" Rose sent a glare in Monty's direction.

"Yes. And he's not perfect. He's a man and, y'know, men will be men and flag-girls will be flag-girls."

"What?"

"I found texts. Nine of them."

"He's having an affair?"

"He says no. But what's he gonna say, really? I never met a man yet who didn't know how to protect his ass."

"What do the texts say?"

Winter paused from her slicing and looked up at the ceiling. In a sing-song voice she recited:

"Hey, sexy, how's tricks? — I didn't bring my lunch, do you have anything for me to snack on? — I have something hard for you to chew on, baby carrots, ha ha — You're bad — You're bad — Is payday Friday? — Yup — If it's hot on Monday, I'm wearing shorts, that cool? — The shorter the better." Winter looked like she wanted to retch.

"Hmmm . . . " Rose said.

"Disgusting, she's nineteen years old for God's sake. Aislyn Tuckanow. The one with that heart-shaped face."

"Doesn't she have a huge mole on her cheek?"

"Yes. Why didn't her parents get that removed? It takes literally minutes."

Rose shrugged.

"Well it doesn't matter, cuz apparently a nice body makes up for a witchy mole."

"So what? She's still a butter face." Rose felt guilty cutting up a teenager but decided that friendship demanded her loyalty.

"He'll be gone by tomorrow." Winter fed the veggies into the salad bowl.

"Really?"

Winter looked at Rose. "What's with the question mark?"

"Okay. I want to say something without you getting mad."

"Not possible."

"But the two of you are having a baby together and babies are wonderful but they are a lot of work."

"I've already thought about that. I can hire one of my cousins and he can certainly afford child support."

"And my second point is, it's just texts." Rose braced herself, expecting something to come flying toward her.

"But that's how it starts! Texting, then sexting, then coffee, then running off to sleazy motels at noon and charging up your credit card that your wife paid down by working overtime all winter and then it's goodbye Winter and your stupid baby."

"Your baby won't be stupid."

"No jokes."

Rose made her face into a frown.

"Now you look like a chubby-faced bulldog. I know he's your cousin and you love him but I've got to think of myself and I know I'm not going to be able to live with him. I can barely stand to look at him. I want to throw things at his head — all the time," she paused to glare at the family room. "I want to see him in great pain."

Rose felt nervous. "I know he loves you very much."

"Stop that. I want to be mad. I need to be mad." As usual, Winter was giving her silverware a quick polish before putting it on the table. "I don't want to be one of those women who turns a blind eye, expecting everything to turn out alright. I'm not that kind of person. I don't put up with bullshit."

As someone who did put up with bullshit, Rose was at a loss.

"I thought this would be the happiest time of my life. Why can't I be happy?"

Rose patted Winter's arm and took a sip with her other hand. This was not turning out to be the relaxing evening she'd been looking forward to.

"Monty!" Winter yelled suddenly, surprising Rose who immediately dropped her glass. The glass shattered and the wine splashed down the front of her shirt onto the counter. Now she had two red wine T-shirts.

"Sorry." Rose began picking up the pieces and throwing them in the trash.

"Use the broom, Rose, you're going to cut yourself."

Monty wandered into the kitchen. Rose looked at his face; he looked tired. He stopped in front of the cooking island, his eyes focused on a point behind their heads. "Did you want something?"

"Set the table. The girls are probably starving — their mom didn't feed them all day."

"How's that different from any other day?" Monty grinned down at Rose as he grabbed a couple of dishes.

Rose laughed harder than she intended.

Winter headed to the stove and pulled out something wrapped in foil. She began slicing and dicing and doing cooking stuff that Rose did not understand.

Rose was in an unfamiliar position. She was the one with the life that looked like an episode of Jerry Springer. Winter was the normal one with the great house, the stain-free clothes, and above all, the good advice. Rose had no good advice to give unless it was about how to get ketchup stains out of your bras.

Rose glanced at Monty as he set the table. He looked terrible. This did not surprise Rose, he was never good at hiding at his feelings. Growing up he was the boy who cried and told people, "You are hurting my feelings." Rose almost expected him to say exactly that when he looked at her.

"Do you need a towel?" he asked instead, and Rose nodded. She had been trying to move the wine toward the end of the table and catch it in her palms rather than disturb Winter by asking for a towel and breaking up this "peaceful" tableau.

∽

Over supper, the play continued. Winter asked Sarah and Callie lots of questions. She teased Sarah about becoming her live-in nanny and Sarah replied by upping her price every time Winter brought it up. Callie joined in and said that she would baby sit for free, if the baby was a girl.

"If it's a boy, I can't help you out. Because boys piss in people's faces," she explained.

Winter laughed. It was short and sharp. So she laughed again as if she was trying to start up a car with a tricky starter. Finally the laughter caught and she held it for a good long while. Callie collapsed into giggles as she always did when people found anything she said remotely amusing. She was on the verge of falling out of her chair when Sarah muttered, "Cool it."

Rose steered the conversation toward Callie's upcoming science fair.

"I'm experimenting on vegetables and cutting them," Callie said through a mouthful of food.

"What is it you're trying to learn?" asked Winter.

"Do other vegetables make you cry like onions do? My mom helped me think it up."

Winter gave Rose a look. Rose shrugged.

"So this is why there were a bunch of potatoes cut up in the kitchen," said Sarah, "I thought mom was making fried potatoes and got lazy."

"Y'know, Callie, onions are the only veggies that make people cry." Winter had barely touched her food.

"What about radishes?" asked Rose through a mouthful of sweet potatoes.

"Not even a tear."

"I'm not sure it's the idea we should go with," Rose said. "We're still thinking about other ideas."

"Maybe Dad can help me when he gets home," said Callie. "He likes cars and fixing stuff."

"Like he has ever helped you with anything," Sarah interjected.

"Sure, he helped me return bottles!"

"And he kept most of the money. Besides, Dad isn't coming home." Sarah looked at Rose. "Is he?"

Rose shook her head as if she had a spider in her hair.

"What about something do with hooking up different vegetables to batteries? Measuring electrical currents, that kind of thing," Monty said.

"Monty could help you, he's great at that kind of thing," Winter said.

Monty looked at her in surprise and then nodded. "One of the guys I play poker with is an electrical engineer, he'll have some cool stuff for you."

"Cool!" Callie rubbed her hands together. "Then I'll kick everyone's asses!"

"Don't swear." Rose and Winter said it at the same time.

"Which one was the swear word?" Callie asked.

While Winter explained the words that could substitute for ass, Rose looked around the table. Monty was hitting the booze pretty hard. Still, his gentle smile was firmly in place.

Sarah had stopped eating and was making a small hill with her sweet potatoes as she watched Winter and Monty from beneath her eyelashes.

They played Pictionary after supper. Winter barely played, she kept going in and out of the kitchen, clearing up stuff. Rose kept following her in and out, offering to give her a hand, but Winter was adamant.

"I invited you to supper, not to clean for me. Besides, I do have a dishwasher,"

Rose stood in the middle of the kitchen while Winter moved around her. She kept opening her mouth but nothing wise was on the tip of her tongue.

Rose sat back down in the living room. "Winter's got it under control," Rose said to everyone gathered around the coffee table.

"You did break one of her wine glasses," Sarah observed.

"She likes doing things a certain way, her way." Monty had opened up one of his fancy beers from a microbrewery that he had to drive three hours to get to.

"Mom, it's your turn!" Callie's voice was somewhat hysterical. She hated losing at board games and her mom was dragging the team down. "And this time, be faster."

Rose turned over a card. Doe. She began to draw a deer head.

"Horse! Dog! Man with big nose!" Callie screamed.

Rose scribbled through the picture and began another deer. She started with the hooves.

"High heels, ankles, skinny girl, anorexic!" Callie was on her feet now.

"How do you know what an anorexic is?" Rose asked.

"I watch TV!" Callie yelled.

"It's a very serious illness that — "

"You can't talk mom," intoned Sarah, her eyes on the tiny sand timer.

"Alien!" yelled Callie.

"Time," said Sarah.

"It was a doe." Rose showed Callie the card.

"What's a doe?" asked Callie.

"Doe, a deer, a female deer," sang Monty. He was looking pretty pissed now. His eyes were on the kitchen. "A female deer . . . " He got up and danced to his own tune.

Callie laughed and Rose put her hand on her arm to shush her.

Rose felt like they were inside of someone's house without anyone being home. She stood up. "Well we should be going."

"What?" asked Callie. "We only got here two hours ago."

Monty nodded while downing the rest of his beer. "It's only been a long time!" he slurred.

Rose called into the kitchen, "Winter!"

Winter was folding up her apron. "What? Who's winning?"

"We're losing cuz my mom sucks!" Callie stalked into the kitchen behind her mother. "You should be my partner, Auntie!"

"We're heading home," said Rose. "Big day tomorrow."

"What are you doing?"

"Well y'know, my run . . . And Sarah has homework."

"You can't leave without dessert," Winter said flatly, and went back into the kitchen.

"No, we should go," Rose replied in a small voice. "We really need to go."

∽

"Omigod, did you have to ask for seconds?" Sarah glared at her younger sister in the backseat. Callie had the collar of her T-shirt pulled over her mouth and nose.

"It was really good," protested Callie through her cotton nose-guard.

Rose squinted at the road. Gilbert's Trixie had terrible lights. "But we had to go and when we have to go then you don't make everyone else wait."

"Where do we *have* to go?" asked Callie. "We're just going home."

"We *had* to leave there."

"Why?"

"Because I said so."

"Omigod, it stinks in here!" Sarah rolled down the window.

Dessert had been long and awkward. Monty, by this time, was too drunk to eat and stared at a spot on the wall and hummed the song, "Friends in Low Places." Winter was quiet too, although she listed all the ingredients and detailed the entire cooking process in a monotone voice when Rose mentioned how good dessert was.

"I wish we could go to Winter's every single night!" Callie said from the backseat.

&

Rose made sure that Callie was watching TV before she went outside. She sat on the steps. Sarah's butt hung out of the car as she scrubbed the car's interior.

"It's not final," Rose said.

"What?" Sarah pulled her head out of the car. She dumped her rag in a bucket and wrung it out.

"They might not break up for sure," Rose said. "I think she's stressed about the baby. Big changes can sometimes do that to people."

"He cheat on her?" Sarah asked.

"No. Well, sort of. Text messages."

"Stupid." Sarah's head went back into the car.

"I want to talk to her but she is so sure about this, it's kind of freaking me out."

Sarah's response was muffled.

"What?"

Sarah pulled her head out and looked at her mom.

"I said it's none of your business."

"She's my best friend, he's my cousin! Actually, she's my cousin, too."

Sarah threw her a horrified look.

"Not so close that they'd have weird kids," Rose amended.

"Don't you have enough things to worry about? It's not like everything is going freaking amazing for us."

"It's not going that bad, either. I have a new job."

"That you don't even know how to do."

"I kind of know how!"

"You always say that you hate band politics. And now you're dead centre in the middle of everything."

Hearing it put that way actually gave Rose a bit of a thrill. "I'm there to help people, plain and simple. I can stay out of the rest." Rose squashed her smoke under her foot decisively. She made a face as she remembered that she didn't have any shoes on. Thank God for calloused feet.

Sarah said something else as she put her head back into the car.

"What?" Rose asked.

Sarah came out of the car. "Nothing."

"You're right, it is none of my business. I can be there to listen but I don't need to get involved."

Sarah lifted her rag to her nose, made a face and then sent it flying into the deep grass.

Rose woke up twice that night. The first time she heard a banging and hurried out of bed. She grabbed the bat from behind the door and walked into the living room. It was dark and silent. She stayed still and listened. She went to the front window and looked outside. She couldn't see anything and silently wished for a dog, a big one. They hadn't gotten one since the last one got killed — the girls felt it would be disloyal. Rose added getting a dog to her to-do list. Then she went back to bed.

A few hours later, she woke up again. The house was silent, and then she heard someone crying out. She jumped to her feet, grabbed the bat again — it was lying at the foot of the bed now — and went into the living room. She heard the cry again, coming from Sarah's room. She opened the door with one hand, her bat in the other. Sarah was sitting up in bed.

Rose saw that her eyes were unfocussed. She hated that look, she'd seen it on Callie before when she was having nightmares and a couple times on Gilbert. She'd read somewhere that night terrors were hereditary — yet another thing to thank her wonderful husband for.

Sarah whimpered.

"You're having a nightmare, sweetheart. That's all."

"She's here."

Rose shivered. "Nobody's here. Just me and your sister. That's all."

Sarah nodded and slowly laid back down.

Rose swallowed. She leaned against the door jamb until Sarah's chest rose and fell, then she crept back to her bedroom where she stared at the ceiling before she was able to get back to sleep.

The next morning when Rose swung her legs out of bed, she noticed something unusual: no pain. She padded into the kitchen to put on the coffee with an extra bounce in her step.

While she was waiting for it to percolate, she attempted a deep knee bend, and was rewarded with two loud knee cracks.

There was a knock at the door and then someone tried the door. Rose exhaled. Only family would be cheeky enough to try that trick. She opened the door. Monty stood there with a hockey bag over his shoulder.

"You lock your door?" He had the nerve to sound annoyed.

"No." Rose pushed the door closed. "No, no, no."

Monty forced his way in and dropped his bag on the floor. "You got coffee?"

"C'mon, Monty, don't do this to me. "

"Do what? I've done nothing." He found himself a cup and waited next to the coffee pot.

"I heard about the flag girl."

His self-righteousness melted into a pool at his feet. "I didn't do anything with that girl. I swear to god. She was, you know, flirty, and I got carried away. Guys talk worse than that all the time at work."

"Women love hearing that. Everyone else is doing it, so I joined in."

"It was texts, nothing else!" He held the sides of his head. "Ow."

"Good."

"I've never said more than two words to her. You know me, I have zero game."

"You're such an idiot."

"Yes! I know! Ow, my head." Monty leaned his large melon against the cupboards.

"Oh, for God's sake." Rose poured him some coffee, which he gratefully slurped.

"Do you have any Advil?" Monty asked in a small voice.

Rose rummaged through a drawer and found a nearly full bottle.

He swallowed a handful.

"That's too many."

"Did you see how much I drank last night?"

"Good point." Rose poured herself a cup of coffee.

Monty sat down heavily. He looked around the kitchen. "Where are your floorboards?"

"Gilbert took them off. He said he was gonna paint the kitchen but he never did."

"Dumbass."

Rose leaned across from him. "So what's the plan here?"

"She asked me to move out," Monty said. "And so I did."

"Do Auntie and Uncle know?"

"No, and I don't want them to know in case, y'know, she changes her mind. This won't last," he said. "You know Winter, she's got a temper but she cools down quick."

"What I know about Winter is that she has very high standards and she lives by them." Gilbert had found that out the hard way. About ten years ago, at a family barbecue, he'd gotten drunk and called Winter a bitch and she hadn't allowed him to enter her house since.

Monty nodded. He'd come to this same conclusion.

"So I was thinking, your house is the same distance to work and you got that extra bedroom — "

"That's Callie's."

"As if she even sleeps there."

"Nope, can't do it. Winter will think I'm picking sides," Rose said. "And I would never pick yours!" she added for good measure.

"But I don't want to end up renting some place in town and then not being near her if anything happens to her or the baby . . . " Monty's voice broke.

Rose fought the urge to comfort him. This situation was all his own fault; he was an adult.

He began to sob.

Rose patted his arm. "It'll be okay, Monty. You can fix this."

"How?"

"You just have to convince her that you're not a douchebag like Gilbert."

"I'm not!" He took great offense to that comparison.

"Of course you're not. But when you act like an idiot, it's hard to . . . convince people that you're not an idiot again. And then there's the pregnancy hormones . . . "

"Is that like PMS?"

"Yes. But it lasts for nine months."

"Did you kick out Gilbert when you were pregnant?"

"I would have if he was around at the time. Being pregnant makes you do strange things. I thought about becoming a standup comedian," Rose remembered.

"But you're not funny."

"Ass," Rose slapped his arm. "I wanted to do jokes about being pregnant like, 'I'm a crime victim: someone broke into my house and stole my feet.' You know, stuff like that. Then I realized, 'Hey, that would mean I'd have to perform only when knocked up.'"

"Yes, that was the only problem with that idea."

Sarah walked into the kitchen. "Hi Uncle Monty."

"Morning Saran Wrap."

"Uh Sarah . . . " Rose began.

"Uncle Monty is going to be staying us." Sarah put two pieces of bread in the toaster.

"Yes," Rose said.

"Of course he is." Sarah banged a cupboard door open as she reached for the peanut butter.

Monty grinned at Rose. "She always did have a temper."

Rose glanced at the clock. "Well, I better get on with my run before it gets too hot."

"It's barely above freezing outside," Monty said.

Rose gestured toward her torso. "It's like wearing an extra sweater."

"Don't overdo it," Sarah said. "If you hurt yourself, you won't be able to run at all."

"Why are you running?" Monty asked.

"The Pesakestew marathon. I'm entering it."

Monty laughed and coffee gushed out of his nose.

"Gross." Rose and Sarah said in unison.

Monty wiped his nose. "You're joking right?"

Rose glared at him, "If you're going to stay here, you could try to be supportive." She looked under the kitchen table where her sneakers sat in the same place from when she had kicked them off the day before.

"You're serious about this?" Monty asked.

Rose refused to look at him.

"Seriously?" Monty looked at Sarah for confirmation. Sarah chewed on her toast and nodded.

Rose walked toward the door and even as it closed behind her, she heard, "Seriously?" behind her.

∽

Run number three, Rose thought to herself. Lucky number three. It did not feel lucky. The pain she felt in her right knee had spread up her femur to her hip and now it ached and Rose knew there was ice in her future. She had no rhythm, her arms were flailing, and she seemed slightly out of step.

Pick a pace, she ordered herself. None of this slowing down, speeding up nonsense. She focused on a point in front of her, "to there, to there, to there," she chanted. Then she reached it and searched for another point, "to there, to there, to there . . . "

She hoped that other runners had more important thoughts floating through their heads.

"To theeeeere." Rose's foot skidded on a muddy spot and she felt her knee slide sideways. She straightened herself. Not good. There was nothing worse than getting injured in your first week of training.

"Staying injury free is the best thing you can do," her dad used to tell her. "Slow and safe is always the best approach."

Lloyd applied this philosophy to his own life. He worked at the same job for the last thirty years, moving slowly up the chain from labourer to manager. His job was not challenging, sometimes boring in fact, but he kept showing up, day after day, for decades. His job held him in place after her mother died, after he moved off the reserve, after he stopped visiting

Rose. The job held him together when family couldn't. Rose felt her feet slow and energy drain out of her. "Good thoughts," she hissed, "good thoughts." She sped up.

Callie's smiling face popped up. Big smile, big teeth, big eyes: Callie was her sunshine. Rose had read somewhere that your grandchildren were your reward for your children, but Callie was an early reward for — well, Sarah hadn't always been bad, only this last year or two, maybe three. When did they begin to grow apart? Rose suspected it was when she began working the long hours at the pig farm. She'd been so happy when she got the job because she didn't need to depend on Gilbert anymore. Or every part-time reserve job that no one else was willing to do.

Her foot slid in another pile of mud. She slowed to a walk and trudged for a few steps with her hands on her hips. Her breath was even; she wasn't struggling for breath. But she did feel this tightness in her chest that she didn't like.

During a rare hot streak, Gilbert's band had booked a four-week tour into the States and Rose had decided to go along. He might have even asked her. No, wait, he had said, "I don't care," when she had asked if he wanted her to go. So Rose had called up Winter and asked her if she could watch the girls for a few weeks.

Winter agreed, although she warned Rose that she wouldn't like it.

"Why are you doing this to yourself?" Winter had asked, "You're going to be bored out of your mind and you're gonna miss your girls."

"It's a chance for us to be a couple again," Rose had replied. Even though she and Gilbert had never just been a couple — she got pregnant two weeks after they started dating.

If she was honest with herself, Rose had gone because she wanted to feel young again. Young and wild, like the perfect groupie/wife. But the two things didn't "slash" well together.

There were groupies and there were wives. Groupies got drunk, slept till noon every day and said everything was "awesome." Groupies sat in the laps of their men and giggled. Rose tried sitting in Gilbert's lap and he made this loud exhale that embarrassed her so much she jumped back up immediately.

The groupie schedule also killed her. Rose's feet hurt by 10 PM. Plus she couldn't stay up all night when she had to be up early every morning so that she could call and check up on her girls. She monitored Gilbert's every expense and nagged him when he bought beer by the case and went off with scummy dealers to score weed and God knows what else for the band. She heard herself nagging and tried to stop but couldn't. After one week, Gilbert had stopped talking to her. After two, the entire band was ignoring her. Week three, she took the bus from Great Falls without telling anyone. Winter picked her up from the bus stop in Regina. Gilbert never called to find out where she was.

Winter had always been there for her. Rose bit her lip. Winter was going to be mad because Rose took Monty in, that was for sure. But what was Winter thinking, anyway? Who spends years trying to get pregnant only to spit out her husband like a stale piece of gum? It made no sense. They loved each other. Not affectionately, not passionately, but they made an excellent team. They went on trips to exotic places like Las Vegas and Niagara Falls and took pictures that were perfectly posed, if not exactly spontaneous or gleeful. (Winter did get a little military when it came to taking pictures. Rose usually hid in the bathroom when Winter got her camera out.)

Maybe Winter would understand; she knew that Rose and Monty had always been close and that Rose would never do anything to hurt her.

"She's going to fucking kill me," Rose sighed and turned around to head back to the house.

Nine

SARAH GLANCED INTO THE LIVING ROOM. Monty was sitting on the couch watching one of the Shreks while Callie babbled to him. Sarah grabbed the phone and pulled it to her bedroom. She tucked the cord under her door and closed it behind her. They had a cordless phone but the batteries kept going dead because Callie or her mom routinely lost it every week.

She dialled. Ronnie picked up on the second ring: "See-rah, what's shakin'?"

"Hey. You sound like shit."

"Stayed out till five. Raymond's party was sick. Where were you?"

"Where do you think?"

"God, your mother."

"I know. Did you talk to your mom?"

"She's not home yet. She went on to some ceremony after the Women's Wellness Conference."

"Shit."

"What?"

"I think my mom saw a ghost."

There was a long pause and Sarah figured Ronnie was surprised, lighting a smoke, or had fallen back asleep.

"She okay?"

"She was scared but she's fine now. But you know my Auntie Winter is acting crazy. And I had a weird fucking dream."

Ronnie was silent.

"Hey? Did you hear me?"

"Sorry, I dozed off for a second. What happened?"

"My dream was freaky. A woman was standing in my room. And I wanted to get past her and she kept blocking me."

"What did she look like?"

"Crazy long hair, smelt like a dog drenched in old people sweat."

"Maybe she was trying to help you."

Sarah shuddered. "I don't want her help. So, who was this Dream Woman?"

"She was like this old woman and people would come to her for healing or if they had a problem, that's all I know."

"Then what happened to her?"

"I'm not sure. I guess she died?"

Sarah took a second to remind herself that she was talking to a hungover teenager. "Yes but what happened to her that she ended up in an unmarked grave all by herself in the woods?"

"Oh. That's like, a really good question . . . "

Sarah waited a few moments before realizing the answer wasn't coming. "So we unburied a woman that you know nothing about?"

"Not nothing. I know her name and that she was real powerful and stuff . . . " Ronnie's voice trailed off.

"Do you think we pissed her off?"

"My mom will know more. I'll call her later. Hopefully she's in a cellphone area," Ronnie said.

"Call her now!"

"I'm fucking tired, Sarah. Oh hey, we're heading to Lowell tonight and gonna sneak into the bar. You up for it?"

"I'm under house arrest, genius."

"I was just being nice."

"Thanks for the invite, but I live in the Nazi-occupied part of the rez."

Ronnie yawned on her side of the phone.

"Go back to bed," Sarah said.

"Like I'm gonna be able to sleep after this phone call."

Sarah hung up. She stared at the phone. She didn't know who to call. If her mom wasn't such a chicken-shit, she might talk to her. But how would a person who got freaked out cuz she thought she heard a voice be any help?

Grandpa Lloyd? He came around at Christmas but other than that they never saw him. She barely knew her other grandparents. They lived in the city and they never visited.

As for her dad, it was like having a frat boy as a parent.

Sarah grabbed her notebook and flipped to an empty page. She forced herself to draw a picture of the woman. The woman had been tall for an old lady. Bony, too. All sharp angles. And she was angry, that was clear. But at what? All she and Ronnie had done was dig some rocks away and light some candles in front of her grave while Ronnie murmured some words in Cree. If they had released her, shouldn't she be grateful to them? Why was she showing up in Sarah's dreams all crabby and menacing?

Of course it hadn't been only the old lady who was angry. After Sarah went back to sleep, her dreams had been only collections of memories about bad times, like standing around the corner while her parents argued, her dad calling her mom things that would make a rapper blush. And knowing that her mom didn't deserve any of that and feeling like such a wimpy bitch cuz she wanted to run in there and help her but she didn't want him to turn on her. And then those feelings of helplessness turned into waves of anger that left her breathless.

Sarah ripped the picture out of her notebook and tore it into pieces.

"That's not me," she said and then wondered why she said it.

She sat back down at her desk and flipped open her algebra book, which she'd been doing a lot lately. Her mom was right; doing quadratic equations was soothing.

∾

Winter walked through the house with the duster. She swiped the top of the TV and the rows of DVDs. She was careful to get all the corners. The house was always dusty, this being Saskatchewan and all. No matter how tightly closed she kept the windows and doors, dust still crept inside. She bent low and found a large, muddy sneaker under the entertainment unit.

"Monty!" she yelled. Then she remembered that he wasn't there to answer. He'd left like she asked him to this morning.

He'd woken up before her and put in a good effort like he always did when they had a big fight. All the dishes and pots had been put away from the night before. The washer was running downstairs and he was folding a pile of clothes on the couch when she made her way into the living room. She had stood in front of him and he'd looked up at her with a hopeful smile that nearly broke her heart.

And she had kicked him out. Winter tried to remember why she did that again.

Aislyn was a dumb kid.

Monty was an idiot.

But he was sorry.

But they always said that.

He'd never done anything like this before.

That she knew of.

Monty loved her.

But he was a man and men do bad things. They can't control themselves. They have urges. They're visual. They think of sex every seven seconds. They were more animals than people. They can't be trusted.

But Monty did nice things without being asked. Winter looked down at her wedding ring, a pretty cluster of gems in the shape of a flower. He designed it himself and when he placed it on her finger, he cried. He loved her.

Or was he making up for something else? What else didn't she know?

Winter jumped to her feet. She moved her head as if trying to shake free the images in there. Monty and Aislyn, and then Monty and every pretty girl she'd ever seen.

Winter needed milk. She went to the kitchen and poured herself a glass.

Her mind returned to the text messages. She went through them in order, imagining how exciting it must have been for Monty to receive each one — he being close to forty with a widening belly and greying hair. He must have felt like a young hottie again.

He liked to think of himself as young. He bought a Tapout T-shirt one weekend while they were in the city and got into a long discussion with the cashier about where to take UFC classes. UFC! He'd never been in a fight in his entire life. What a joke. And of course, she wasn't consulted. Even though it was her money that would have been wasted on a stupid hobby.

Winter finished her milk in one long swallow.

Waste. That's all he ever did. He wasted her time, her money, and her life. She opened the dishwasher to put her glass inside but instead it flew across the room and hit a framed picture on the wall. It was Monty's favourite picture — his parents and Winter and him at their favourite Mexican resort. The picture tilted, hung in the air for a second, and then fell to the ground, shattering again. Winter hadn't meant to knock it down. She had meant to put the glass in the dishwasher. It must have slipped.

Ten

Rose congratulated herself on a smooth morning. Both girls woke up and got themselves ready without being prodded, nagged, and finally screamed at. They sat in the kitchen while Monty served them sausages and eggs, which put her no-name dry cereal and week-old milk to shame.

By the time Rose got out of the shower — she never got to be first in the shower, not once, ever — the girls were giggling at Monty's impression of Rod, the half-blind carpenter who was always making mistakes on the work site because he was too vain to wear his glasses.

The bus came on time, Monty was out the door and Rose left the house in plenty of time to show up early for her first day.

Then the car conked out a short way down the road, giving her a sweaty one-kilometre walk to work in her best shoes and dress pants. "This is what I get for trying to look professional," Rose mumbled to herself. "A nice glaze in a pair of polyester pants."

About ten minutes into her walk, Gladys honked the horn behind her and Rose jumped in, turning to say hi to Gladys' chubby-faced grandchildren — she always had at least two or three with her. Gladys was upbeat, excited by a big win at bingo the night before. She was on her way to lord it over the other old ladies.

"And if they think I'm gonna be suckered into a card game, they got another thing coming."

Rose assured her that she had the willpower to withstand their bullying, but they both knew she'd be in the game before noon. The games were too entertaining to pass up.

Gladys asked her about the new job and Rose didn't have much to tell her, only being on the job for a few days. They both pondered the question of where her predecessor had gone and if she'd ever come back. Apparently Liz's kids were thinking of hiring someone to go down there to look for her.

"You been having any strange dreams?" Gladys said casually as they pulled into the band office parking lot.

"No, not having any dreams at all. I think I'm too damn tired."

"Some of the old girls been talking about strange dreams lately. I was wondering if anyone else was having them."

Rose thought about telling her about hearing her mom's voice but decided against it. Scary dreams were in the realm of normal, hearing voices was in the area of psychiatric medicine.

The cars in the parking lot were laid out in jagged lines in front of the band office. She held open the front door of the band office for Gladys and her little ducklings with a heavy sigh, the movement giving her a glimpse of her pit stains.

The lobby was half full and people called out "Hi" to her as she went straight for the coffee machine and poured herself a cup.

Rose walked past the community services area. The government nurse was in and people were hanging out in the makeshift doctor's office. She was giving inoculations to the infants and toddlers. If she had time, she also gave rudimentary physicals, which always came out the same way: "Lose weight." Then at the end of the day, the nurse would drive away in her Toyota Tercel; people would talk about trying to eat better and make some earnest efforts, for a few weeks or so, until the siren song of Pepsi and KFC overcame their good intentions.

For her part, Rose put vegetables into her girls' food every meal and watched them stack them in the corner of their plates. But they never got KFC and they never got pop so maybe things were balancing out okay.

Rose flicked on the light in the social welfare office. Liz's absence was immediately felt. Gone was the welcoming vanilla smell. The office that once felt like a softly-lit womb was now dank and cramped. She looked up at the ceiling and saw the brown stain of a leak. Where the hell had that come from?

Someone had stolen Liz's comfortable black leather chair. However, they had taken the time to replace it with a hard wooden one from the lobby area.

Rose put her bag down on the desk and looked around. The bookshelves had dark rings where Liz's flowerpots had sat. Those had also been liberated by one of her coworkers.

Four filing cabinets were behind her. Rose tried to open one of them. It was locked. That was good, as all the information was supposed to be confidential and secure. Except Rose didn't know where the keys were.

She looked on the wall and saw a poster that had always bothered her. It was of a young Aboriginal girl standing there with a huge smile lighting up her nut-brown skin. Underneath a caption read, "I'm Tiffany, I'm seventeen, and I'm not pregnant." *Way to aim high Tiffany,* Rose thought, and ripped it down with a great deal of satisfaction.

Rose sat down in her desk and traced her hand in the dust on her desk. What the hell was she supposed to do now? She leaned back in her desk, took a sip of her coffee, and then went to the back to find some cleaning supplies.

She was standing on her desk, scrubbing the ceiling of its rainwater stain when Taylor walked in. "Whoa," he said, "I don't think we're insured for broken necks."

Rose smiled down at him, "But Chief, a broken neck is my retirement plan."

Taylor surveyed Rose's desk, she had placed a notepad and a pen on her dust free desk. "Looks like you're getting settled in."

"I guess," Rose said.

"Cool, cuz you're open for business tomorrow."

"Great." The violent roll of her stomach expressed the opposite sentiment.

"Also, and I hate to spring this on you — "

Rose looked down into his eyes and already felt helpless — no matter what he asked, she was going to say yes.

"We need you to handle some other duties. Nothing major. Just, you know, community relations."

"Whassat?" Rose climbed off the desk. She pretended not to see Taylor's offered hand and scampered down on her own steam.

"It's organizing intramural sports for the reserve."

Rose looked bewildered.

"Remember when we were kids and how families used to go hang out at the school gym and play sports and stuff? I want to start that up again." Taylor perched on the edge of her desk.

"What happened to Rob?" Rob Cardinal had handled sports for the kids for years. He had a tendency to blow the budget on hockey and soccer for the boys, which had always annoyed the parents of girls like Rose. But at least half the kids were involved in sports.

"Him and his wife moved to the city, their son got drafted by some Triple-A team."

Rose sighed and looked at the ceiling. "You're sure you can't find someone else?"

"Everyone has a full plate. It's not forever, only until we find someone else. And I'll help you out however I can. I know a little about sports."

Rose imagined drawing up tournament lists sitting next to Taylor. "You're right. It has to be done."

"I want the first game this week."

"This week?" she squeaked.

"I kind of promised the council," he said sheepishly.

Rose frowned. "I better start calling the parents and figuring out how many kids and how many rides I'm gonna have to organize."

"Rides?"

"People aren't gonna walk to the gym. I mean that would be great and all but by the time they got there, we'd have fifteen minutes to play before they had to get ready for their walk home. There's a bunch on the east side of the reserve that don't have cars, so we could send the reserve van to pick them up. I'm gonna need a budget."

"More money," sighed Taylor.

"It's not like the city," Rose agreed.

"You draw up the schedule and I'll make sure that the band finds the funds. I wonder if there's another program I can tap into . . . "

Rose admired the way his brow furrowed. How is this man single? He is like a chocolate sundae on a hot day. He was so fine, she couldn't even imagine herself having sex with him. The best she could imagine was giving him a haircut.

"What's wrong? You look like you're in pain." Taylor asked, interrupting her scissor/Taylor naked fantasy.

"Feeling light-headed. Probably because I'm hungry. With training and stuff I feel like I can never get full."

"I remember those days." Taylor looked wistful. He glanced at his watch. "I brought a tuna fish sandwich I was planning to eat outside. You can have half if you want."

"No, no, no! How has no one told you?" Rose punched Taylor in the chest.

"Ow!"

"Kaylee's mom, Frances, runs a lunch buffet next door in the old band office. We're talking fried bannock, baked bannock, rabbit stew, Saskatoon berry pie."

"That sounds like heaven on earth."

Rose glanced at the clock, "Crap, we're gonna be late. If you don't get there soon enough, she sells out."

Rose grabbed her purse and pushed him out of her office.

"I was wondering where everyone went at lunch," Taylor said.

"Thank God I'm here to teach you."

Taylor glanced at his reflection as they passed a window (Rose studiously avoided hers). "This place is gonna make me fat," Taylor said. "Do you mind if I join you for a run?"

Sure, I'll pencil you in for never. "Yeah that would be great."

They walked into the lobby where Tisha stood, her smile tight across her face like a belt on a fat man. She did a sitcom-worthy double take at seeing them together.

"Taylor, where have you been?" she asked, even though it was fairly obvious.

"Talking to Rose about the intramural sports. Where's the reserve van?" he asked.

"Uh ... well, my mother is using that right now, she uses it to deliver baked goods to the elders," Tisha said.

"Donating baking to elders? I wish we had a hundred people like her," Taylor said.

"Isn't there a small charge for that baking?" Rose asked, "Y'know, like, a price?" Rose's smile was downy fresh innocence.

Tisha glared at Rose. "She has to cover her expenses."

"I'm glad the band is helping your mom's business, but she'll have to keep her deliveries to a day when we don't need the van," said Taylor.

"What do we need it for?" Tisha asked.

"Picking up families for sports," said Taylor. "Rose will work out the schedules and pass it on to you."

Tisha looked pissed, but said nothing.

"Coming over to Frances's for lunch?" Taylor asked.

Tisha pretended not to hear him as she went into her office and slammed the door.

"Whoa, someone's not happy," Taylor said.

"She'll get over it," Rose commented, not really caring if she did or not. Then she focused her attention on enjoying every nanosecond of the next few minutes she was going to spend in Taylor's presence.

∾

Rose spent the afternoon cleaning up the gym. The band had a janitor, Neil, but he had hurt his back a month before and his doctor hadn't cleared him to work. Rose found this out when she called his house and spoke to his oldest daughter, Cara. The daughter was having a hard time selling the excuse; she probably wanted her dad out of the house as much as Rose did.

Rose got off the phone and raided the cleaning supplies.

The gym was regulation size. When it had first been built, there had been volleyball games every night and floor hockey on weekends. Family reunions had been held there and badminton tournaments and then, somehow, it had faded from people's memories and became as disused as the ball diamonds and rodeo grounds. It's like every place had a spirit that would keep it alive and then the spirit moved on to somewhere else. It was too bad that even great things lost momentum.

Rose pushed the broom across the gym and beads of sweat spread across her forehead, then across her cheeks, then even on her chin. When she reached the other side of the wall, she stopped to take a few deep breaths. She felt the underside of her hair it was wet with effort. "Fortunately, I'm built for hard labour," she assured herself.

The pig farm had been nothing but lifting and carrying for hours and hours. It was a wonder she wasn't a skinny little thing, but Susie had always fed her staff well. They all had as much pork chops, bacon, pork rinds, and mashed potatoes speckled with bacon bits that they could eat.

I should call her and thank her for my fifteen-pound weight gain, Rose thought.

As she pushed along the mop, its strings reminded Rose of the pigs and their dainty tails and their intense little eyes. Pigs were smarter than dogs, people said, and Rose would have to agree. Rose used to talk to them for hours, and it was like they listened to her. Rose's eyes grew wet. "I can't cry about goddamn pigs," she told herself, and then cried anyway.

Eleven

MONTY DROVE ROSE OUT TO HER stalled car the next morning. They stopped at the car and Monty looked under the hood.

"What do you think?" asked Rose.

"Pretty sure a boost will get you started. But you definitely need a new battery. I can pick you up one today," Monty said.

"Whatever you think is best," Rose said, instead of saying thank you like a normal person.

Monty boosted her car, took off the cables and handed them to her through the car window. "You'll need these again," he said, and then drove off to work.

Rose settled into her office nice and early. But even so, there was already a formidable lineup outside her door. Rose threw a scared look at Kaylee, who shooed them away.

Rose frantically rummaged through her desk for a pen. Kaylee stuck her head in.

"Ready?"

"I need a pen!"

Kaylee pulled the pen stuck into her cleavage and flicked it at her. Rose caught it in her right hand.

"Lionel Cardinal, your ass is up," Kaylee called out the door.

Lionel appeared in the doorway and stood in front of Rose's desk, his hands folded in front of his crotch. If he'd had a hat, it would have been in his hands. Lionel's long hair flowed down both his shoulders, thick, scraggly, and highlighted with grey. He was tall and thin no matter how much fried bannock he chowed down on at fall suppers and feasts, the Cardinals had that body type. *Lucky assholes,* Rose thought. Lionel had been a carpenter until he lost his driver's license earlier that year to a DUI.

Kaylee shut the door.

"So, uh, what do you need?" Rose asked, hoping that her awkward abruptness could be mistaken for brusque professionalism.

"A place to live. My brother's wife kicked me out. Again."

"Oh. Well. Sandy, right?"

"Yeah. She said she was sick of Dan's relatives always hanging around."

"Do you have a file open already?"

Lionel shook his head. That was a good thing because Rose hadn't figured out how to open the file cabinet. She grabbed a file folder and took down his particulars. She raced through the intake process, mindful of the line growing on the other side of the door.

After a few phone calls, Rose found Lionel lodging at his cousin Lauren's house. Lauren wasn't crazy about the idea but when she found out she'd get a rent cheque immediately, her yes came out as a happy squeal.

"That okay?" Rose asked Lionel.

"You know she's got five kids, right?" he said.

Rose nodded. "Yeah."

"And she won't want me to drink," he added.

"But it's a place to stay, right? And maybe you can get your buddies to pick you up if you want to go boozing."

Lionel nodded, his eyes on the cheque in front of him. Rose signed it with a flourish and ripped it off and handed it to him. He thanked her and headed out the door.

Before the next person could flow in Rose yelled for Kaylee. She came and filled the doorway, her left hand on her hip.

"What?"

"I can't get in the cabinets."

"Use the key."

"I don't have the key."

"Oh right. I forgot." Kaylee fished a keychain out of her pocket and took a key off of it and tossed it on the desk.

"Thanks."

"Whatever. Better hurry it up. That line ain't getting any shorter."

"Can I get a coffee when you have a chance?"

Kaylee looked for a second like she wanted to tell Rose to shove it in a creative, yet violent manner, but then she noted Rose's pale cheeks and sweaty forehead and relented. "Yeah, whatever."

Thirty-four appointments later, Rose sat at her desk and stared into space. In the last five hours, she had heard more tales of general woe than she'd heard in her entire life. Bad stuff happened with alarming regularity. And people were fucked up. They made bad choices, consistently and consciously.

"Why'd you go to that party when you knew that you had to get up early for your apprenticeship exam?"

"I dunno."

"Why didn't you report your boss' sexual harassment instead of quitting?"

"Beats me."

"Why did you take him back when he stole your welfare cheque and spent it partying with his mom?"

"Wasn't thinking, I guess."

Rose's hands shook. She'd consumed nothing but coffee whitener and sugar all day long. She got up on her unsteady legs. The band office was closed now and she was so grateful to see the couches empty, the card playing table devoid of people. She was alone, blessedly alone.

"Hey Rose."

Rose shrieked.

"Sorry," Taylor said.

"No it's not . . . It's that . . . I'm . . . well, my day was . . . ver y . . . y'know . . . " She waved her hand as if trying to pull the word out of the air. " . . . Bad."

Taylor nodded. "Yeah, I saw the line."

Rose nodded and reached for the coffee pot. It was cold. She poured herself a cup, slopping it over the sides.

"So how are those intramural forms coming along?"

Rose grabbed an empty pop can from one of the tables and threw it at his head. It bounced off the wall behind him.

He threw his hands up in defense. "I was kidding!"

"I don't know why I did that. I never throw things . . .at anyone other than my husband." Rose stared at the coffee in her hand. "I feel like everything is hopeless. Everyone wanted more and more. Five people cried. Or maybe it was six. I don't even know anymore."

Taylor laughed. "You got stuck with the tough cases today. So you met twenty-four — "

"Thirty-four"

" — people going through a rough patch. This reserve has 564 people, that means 530 are doing okay."

"Most of these people have kids. Omigod! I have to make sure they don't ruin their lives. Every single kid is going to post-secondary. I'm going to make sure." Rose took a sip of the murky liquid in her cup and winced at the taste.

"We actually can't afford to send every kid, so some of them need to slip through the cracks."

"I'm being serious!"

"Well, stop it," Tayler smiled, that slow one that drew across his face like a bow. Rose sat down in her chair and pointed her eyes at the back of the lobby couch. She examined the hole in the back, the coffee stains, the dust stain at the bottom. Maybe she should say something, like how he was so confident that she felt stronger being around him, or how it was nice that he asked questions and looked at you like he honestly cared, or how his jeans made his ass look like it was sculpted from stone.

Taylor pushed in chairs around the community cardplaying tables. He grabbed a few cups off the table and tossed them in the garbage.

"What are you doing?"

"The janitor is still off sick. Do you know he has seven sick days a month? Guy could go to Europe once every two months."

"Maybe he'll bring you back a tiny Eiffel tower."

"I'd rather have a clean toilet." Taylor tossed an empty pack of smokes at her.

"Cleanliness is overrated." Rose deflected it into the garbage.

"I heard that was the motto of the black plague." Taylor tossed a Styrofoam cup at her. It hit her on the boob and ashes poured out of it.

"Taylor, shit!" Rose dusted her shirt and spread the ashes further.

"Sorry," Taylor looked sheepish.

"This is my best work shirt." It was true, the rest of them were T-shirts.

Taylor reached out and flicked some ashes from her shoulder.

"Was there more there?" Rose said. Her heart rate began to increase.

"Yeah, or it was just dirt." Taylor said.

Rose stared at his face. His lips were so rosy. Like a little girl's.

"What are you smiling at?"

"Your lips. Do you use strawberry shortcake lipgloss on them?"

"Yeah, but only for the scent."

Taylor kept coming closer. The distance between his pouty lips and hers was closing in tenths of a second, but to Rose, it felt like the same length of time as evolution. The oceans were covering the globe, then small leech-like animals were crawling out, then a reptile laid an egg, then a monkey picked up a tool and started banging a car together . . . and, then, their lips touched.

Her thoughts spun like a tornado: I'm kissing Taylor. This is happening. And I smell like an ashtray but that's okay because he seems to be into it. Oh my God, I'm still kissing him and he's kissing me and I'm married. But not really. And besides this is only a kiss. With Taylor. Who is handsome. And the chief. Such a sexy word.

Her mind continued along those lines as Taylor's left hand moved in the general direction of her boob, the soot-covered one.

The reception phone rang. Once. Then twice. Then three times. Rose broke free and answered it.

"Mom?"

"Heyyyyy Callie. My daughter."

"Yes that's me. So when you coming home?"

"Five minutes. Did you eat?"

"No."

"What? Let me talk to your uncle."

"No, no I mean I did eat. But only some wieners and beans that Uncle Monty made. And some cake. And an apple. But that's all."

Rose rolled her eyes. "Okay, well, I'll be home right away to make you something. Bye, Callie." Rose smiled as she put the phone down.

Taylor was locking his office and then went to lock Rose's. Their offices held the most confidential information. Tisha also locked her office but that was just because she was a dick. Taylor held the door for Rose on the way out. He punched in the alarm code.

It was starting to get dark and the crickets were already making a racket. The air tasted frosty like winter hadn't given up yet, and Rose shivered and wished she'd brought a sweater.

"Good work today, Rose," Taylor said, professionalism creeping back into his voice. "But I knew you could handle it."

"I don't know how you knew that."

"I read your resumé. You stick with tough jobs that nobody else wants to do."

Say thanks, Rose commanded herself. Stop, look him in the eye and say a heartfelt thank you.

"I hope I don't fuck up and make you look bad." I guess that's a type of thanks, Rose sighed to herself.

Rose opened her car door, Taylor moved as if to walk away. "Just a sec, Chief, I might need a boost," Rose called out.

Rose tried the car and, as predicted, it refused to turn over.

"I got cables," Rose said and popped the hood. She kept her voice neutral and her movements smooth despite her embarrassment.

Taylor went to get his car.

Rose did a few leg stretches while she waited. She turned as she heard a car pull up. It was a pretty thing, royal blue and curvy. As the car pulled closer, Rose saw the horse perched on the hood. "Nice," she thought, and made a mental note to buy a shiny Mustang as soon as her lottery numbers hit.

Taylor got out of his car. He stared at the car and Rose saw his mouth move in the shape of "Oh shit."

Then the car door opened and Rose saw a collection of hair emerge: thick, long, wavy, sort of moving everywhere in the breeze. Then she saw the face under it, a perfect Disney Pocahontas princess face. Rose's eyes moved south and saw them: the breasts. They defined perfection: big but not too big, high and perky but not all in your face. Hell, these breasts even had personality! They said, "Hey, wanna go do shots?"

Rose let out the deep breath she'd been using to suck her gut in all day. Taylor did the opposite move and seemed to grow two inches taller.

"Megan."

"Hey Taylor, you look good." Her words fell out of her mouth like perfectly formed diamonds, all white and clear.

Rose made a sound that was a cross between a cough and a grunt. Megan flicked a glance in her direction and as quickly dismissed her.

"What are you doing here?" Taylor looked constipated, Rose noted, but somehow even that expression looked hot on him.

Megan shrugged.

"That's not an answer Megan."

Megan looked down at the ground. Rose looked down to see what she was looking at and saw Megan's brown leather, pointy boots. They had a slight heel but nothing that would make you say, "What a dumbass," for wearing them out in the country.

"I'm sorry you came all the way out here but I don't want to talk to you. I made that clear when I left," Taylor said. Then he grabbed the cables out of Rose's hands and turned his attention to the sickly battery.

"My car is acting up," Rose explained to Megan, who acted like she didn't hear.

Megan took a step forward. "Taylor, we need to talk."

Taylor kept his back to her as he put the cables on. Rose watched his movements, a little surprised to see that he knew what he was doing. She snuck a glance at Megan and saw her pretty face crumpling.

Megan blocked her face with long, thin fingers and a wet, sniffling sound leaked out from behind them.

Whenever Callie tried to use tears to get her way, Rose would pretend that she wasn't crying: "Are you sick? Did you swallow a hairball? Are you sweating through your eyes?" Rose had a feeling that wouldn't work on Megan.

Of course, Rose wasn't quite sure that Megan was even part of the human species because no *Homosapiens* she'd ever seen had skin that glowed like that.

"That's not going to work," Taylor grunted, without turning around.

Megan continued to cry. Rose noted that she was a very pretty crier. No red nose, no blotchy cheeks, just big voluptuous tears rolling down her face. And she wasn't even wearing make up! *Oh, c'mon God, that can't be fair,* Rose thought.

"You want to try it?" Taylor asked.

"What?"

"Try your motor," Taylor said.

"Oh right." Rose scurried to her front seat and turned the ignition. The car turned over. She hit the gas a few times and the motor revved.

Rose rolled down her window. "Thanks! See ya tomorrow!" Then she hurriedly rolled it back up.

"Wait!" Taylor called.

"What?"

"Your cables." Taylor came round to the passenger side. "Can you stay?" He asked under his breath.

Rose's mouth fell open. "Why?"

"I don't know what to do with her," he said.

Rose glanced into her rear-view mirror. Megan had climbed back into her car and was full out sobbing. Her big head of hair was one with the steering wheel.

Rose's first answer was "let the bitch cry," but she didn't know the backstory so she took the diplomatic route. "You could always go for coffee with her. Petro-Can out near Lowell is open until ten."

Taylor shifted his weight from side to side; he looked like a little boy who was too afraid to ask to go potty. "You sure you can't stay?"

"I have a very spoiled eight-year-old who wants me home now. Sorry."

"Yeah. Okay. Have a good night." He closed the door.

Rose pulled away but watched the couple in her rear-view mirror. Taylor stood between the two cars with his hands jammed in his pockets while Megan kept her head down. They both looked so damned forlorn that Rose hoped they'd be able to work things out. But, then again, not really because Rose Okanese didn't get kissed by good-looking chiefs every day and goddamnit, she deserved a win.

Rose wanted more than anything to talk to Winter and dump out this situation like an over-packed purse. Winter always knew how to tidy up Rose's thoughts. Rose turned the music up loud to drown out her guilty feelings.

Rose got in extra-extra early the next morning and started working on her intramural schedules. She'd decided the night before that volleyball would be the best sport to start with because it was something people of all skill levels could play together. And, also because she found a bunch of volleyballs in the storeroom. She made a couple of sign-up sheets for different ages, and at lunchtime she marched into the lobby area and tacked them to the community bulletin board.

People's eyes drifted over from the poker game going on at the table.

"What's that?" mumbled Annie, an elder who refused to wear her dentures.

"Volleyball sign up for kids and families," Rose said. "These are friendly games, no spikes to the face."

Annie had over a dozen grandchildren, "Good, sick of them playing their damn video games."

Other people chimed in. "What about the younger kids?" "How the kids supposed to get there?" "Who's gonna feed them?"

Rose explained that she'd be figuring out what to do with the little kids once the funding kicked in. She told them she'd be organizing rides if they left their numbers. And finally she told them that they'd have to feed their own damn kids.

Before Rose finished pouring herself a cup of coffee and mixing in her sugar and whitener, the list was already half filled with names.

Rose walked over to Kaylee's desk. "Chief in yet?"

"No. He called in sick."

A deep sad sigh expressing the predictable unfairness of this vale of tears escaped Rose's lungs.

Kaylee looked at her suspiciously. "You know something?"

Rose shook her head. "Nope. I'm surprised cuz, you know, he's so healthy and all."

"Uh huh."

"That's all."

"You got twenty-five appointments today. You wanna start or keep gossiping?"

Rose grabbed the stack of files on Kaylee's desk.

∾

Rose spent her lunch working on the teams. She paused for a second to call Winter's house and was disappointed to get the answering machine again.

"Hey, it's me. Again. Call me at work. Or at home. I thought you weren't working this week? Don't let them work you to death. Okay? Call me." She hung up the phone. Two days was the longest the two of them had gone without talking since they were in grade two and Rose got that ear infection from a woodtick that her mom had missed.

Rose dived back into her scheduling. She was on a roll when there was a knock on the door. She looked up to see Gilbert's broad shoulders filling the doorway. He looked dog-eared as he always did when the bender ended and the hangover kicked in. Then he'd spend the next week hanging out on the couch, grouchy as a bear and ordering Rose and Callie to grab him food and water. (He didn't try with Sarah because she'd just tell him to go fuck himself.) Mostly Rose tried to keep the girls out of the house during that week.

"Hi." His voice was deep and warm, like a dugout filled with sewage water.

Rose wanted to growl. And maybe she did. Definitely an ornery sound left her mouth.

"Came by to pick up my last paycheck and heard you're working here now. Thought I'd say hi."

"Why?"

Gilbert shrugged. Rose's eyes narrowed. The patented Gilbert-shrug was his way out of every hard question.

Gilbert ran his hand over the inside of the doorway and examined the wood. "I know I did some bad things," he said finally.

Rose laughed. It came out like a bark. "Are you fighting with Michelle? Did that cunt kick you out? Cuz I can't think of another reason why you'd want to talk to me."

Gilbert examined the wood even more closely.

Rose had a dozen things to say, bubbling up like bingo balls. Then she stopped herself. This was not going to go like every other fight they'd ever had. She'd talk and talk and he'd look sad and eventually she'd run out of things to say and then they'd both be silent. Then he would stay and gradually she'd accept that he was back in her life, like a mould growing on baseboards — if she had baseboards, that is.

Gilbert would get her back by standing still and doing nothing. It never fixed anything but she was so damned stupid that she'd fallen for it every time.

She stared at him. He stared at the wall. Finally he looked over at her, confused.

Rose shrugged. Then she looked down at her schedules again and started writing out names with shaking hands.

"I'm sorry." His voice was little more than a whisper.

She kept writing. She knew he was gone when his shadow left her desk.

For the rest of the day, Rose kept an eye out for Taylor. Her appointments went quickly and she tried to keep a few people in her office chatting about their lives and hers, but it was clear they wanted to be on their way. "The bank closes early today," was their constant refrain.

Rose wandered over to Kaylee's desk and kept getting sent away. Kaylee was playing online poker and had been on a red-hot streak all day.

"Get away, you're my bad luck charm," Kaylee told her when she lost a hand.

Rose got so desperate she even looked in on Tisha, who reminded her of ten tasks that Rose hadn't completed yet. So Rose ambled back to her office, but kept the door open.

∾

Winter called as Rose was setting out the plates for supper. Rose saw the number and froze. She didn't feel like having "the talk" at that particular moment. Sarah walked by, saw the number, and made a "tsk" sound. Callie ran from the other room and picked up the phone.

"It's Auntie!" she yelled to the entire house.

She chattered to Winter about schoolwork and what they were having for dinner and how come she didn't come and join them. Monty and Rose exchanged guilty looks across the table. Sarah looked up from a novel she had propped in front of her plate to give Rose a dirty look. Finally Callie passed the phone to Monty.

"Okay. Yeah I'm staying here . . ."

Rose cringed.

"Since you kicked — since you asked me to leave . . . nobody is ganging up on you, it's not like that . . . How's the baby?" Monty looked at the phone in his hand.

"How is the baby?" Callie asked.

"She hung up."

"That's kinda rude," Callie replied.

"She's all alone over there and we're all over here. Of course she's gonna be mad," Sarah said.

"How come Winter doesn't come here?" asked Callie.

"Your dad stopped by my office today," Rose said to distract her.

"Did he ask about me?"

"Course he did," Rose said and shoved a forkful of mashed potatoes into her lying mouth.

"Did you tell him that Mrs. O'Watch said that my experiment idea was the worst she ever heard of?"

"I told him about how you were riding your bike with me every day."

"That's good."

"He said he was proud of you," Rose added. Callie grinned and sat straighter in her chair.

Rose glanced at Sarah, who was piling her mashed potatoes into the shape of a pyramid.

∽

Rose followed Sarah into her bedroom after dinner. The lair had more pink than most people might imagine tough girl Sarah would have. Rose knew that she was also hiding a Hello Kitty jewelry box in her drawer. Sarah sat at her desk chair and spun in a circle.

"You were right," Rose said. "Letting Monty stay here was like picking sides."

Sarah nodded.

"But he's my cousin and I couldn't say no to him. And — I hate to say this — even with how good stuff is going for us, his rent is helping us a lot."

Sarah looked at the carpet.

Rose sat down on Sarah's bed. "So are you gonna help out at volleyball?"

Sarah spun in a circle three times before answering. "Yes."

"Thank you."

"So . . . " Sarah traced a circle on the floor with her big toe. "Did he ask about me?"

Rose shook her head.

"I wish he wasn't my dad."

This is where Rose usually supplied some emotional salve like "He's an addict. This is the way he was raised. He doesn't know any better." But she didn't feel like it. She was sick of apologizing for Gilbert's bullshit.

"He's not a good father," she agreed.

"He's worthless," Sarah said.

"Well . . . " Rose rifled through her brain for proof of Gilbert's value.

Callie called, "Mom! It's six!" from the living room.

"I gotta go for my run."

"Really?" Sarah asked. Rose thought she saw some disappointment in Sarah's face.

"You can come if you want."

"Nah," Sarah said, "I got homework."

"Anything interesting?"

"No."

Rose got up to leave.

"I got an *A* on my English essay."

"Really!"

"Don't sound so surprised."

Rose smiled. "I mean, good job."

"It was on *The Old Man and the Sea*."

"I liked that book," Rose said. It had made her hungry for seafood the entire time she was forced to read it.

"He works so hard and then he gets nothing in the end. That sucked."

"We all get nothing in the end." Too late, Rose remembered that she was talking an already cynical teenager and that there was no need to throw more wood on that fire. "Except for your *A*, I mean, it's those happy moments that make it all worth it in the end."

To her credit, Sarah restrained herself from rolling her eyes. As a reward, Rose restrained herself from patting Sarah on the shoulder.

∾

Callie kept Rose busy asking questions on the run. It was their third time bike-running together. At first, Callie had trouble biking slowly enough but she was learning how to loop around Rose and peddle ahead, "because you are so slow, Mom." Rose was grateful for the company. Running was boring, and Callie's chatter helped pass the time.

Cars honked as they passed. Sometimes the people would yell out some teasing encouragement like, "Keep it up Rosie!" "Shake it girlie!" or "Do you want a smoke?"

Rose was noticing changes in her body. She had trouble keeping her jeans up and had to borrow a belt from Sarah to keep them from slipping down her ass like a teenage boy. She had blisters all over the soles of her feet and on the tips of her toes. They weren't healing but they weren't getting worse. She didn't even mind looking at them so much anymore. The worst of it was an angry-looking rash underneath her arms from the loose skin of her upper arms rubbing against the sides of her torso. Callie had described it as gross and Rose had to agree.

Sometimes Rose and Callie went all the way to the dugout where they would see kids swimming. The water was black and muddy, but they were happier than pigs in shit. Rose was sure that their mothers were going to lose their minds when they got home.

Rose ran extra fast past the dugout so that Callie wouldn't get any ideas. But the days were getting longer and warmer; it was only a matter of time before Callie came home covered in mud.

A couple of times they ran past the dugout all the way to the band office where Rose took a breather up against the building and Callie practiced her wheelies in the parking lot. Then they'd turn back around and head all the way home.

They were only twenty minutes into their run when a truck pulled up beside them. Rose was preparing herself for another cheeky remark when the driver called out, "Rose!"

She glanced behind her. It was a worn-out looking truck, so rusted and beat up that you couldn't tell its original colour. Rose strolled up to the passenger window, annoyed and grateful for the distraction. Then she saw Lloyd's hawk nose and high cheekbones under his oversized cowboy hat and was plain ol' surprised. Lloyd looked handsome sitting there and for a second she wondered if he had a girlfriend.

"Hey, Dad."

"You should be doing hills."

"Kind of hard, this is Saskatchewan."

"The marathon has four hills."

"Yeah, that makes sense."

"You drinking enough water?"

"Keep forgetting."

"Hi, Grandpa!" Callie said, popping her head into the window.

"Hi Callie." He said her name awkwardly; it sounded more like Kelly. "How's school?"

"Our teacher is so mean she won't let us wear Justin Bieber T-shirts to school!"

"That's too bad," Lloyd agreed, even though he clearly didn't know who that was.

"No, that's perfect," Rose said.

"Mom!"

Rose was on the verge of inviting him back for coffee when Lloyd said suddenly, "I entered you in a race. Next Saturday."

"What?"

"It's only 10K, six miles. You'll be fine." Lloyd took a sip from the Coke can in his lap.

"I'm not ready for that."

Lloyd shrugged and then put the truck in gear and drove away.

Rose looked at Callie. Callie looked at Rose. "How far is 10K?" asked Callie.

"Like twice as far as we went today."

Callie bit her lip. "Yikes."

"No shit yikes."

Callie looked down the road. "Let's do another kilometre tonight, then. To see how it feels." Callie took off on her bike, her short legs pumping with determination.

Rose turned in a little circle in one place, feeling her hips and muscles express their specific complaints, and then followed her daughter down the road.

Twelve

ROSE SAW WINTER IN THE IGA and felt torn — this was reflected in the way she stepped toward her gleefully, then took a step backwards hesitantly, then forwards again, like a nervous Salsa dancer. Her first thought was a joyous, "Winter!" then an afraid, "Oh shit," and then finally, "I have to do this now." Rose rushed over with her squeaky cart before her courage could abandon her.

"Hey."

Winter frowned when she saw Rose. "Oh, it's you."

"Yes, me." Rose bent low and addressed Winter's belly: "How you doing, kid?"

"Don't do that."

"Did you find out the sex?"

"Are you crazy? I'm only nine weeks." Winter put a block of cheese up to her nose and then put it in her cart.

"Right. Plus it doesn't matter. Boys are easy. And, girls are a lot of work but she'll be your best friend." And then your worst enemy when she turns fifteen, Rose added silently. "When's your ultrasound?"

"Three weeks from now."

"Do you want me to tell Monty?"

Winter threw a can of lentils into her cart. "I suppose I don't have a choice about that."

Rose reeled back like she'd been slapped. Her face went warm. "I won't tell if you don't want me to."

Winter pushed her cart past her. Rose turned hers around in the aisle and followed behind her.

"Are you gonna come visit?" Rose asked.

"No." Winter grabbed a few different herbs off the shelf. Rose had no idea what they were for, but didn't think this was the time to ask.

"Callie wants to see you. She has this idea for making a traditional poultry — poulter — I dunno, some kind of salve out of bark, and I told her you would know more about that me. Doesn't your mom make traditional medicines?"

Winter had no reply to that.

"I suppose I could ask Jane — Ronnie's Mom — she's always been the expert on that kind of stuff, but damned if she's ever around."

Winter turned the corner. Rose edged her cart in front of Winter's — a bold move, but she was desperate. "I'm sorry. I didn't want him to stay with us. I told him no but he — "

"He's a lying, cheating pig and you took his side because you're weak."

The force of Winter's anger knocked the wind out of Rose. Frozen, Rose watched her continue down the aisle. "You're thinking Monty's like Gilbert," Rose replied finally. "But he isn't. He made a mistake and he is so sorry."

"I'm not going to be one of those women who stands by while her husband fucks every skank from here to the States."

Rose didn't know what to say because she was the kind of woman who stood by while her husband fucked every skank from here to the States. Maybe even Central America for all she knew. (But not Europe because Monty couldn't leave the continent on account of his criminal record.)

Winter had never been this mad at Rose. Not even when Rose spilled mustard on her white suede lampshade.

Winter bent low to grab a huge bag of wild rice. Rose
rushed over and bent with her. "Let me grab that for you."

"I can do it."

"But I want to help you."

"I don't want your help."

"You're mad, you don't mean that."

"I'm not mad!"

"You shouldn't get so excited when you're pregnant."

"Fuck, take it like you take everything!" Winter hissed. She
heaved the bag of wild rice at Rose who caught it in both her
arms and stumbled backward.

Rose started crying.

Winter saw the tears, turned and pushed her cart away. So
of course, Rose cried harder.

Rose took a Kleenex box from the shelf next to her,
punched a hole in it and grabbed a few tissues. Annabelle
popped around the corner. Rose nodded at her. She had long
ago stopped feeling embarrassed over crying in public. Being
married to a jerk did that to you.

"Hey Rose, you okay?"

"Yup." Her voice was thick with snot and tears.

Annabelle pretended to read the side of a toilet paper
wrapper while she waited for Rose to compose herself.

Rose blew her nose. "Where's Mariah?"

"My mom's."

"I thought you were in the city now?"

"The daycares were all full up and my cousin said she
would babysit, but then got a job at the casino so that fell
through. Plus Jason Six kept calling all the time telling me to
come back. Don't know why, haven't seen hide or hair of him
since I moved back to the rez."

"Maybe he's working?"

"He better be. Cuz I'm broker than a stripper with scabies. Spent all my money on bus tickets, babysitters, and a few bad bingo investments."

"The city's hard with a kid." Rose wiped at a couple of stray tears.

Annabelle nodded. Then she glanced around the corner and moved in close to Rose: "So, I heard you and Winter going at it."

"It would be hard not to. It's a small store." Rose hiccupped on the last few words, and a few more tears burst out of her eyes.

"What's the deal there?"

"Monty was texting a flag girl so she kicked him out and I let him stay with us," Rose whispered.

"Texting?"

"I guess they call it sexting these days."

"I don't know if I'd kick a man out for that. But then again Winter and I have different standards. Like she probably wouldn't date a man who got arrested for stealing a tattoo gun even if it was the best Christmas gift ever."

Rose was curious about the details but didn't have the energy to ask about it. Annabelle smacked her gum.

"So I heard you're running a marathon?"

"Well, yes, I guess."

"That's cool. Oh, and I heard you got Liz's job at the band office."

"Yeah," Rose wiped at some more tears and blew her nose on another tissue.

"And I heard you're working with that fine-ass chief of ours?"

"He's very nice," Rose hiccupped.

"See, then, you don't have anything to cry about. Shit, I'm the one who should be sobbing in the fucking IGA. No job, no man, haven't been laid in a month."

"A year for me."

Annabelle laughed. "Jesus, Rose, I'd be bawling too."

❧

Monty went to see Winter after supper.

Rose had mangled the wild rice, but she and the girls enjoyed a bowl of popcorn on the couch while watching a horror movie that was too old for Callie and too young for Sarah.

"Are you allowed to eat this?" asked Sarah.

"She's carving up." Callie said. "Big race tomorrow."

"It's carbing up," Sarah corrected her.

"I've been carbing up my entire life," Rose said. "So this race should be a breeze."

The door opened and Monty walked in. His dark mood filled the room and nobody said a peep as he walked through the living room on his way to the bedroom.

"I need to talk to Uncle 'bout my science project," Callie said.

"He wants to be alone."

"He was gonna show me how to make a really good volcano."

"Even I know that: vinegar and sugar," Rose said.

"Vinegar, baking soda, and dish soap," Sarah piped in.

The phone rang and Rose jumped at the sound.

"It's just the phone, Mom, relax." Sarah said.

"I know," Rose said, throwing a bit of annoyed teenager tone into her voice. She clambered up from the couch and grabbed the phone. She didn't recognize the number so she answered a bit hesitantly, trying to remember what bill she might have forgotten to pay.

"Rose, it's Taylor."

Rose's heart leapt like a lamb in a field of flowers. "Yeah?"

"Albert had a heart attack."

"Oh my God, is he okay?"

"Sergeant Martin found him on the side of the road and drove him to the hospital."

Rose went around the corner and sat down on a kitchen chair. She'd known Albert since she'd been a kid.

"That really sucks," Rose said. "He's one of the reserve's only elders."

"I know. Anyway I'm on the way to the hospital. His family is all there and well, I want to be there with them." Taylor's voice went up at the end of the sentence and Rose smiled in the dark, hearing his nervousness.

"I can come with you. I mean I have a race tomorrow but — "

"You can't miss your race." Taylor's voice was firm.

"I could cancel it, though, if you need some help." Rose was actually pretty excited about the idea of not running ten kilometres at the crack of dawn.

"No, absolutely not, do your run. Good luck tomorrow."

"Thanks."

Rose put the phone down. Then she said a silent prayer for Albert. As she headed back into the living room, she was struck with that nagging feeling like when you're at the movies and you feel like you've forgotten to turn off your stove.

Thirteen

THERE WERE A LOT OF PEOPLE in the parking lot: long, lean men with hips the size of ten-year-old girls, women with legs the size of Rose's arm, and an army of volunteers with eager smiles and matching T-shirts. Rose watched the runners kick out their uncooked spaghetti legs in the cold morning air.

Rose had not yet left the warmth of the car. She chewed energetically on a piece of gum. Callie sipped her hot chocolate in the passenger seat; Sarah was stretched across the backseat, wrapped in the quilt from her bed, her eyes clamped shut.

"I'm not ready."

"Kinda too late, Mom."

"We could go to Timmy's and you could get a donut. And we could say that I ran the race."

"I don't like lying for you, Mom." Rose knew that was a lie.

"It's gonna hurt. A lot."

"Yeah."

Rose peered at the sky. "It's still dark out, is it even safe to run in the dark?"

"Probably not." Callie blew on her window and etched her name in the fog.

Rose opened her car door.

"You're not wearing those, are you?" Sarah's voice was drunk with sleepiness and judgement.

Rose looked down at her purple sweat pants. "It's cold."

"Take them off."

Rose obeyed. Underneath she wore a pair of nylon basketball shorts that Gilbert used to wear around the house. They hung to her knees and were too big around the waist but they had a drawstring that would keep them up. At least Rose hoped it would.

"Okay, then. This is it." Rose looked into the car, the warm air inviting her back inside.

"Good luck, Mom," Callie said. "Run fast."

"Y'know, maybe I shouldn't do this, I could always do another run in a couple of weeks — "

"Shut the door, it's frickin' freezing!" Sarah commanded.

Rose slammed the door shut and made a face at Sarah through the window. Sarah had already closed her eyes. Callie bounced into the driver's seat and knocked on the window; she gave Rose the thumbs-up sign.

Hordes of runners were walking past the car and Rose followed them, unsure of where the start line was supposed to be. She listened to a pair of matchstick-thin women talk about how hard it was to find good entertainment for toddler's birthday parties.

"You have to turn over every stone to find a good clown and then — the pay they want! It's like extortion!"

"Have you considered a juggler?"

"I assume every good clown can juggle."

Rose's nylon shorts clung to her legs and ass. She figured there'd be no static cling at five degrees Celsius on a misty day, but then her bad luck always defied science. She stuck out like a sore thumb, but she also knew from years of being a sore thumb that people punished the below-average by ignoring them, not by singling them out.

The start line was thirty metres from where Rose stood. Rose let the crowd form around her. The matchstick women were on her left side, slightly in front of her. Their conversation had turned to organic, gluten-free birthday cakes. To her left, tense middle-aged men checked the thick black watches on their wrists. A few people jumped up and down and made Rose nervous that they would land on her feet, thus forcing her to get angry and say something sharp which would of course draw attention to her ridiculous shorts.

She glanced down at her shoes and noticed another hole in the netting of her sneaker. Her mind flicked back to elementary school and having kids calling her "Holy Rosie" because of the holes in her shoes, her jeans, and her school bag.

Those were not good days. One time Rose was so upset that when she got home from school, she marched into the kitchen and balled out her mom: "It's your fault I look so stupid!"

Rose remembered how her mom had spent the night sewing up the holes in her jeans with thick black thread which, if you know anything about denim, made them look a thousand times worse. But Rosie wore them anyway because she felt so bad for yelling at her mom.

Fuck this stupid race for bringing up issues, she thought. *Positive thoughts only now. Healthy kids, healthy body, okay tits, a house, a car that worked most of the time, a job, and a hot-looking boss.* Rosie grinned at her list, wishing she could share it with the Popsicle stick twins — its meager happiness would probably stun them into silence. Then a gun went off and the runners began to move forward. And that was that; Rose was in a race.

❧

Once the runners got past the muddled up stage, they started to thin out. There were the front people who Rosie saw briefly and never expected to see again. Then there were the people who passed her. There were no other types of people. So far she had passed no one, which meant that if she didn't speed up that she would end up being the last person to cross the finish line. She hoped there was at least one inspiring centenarian in the race — one that she could beat, of course.

At the top of every kilometre, there was a table set up with volunteers handing out Gatorade and water. Rosie thought maybe the runners had bought the drinks beforehand. What if the runners who had purchased drinks were wearing some special kind of tag on their bib? And what if she went up to the table and volunteers were like, "Sorry, but you have to pay for this . . . " and then Rose would have to slink away. So this is why she didn't drink any water for the entire race.

She walked at least a kilometre, maybe even two. Whatever it was, it felt long. She didn't even walk fast, she walked slowly and held her hand to her aching left side. People passed her and gave her encouraging remarks like, "You can do it," "Good run," and "Be strong." She wanted to trip them. It was like they were pointing the opposite out of the obvious. She could not do it, but she would do it because there was no other way to get home. She was not having a good run — she was walking. And she may have been strong but how would they know unless she placed her hands around their necks and showed them?

All she wanted was her bed and a water bottle and a pack of smokes.

Her body parts took turns plaguing her. Her left knee ached until it popped. Then it would relent until it started to ache again. Her lower back hurt. It was like menstrual cramps but not as pleasant. Her stomach hurt — from hunger, of course. Apparently half a coffee and a piece of toast wasn't enough fuel for a ten-kilometre run. And, her lungs — could they hurt any more? Breathing felt like someone had stuck a straw into thick mud and asked her to suck on it. Was the bottom of her lungs like tar? Rose thought of people she saw on the street dragging their oxygen tanks behind them. That would suck. Nobody ever tried to pick up someone with an oxygen tank.

Rose began to jog, but it was a pathetic sort of movement, like her hips were dragging her legs behind her. Strange words began to reverberate through her brain. "Pickles, bikini, remote, steam cleaner . . . " Her mind wasn't making a whole lot of sense. She was ready to pack it in and sit on the sidewalk, hoping that someone would send an ambulance back for the "old lady in the boy shorts," when she heard her mother's voice.

Same as last time, Callista sounded like she was right there with Rose, walking beside her, calm and composed. "You can do this."

"No, I can't," Rose grunted.

"You can, and you will," Callista replied in a tone that suggested that a spanking was on the way.

Rose moved her feet in the direction of her mother's voice, which was always slightly to the right, slightly ahead of her.

I miss you, Mom, Rose said in her head.

I miss you, too.

Dad and I fell apart. I don't know how to put us back together.

It'll be okay.

I wish you never had to die.

I wish that, too.

Callista's voice wasn't sad. Just practical and kind as she always was when Rose stood beside her every night while she cooked dinner and Rose nattered on about school.

And then the blue shadow was there again. Rose veered away from it and felt a pain as her knees disagreed with her quick turn.

She nearly tripped and called out "help," although with the pain in her throat, it came out, "haw." There was no one around to hear her anyway. She looked back at the blue shadow, the form was a little more true. She saw her mother's face. Then beside her Rose saw another figure, a small man with jet black hair, despite his age. Albert. He smiled sadly at her.

"Holy shit," she muttered, although it came out, "hoe-wee sheet."

"She's here." Her mother's voice was solid.

"Who?"

"Protection," Callista pointed at her heart.

"What the hell are you talking about?" which came out, "whuh arr you talhing aboo?"

Then they were gone. Rose was flummoxed, what the hell did that mean? Was she finally going crazy? Everyone had told her that living with Gilbert would eventually do that. But she always thought that when someone went crazy that they didn't know it was happening, like being possessed by a demon. Everyone else would be scared shitless, but you'd be blissfully unaware.

Rose let out a deep breath and stuff flew out of her nose, reminding her that in a few moments, someone would come around the corner and see her standing there covered in her own snot.

She turned and trotted in the direction of the finish line. She would ponder supernatural matters later, right now she had to get herself home.

∼

After a few thousand years of "only one more step," Rose turned a corner and saw the big banner hanging above the road. It proclaimed the end of the race and Rose had never been happier to see a banner.

"Bes bannah in a worl," she muttered to herself.

Callie stood at the finish line. She clutched a Canadian flag in her hand — God knows where she found that — and waved it.

"Mom!" she screamed when she saw Rose coming up the hill. (Yes, a hill at the finish line, could the organizers be more cruel?)

"Mom!"

Rose nodded at her; speech was well beyond her.

"Mom! Mom! Mom! Mom!" Callie yelled.

Rose waved a finger at her. Fortunately, her weak gesture was enough to mollify Callie.

As she crossed the threshold between running and not running, Rose would have liked to have sped up, straightened up and generally looked more like an athlete than a broken down collection of limbs and stiffening joints, but that boat had already sailed about five kilometres ago. Instead, she staggered across the finish line into the arms of the volunteers, who were delighted at her degradation — at last someone needed them! They wrapped her in a metallic blanket and spoke words of encouragement, "You made it! You're amazing! You rock! You're a hero!"

Rose tried not to puke on them.

The volunteers quickly conveyed her ravaged body to the medical tent.

"Count to ten," said the female paramedic who looked barely out of high school as she grasped Rose's wrist for a pulse.

"Thro hurs," croaked Rose.

"Good enough."

The paramedic declared her still alive and eighty percent likely to stay that way.

Callie stood beside her, and when Rose made it to her feet — this was a five-second feat of mind over pain — Callie immediately demanded a donut.

Rose nodded her agreement and then limped to the parking lot. It was a long, quiet journey.

By the time they reached the car, Sarah had reclaimed her front seat and had her feet up as she bobbed her head to some kind of music. She looked surprised when Rose opened the door. She checked her watch and was about to proclaim a time when Rose held up her hand, "Doan teh me."

"But it's really bad — "

Rose nodded as she began her descent into the driver's seat. "I doan wanna know."

"But how will you improve — "

Rose glared at her; Sarah slouched back down in her seat.

"Well, I would want to know," she muttered to the passenger window.

Rose's hands shook as she grasped the steering wheel. She wanted to tell the girls what she'd seen but she was too tired to talk, too tired to think, and so she eased her aching legs into the car and drove in the direction of donuts.

Taylor's black car was parked in the front yard when they pulled in. He was leaning against it, his hands in his pockets. Callie whistled from the backseat. "Holy moly, now that's a car."

Rose took a long time getting out; she had to lift each leg out in turn. By the time she managed to get her body into an upright position, Callie was already rubbing her chocolate-stained hands over the car and peppering Taylor with questions. Sarah was off to the side, conflicted by her natural instinct to never be impressed by anything and her genuine admiration for pretty things.

"How much did this car cost?" Callie asked boldly.

"Callie," Sarah and Rose said at the same time.

Taylor smiled crookedly. "Too much."

Callie did not look impressed with that answer. "That's not what I asked," she muttered, checking her teeth in the side mirror.

Rose hobbled closer before anything else rude could tumble out of her youngest's mouth.

Taylor pointed at the numbered bib attached to the front of Rose's T-shirt. "Good job."

"Thanks."

"So, I have some bad news."

Rose looked meaningfully at Sarah, who nodded. "C'mon mouth breather," she said as she pushed a protesting Callie up the steps.

Rose wanted to tell him that she already knew but that would be certifiably weird so she stood there and waited.

"Albert passed away this morning. His family — or I guess, families — called me and said they want a traditional ceremony and I said, of course, but I don't know what to do."

"Call Cote and Sons, first of all. They're the only funeral home in town that knows their way around the reserve. Gladys will handle the rest; do what she tells you."

Taylor let out a deep breath. "Okay, cool. Thanks."

Rose changed position and winced.

"You okay?"

"I'll be fine. You want to come in for some ..." Rose rummaged through her mind for some kind of food that wouldn't take any effort to prepare, "apples?"

Taylor smiled. "No that's okay."

"Good, cuz my immediate plans are to crawl into bed and die."

"You deserve it — the rest, I mean. Don't die or I'll have to fire you." He looked like he regretted the joke as soon as he said it. "I'll let you go."

Rose watched him drive away (unwilling to let him see her limp across the yard and drag herself up the stairs) and thought about his last phrase, because it sort of meant that there was an alternative to letting go, and dog-tired as she was, she wished he'd decided on that instead.

Rose's stomach growled, and she pondered the strange fact that she was incredibly hungry but so tired and sore that she could not make it to the kitchen to get food. She was beginning to see how those marathon runners got so damned skinny. She was so hungry, but so tired, but so hungry! Rose took a deep breath and bellowed, "Callie!"

∽

Rose packed up the girls around eight to head over to the wake. It was held in the band hall where every wake, wedding, bingo, and cabaret was held. She and the girls walked up to the people smoking outside and shook hands with everyone. Before going inside, Rose and the girls stopped at the fire where a group of young men and women were keeping the fire going. It was the first night and the fire was bright enough that the teens could share flirtatious glances over it.

Sarah was waylaid by some teenage girls. Rose gave them a once over, they were good girls (although what did she know, really?), and ushered Callie inside. Callie's energy was bubbling through her — Rose could feel it through her fingertips perched on Callie's shoulders. The kid always loved crowds. Rose was not such a fan. She generally babbled around people and usually depended on Winter's calm to steady her.

At the threshold to the hall, Rose stopped to survey the mourners. The hall was crowded, every folding chair was occupied and still more people were leaning against the walls. The hall was loud with the sound of people telling stories about the old man and cracking inappropriate jokes that made the laughter both loud and guilty. Even louder were the kids running around a corner of the room, playing a fast-paced game of "not-it" with incomprehensible rules.

Albert had lived on the reserve his whole life but he'd also travelled as a powwow dancer so there were many faces that Rose didn't recognize. Then she saw two that she did —

"Dad!" Callie leapt forward like a colt and launched herself at his waist. Gilbert looked down at her, surprised as usual at his younger daughter's joy. He patted her on the head absently.

Rose had no time to ponder his lack of parenting skills, her attention was drawn instantly to Michelle standing to the right of him. Their eyes locked. Rose saw the fear in her cousin's eyes and sent back a brief blink of her rage. Michelle looked away.

Rose stayed completely still, not exactly by choice. Her feet were rooted on the spot even though her heart was beating so fast she could hear it in her ears.

Michelle turned back toward her and half-smiled, "You lost lots of weight, huh?"

"Like a tonne," Gilbert added.

Rose and Michelle glared at him for different reasons. He feigned interest in a story Callie was telling him.

"I can't believe he's gone," Michelle pointed with her lips at the casket near the stage.

"I can't, either." Rose's words were barely above a whisper. She was technically talking to Michelle the cunt but nobody could really prove it.

Callie looked up at her dad, "Did a ghost kill him?"

Gilbert shook his head. "His heart broke."

"People's hearts can break?" Callie looked fearful.

Rose grabbed the back of Callie's hoodie and hauled her back. "Only people who've lived long, long, long lives."

She moved away from the adulterous twosome, towards where Albert's two wives sat on folding chairs next to each other. She gave Gladys a kiss and then Edna. They smiled at her and pinched Callie's cheeks, who complained loudly even though she secretly enjoyed it. Children were always a treat at funerals for the elders. Gladys grabbed Rose's hand and pulled her close. "He almost made it."

"Where was he going?"

"He was heading for the reserve boundary. She can't make it across."

"Yet." Edna's voice was sharp.

Rose had more questions but the line of people pushed her past them.

At the end of the line, there was only one more place to go. The coffin stood alone at the end of the room, flower arrangements placed around it. Rose readied herself. She pushed Callie back and for once, she stayed. Rose took the longest walk alone. Albert's eyes were closed, his hands were folded in the middle of his chest. Smokes and tobacco pouches were tucked in around him. Rose gave him a kiss on the forehead.

Fourteen

Rose drove to Winter's house the next morning. The car was gone, so Rose left a card tucked in the door. It was an old unused birthday card that she had found in a drawer. Certainly it wasn't Winter's birthday, but it was a cute card with a kitten on the front of it. Rose had gotten Callie to write, "Miss you so much, Love, your niece Callie." What good were children if not to emotionally blackmail people?

Monty was stopping by again after work. They were hoping that the two-pronged approach would get them some results. Monty still hadn't told his parents, which made Rose nervous. What if the gossip got to them first? She wasn't worried about Winter's parents, who lived hell and gone up north. Someone would have to dogsled the news of the pregnancy and subsequent break-up to them.

Rose peeked in one of the windows. She noticed a black mark on the floor. She leaned closer — it looked like a burn mark. Rose tried the front door; it was locked. She headed around to the back door. It was locked, too. She looked in another window; there was another black mark on that floor. In fact, they were everywhere.

Rose wished she had a cellphone. She climbed up the verandah and tried the patio doors. Locked. Rose looked inside, there were even more burn marks on the floor. She also saw a broken plant. What the hell was Winter doing? Winter loved her bamboo floors more than she loved Monty. She rattled the patio door, hoping to jar something loose.

∾

As soon as Rose got to work, she left a message on Monty's cellphone. Then she dialled one of her least favourite phone numbers.

"Police, Sergeant Nolan at your service."

"Hi, this is Rose, I want to report — "

"Well if it ain't a whole lot of Rosie . . . I've been waiting for you to call . . . " Nolan sounded even creepier over the phone than in person.

Rose heard a bit of distortion on the line. "Are you in the band office?"

Nolan stepped into her doorway. He closed his cellphone with a snap and winked: "What's going on, gorgeous? I hear you are officially in the single game. Are you ready to send a new quarterback into the end zone?"

Rose stifled a shudder. "Winter is missing."

"What are you talking about? I saw her yesterday."

"Where?"

"Driving down the road, looked like she was coming from your place, now that I think of it." Nolan scratched his belly through the buttons of his shirt. "Is the lack of sex affecting your memory? Cuz I can take care of that."

"Oh shut up. It's not that she's missing, it's that she's acting strange. She won't talk to me, she won't talk to her husband, her house is all messed up."

"A woman who won't talk to her husband? Jesus, call in the SWAT team!" Nolan laughed.

"I'm serious, Nolan. She's not herself."

"She's mad. Women get mad. I can't do nothing about that. Even though I know how to make them real happy," he purred and came halfway around her desk.

Rose sidled around the other side, moving the desk as she did so. If she was slimmer, it would have been an easy slide but she was still five pounds away from making a quick getaway. *Soon,* she thought to herself, *I'll be able to wriggle away from guys like this much faster.*

"Can you check on her?"

Nolan rolled his eyes. "If it will make you feel better."

"It would."

"Remember I did you a favour, now you owe a favour."

"It's your job."

"I think we have to stop this song and dance," Nolan said. "We need to give in to these feelings."

Rose picked up a pen. "Come a step closer and I'll stab you with this Bic."

"Funny, I was going to say something very similar to you."

Rose restrained herself from throwing her stapler at his head (mostly because it was only one of two in the entire office that worked). She settled for "Gross."

"Eventually, you'll realize that I am the best option." Nolan sauntered out, his wide hips undulating from side to side in a hypnotic fashion. Rose had to tear her eyes away.

The phone rang and Rose picked it up on the first ring.

"What's wrong?" Monty sounded annoyed.

"Have you been inside the house lately?"

"I didn't make that mess in the bathroom, that was Callie. That kid is gross."

"I'm talking about your house." Rose told him about the stuff she'd seen. He told her that he would head over to the hospital at lunch to check on Winter.

Then she quickly got off the phone because her peripheral vision told her that the line-up outside her door was gathering in size and rage.

For once, Rose did not feel her usual heart-pounding fear. Instead, it was a slightly elevated heartbeat and a mild stress sweat.

Twenty-five cases later, Lionel Cardinal stopped in and plopped himself in the chair.

"And how are you doing?" asked Rose, bracing herself for disappointment. His next appointment wasn't for two weeks.

"Pretty good, actually. My cousin's happy to have me there. Got my own room and everything. And last night I made lasagna for the kids."

"They must have loved that."

"They would eat lead if you poured cheese on it. These are eatin' kids. Anyway, wanted you to know that I'm working again."

"As a carpenter?"

"Yeah, turns out one of Lauren's baby-fathers works on a construction site and they needed some journeyman carpenters. I went in on Monday and they hired me on the spot. He's gonna drive me in every day until I get my license back."

"Lucky duck. But what if Lauren and him start fighting?"

"Well, I guess I'll have to find another ride, and if I can't, then I'll walk."

"For real?"

"I seen you running down the roads a few times and I thought well, goddamn, if she can do it, so can I."

Rose blushed and pretended to make a note in his file, but instead drew a cat face.

"I hear you're running that big marathon."

"Yeah, well, it's not looking good these days. I ran a 10K this weekend and nearly killed myself."

"How many more weeks?"

"Four."

"That's more than enough time," Lionel said. "Just gotta stay consistent. It's only a race, one foot in front of the other."

"It is," Rose agreed. She told him about the family volleyball night.

"I'll make sure Lauren knows, it would be good for her to get those kids out of the house. They're big kids, you know. Really big." He held his hands out wide in front of him to suggest something the size of a Smart car. Apparently, the Cardinal gene had skipped a generation.

∽

"Sarah!"

Sarah saw Ronnie beckoning from around the corner of the school. Sarah tossed her smoke to the ground and stepped on it.

"That's littering!"

Sarah looked in the direction of the voice, which was in the general vicinity of a black truck. The Ewchuk cousins stood in front of it, arms crossed, smirks on full beam.

She ignored them.

"Pick it up," Jonah yelled. Or maybe it was Brendan. She'd never seen the point in learning which asshole was which.

She looked over at them and gave them her best bitch face. "Go fuck yourself."

"Whoa, big words from a little girl."

She kept walking.

"Native slut."

Before she thought about it, she reached down, picked up a stone and flung at them. It hit the windshield and Sarah smiled as she saw a divot in the glass.

"Fucking bitch!" "Cow!" They were yelling over one another now.

She picked up another stone and flung it at one boy's head. He ducked and it flew over him and dinged the hood of the truck.

She threw another stone, this one took out their left headlight.

"What the fuck?" One of the cousins was backing up toward the driver side.

Sarah picked up another stone and smiled as she lightly tossed it in her palm.

"Crazy bitch!" The other one jumped in on the other side.

Sarah turned away and heard them peeling out of the parking lot behind her. Ronnie came out from behind the corner, the dark circles around her eyes threatened to swallow them completely.

"Good job."

"They deserved it."

Ronnie nodded slowly. Her movements seemed sluggish, like she was barely awake. "The Dream Woman is coming for us."

Sarah blinked suddenly and looked around in a panic. "The witch?"

Ronnie looked hurt. "She's our friend. Who do you think gave you the power to do that?"

Sarah looked down at the stone in her hand and dropped it. "We have to reverse this. Can we go back to your house and undo it? We can rebury her! Or bury her deeper? Maybe we can borrow a backhoe!"

Ronnie shook her head.

"So what do we do? What's she gonna do?"

Ronnie shrugged. "I don't know. I'm so tired."

Sarah felt her forehead. It was clammy. "We should take you to the doctor."

Ronnie shook her head impatiently. "She wouldn't like that. She doesn't want people to know she's here yet. She's still testing things out."

"And you're telling me this now?"

Ronnie slowly slunk to the ground. Sarah plopped down next to her.

Ronnie rubbed her eyes. "I wanted to make something happen. If I could get one kind of magic to work then maybe I could get another kind to work and then y'know . . . my dad . . . "

Sarah patted her friend's leg. "Did you talk to your mom?"

"She's in Ottawa now."

"Fuck."

"What about your mom?"

Sarah thought for a moment. "My mom doesn't know anything about spiritual stuff. That's kind of why her and my grandpa don't get along anymore."

"What about him?"

Sarah brow wrinkled. Lloyd wasn't one of her favourite people. The last time she'd seen him he was yelling at her mom outside the band office because she let Callie make her first communion at the church. It had all been Callie's idea. Sarah suspected it was because she wanted to wear a pretty white dress and be the centre of attention.

"Or, what about your dad? He sings with a powwow group doesn't he?"

"He has, yeah."

"Let's call him." Ronnie pulled out her cellphone and handed it to Sarah.

"I don't know his number," Sarah said.

"Then call your mom and ask her."

Sarah inwardly groaned but dialled the number to the band office and asked for her mom.

"What's wrong?" Rose's voice was already verging on the hysterical. She always assumed the worst when Sarah called. Though to be fair, thought Sarah, this time her mom was actually right.

"Nothing. I need Dad's number."

"Why?"

"Because I want to ask him for money."

"He's probably broke."

Sarah made a face at Ronnie. This was already turning out to be way too much work. "I need to talk to him, okay?"

"What's wrong?"

"Nothing."

"Then why do you want to talk to your dad?"

Sarah wanted to throw the phone at the wall. "I want to talk to him, alright? I thought you said that if we wanted to have a relationship with our dad then you wouldn't stand in our way."

"I never thought you actually would."

"Mom!"

"All right, don't freak out."

Her mom told her that Gilbert was staying in his brother's house on the west end.

"It's great that you want to talk to him." Rose added. "Say hi to the cunt for me."

Sarah hung up and then looked at Ronnie, who was chewing on her black fingernails. "Got it."

"Took long enough," Ronnie said.

Sarah burned Ronnie with her glance as she dialled the phone. Nobody picked up so she left a short message.

"That's that. Maybe we should go see the police, too."

"Why?"

"Dude, we're being haunted."

"You can't arrest a ghost. We'll look crazy and they'll arrest us for being high. And besides, she would be very angry."

Sarah shivered. A tone kept creeping into her friend's voice that was not-Ronnie.

Ronnie sat up straight. "Hey! Do you think your dad can get us some weed?"

Sarah glared at her but was inwardly relieved. That was 100 per cent Ronnie.

Ronnie put her head on the wall. "Hey, I'm gonna sleep for a while, okay?"

"No problem."

Sarah looked down at her hands. Her palm tingled from where she had palmed the rock, the sensation was moving up her arm and spidering through her body.

∾

Rose went to the café for lunch. She spotted Tisha sitting at a table with the other councillors and pretended not to see them. She looked around for a certain dark head and was disappointed when she didn't see it. She went up to the counter.

"Rose Okanese — what the hell happened to you?" asked Frances Adams, who ran the lunch counter. Rose's face turned red as people turned to look. Frances had the same commanding voice as her daughter Kaylee.

"What do you mean?" Rose checked her blouse for coffee stains. There were none, but there was a small hole near her armpit. She kept her arm to her side.

"You have AIDS or something?"

"Hell, no. You have to have sex to catch that."

"You turn sideways and you'll disappear. You're a goddamn bone rack."

Rose still had a formidable amount of jiggle on her, but Frances' comment put a grin on her face.

She sat down next to Kaylee, who was texting and talking to a table full of people at the same time.

"I woke up like four times last night and I need my sleep," Kaylee was saying. "You may not believe this but I get fucking evil if I don't get my rest."

"Why'd you keep waking up?" Rose asked.

"Nightmares."

"For real?"

"Yeah, it was fucking weird. I had this one where this big dog was chasing me and it smelled so bad. Then I woke up and had an even worse dream."

"'Bout what?"

Kaylee made a face as she tried to remember. "Not sure, but it was scary. Someone was coming for me, like, I could hear it crunching on the gravel and everything — not even fast either, like, slow but unstoppable."

Rose took a bite of her sandwich and tried to make herself chew gracefully. She'd gone for a short run that morning to loosen up her muscles and as usual she was ravenous.

Kaylee changed the subject and was midway through a story about how her tattooist was going to jail for selling stolen computers when a familiar smell wafted into the room. The scent of Polo was accompanied by hoots and wolf whistles from the women at Rose's table. A second later, Taylor slipped into the seat next to Rose.

"Hi, ladies," Taylor said.

"Bossman," Kaylee purred. "Where you been keeping your sweet self?"

"Flu kicked the crap out of me." Taylor did look pale, but Rose knew he was full of shit. Thanks to all those years with Gilbert, she was a human lie detector.

"I'm gonna keep an eye out for who gets it next, then I'll know who you've been messing with," Kaylee joked.

"Kaylee, he's the chief, have a little more respect," Tisha intoned from the next table.

"Oh, calm down, *Kokum*," Kaylee replied. "Don't get your corduroy panties in a knot."

People snickered.

Tisha looked ready to smack Kaylee, so Rose spoke up: "Volleyball tonight, everyone. Bring your kids."

"How much?"

"Free," Rose said, "but don't expect me to watch your kids. It's family night, not free babysitting night."

A few people indicated that they would be stopping by.

Kaylee told Rose that she'd be bringing her kids, her sister's kids, and her neighbour's kids around 8 PM. Then she headed back to the office, as she was scheduled to Skype with some guy she used to date but who was now living in Thunder Bay with his mom.

Taylor watched Rose finish her lunch, which was disconcerting, to say the least. She tried to pretend that he was like a cousin or a brother, but her body wasn't fooled. Pheromones rose off her skin like a warm steam. She pushed her food away before she was even half-finished.

When most of the people had drifted out, Taylor leaned close to Rose. "She won't leave."

Rose didn't need to ask who *she* was. "Well I guess then you have two options."

"Which are?"

"You get the police involved or you buy matching pajamas."

"I figured I'd outwait her."

Rose laughed. Like any man had ever beaten a woman at that game. "She is not going anywhere, I can guarantee it. Might as well go get a priest," Rose said.

"She's so . . . frustrating," Taylor said.

"And beautiful."

"That wears off."

"Does it?" Rose looked skeptical. She knew the signs of sexual chemical poisoning, having suffered from them for most of her adult life. Taylor was sweaty, confused, and too open with his problems.

"I told her to go, but she won't. What am I supposed to do? I can't force her out or else I'll look like a bully and she says she has no place to go — she got fired from her cheerleading job, y'know."

"Cheerleading is pretty cutthroat from what I see on reality TV." Rose cleared her tray in the garbage and poured herself some more coffee.

"She's never been good at saving money, so she's broke now. Do you know how it feels to have someone completely dependent on you?"

"I can ask my two *children* if they know how that feels."

"Right, of course. And if I call the tribal police, then everyone will know I can't handle my own business and that'll look bad."

"Plus, everyone around here has a police scanner so it'll be all over the reserve in matter of seconds."

Taylor rubbed his forehead. Even in bad shape, he still looked good.

"There might be something you can do," Rose said, even though she couldn't think of anything other than packing a tiny body attached to a pair of big boobs into the trunk of her car.

As they walked over to the band office together, Taylor noticed Nolan sleeping in his police car.

"Well, that inspires confidence," he commented.

"That's when he does his best police work," Rose joked, and then felt disloyal. Nolan was family, after all (despite what he thought).

❦

Rose and Callie left the house early for the volleyball night. Monty was following with Sarah and Ronnie because they didn't want to show up too early.

"Teenagers think it's not cool to be early," Rose explained to Callie.

"Who cares about being cool, I want to be first!" Callie said as she pulled her seatbelt on in the front seat.

Rose and Callie discussed her science project. They had decided to make a volcano after all. Monty had described some of the ingredients needed, and it seemed like it wouldn't be so hard. Rose spotted a woman walking on the side of the road and slowed down. She honked the horn and the woman stopped but did not turn around. Rose suddenly felt wary.

But Callie was already rolling down her window.

"Do you need a ride?" Callie called out.

The woman turned. Rose fought the urge to gasp. This was the oldest woman she'd ever seen. How could someone be so old and still walking? And fast, too. From behind, she'd looked like a woman in her prime.

The old woman strode toward the car while Rose fought the urge to peel away.

Callie was unbuckling her seatbelt to give the hitchhiker the front seat but Rose threw her hand over Callie's. "Stay put."

The back door opened and the woman slid in. Rose felt the car sink like a huge weight had been added to it. Callie turned around in her seat and smiled at their new passenger.

"Hello, I'm Callie," she said, "I'm eight years old and in grade five."

"Grade two," Rose corrected. "How far are you going ma'am?"

"As far as you can take me." The voice was gravelly. Rose didn't want to be one of those people who got freaked out around old people, but she was seriously freaked out. *Same as a young person, only with a different skin on,* she reminded herself.

She didn't smell like a young person, though. She smelled like smoke and damp at the same time. Like when someone poured a beer into an ashtray. Unclean. The word popped into her mind unbidden.

"Where you coming from?" Rose asked.

The woman did not answer, so Rose glanced in the rear-view mirror and flinched when the woman's eyes were waiting there for her.

"I've come from a long ways," she growled.

"You got family here?"

The woman shook her head. "All dead."

Rose would have said the obligatory "I'm so sorry" here but the woman's voice was hardly sad, she sounded almost gleeful.

"Then who are you visiting?" Callie had turned around completely in her seat.

The woman's white lips curled into a smile. "Whoever will have me."

Rose prayed that Callie wouldn't offer their house to her. She threw a quick glance at Callie, hoping to communicate this to her.

"You could come stay with us. It's crowded but you could sleep on the couch."

The woman laughed sharply. "I already have a place to go."

Rose sighed with relief.

"How is that husband of yours?" the woman asked.

"You know Gilbert?"

"Everyone knows him," the woman said slyly.

Rose couldn't disagree with that. "He does perform a lot. Do you want one of his CDs? There's some rolling around in the trunk. And if you head to any sleazy bars in the area, I'm sure he'll autograph it for you."

"Or I could autograph it for you!" Callie offered. "I'm his daughter."

"Your dad is a bad man for leaving a little girl as sweet as you," the woman breathed.

Rose inhaled sharply, wanting to tell off the woman but unable to because she was an elder. Callie spoke up.

"Oh no, I know he loves me," Callie replied. "But he's not connected to his feelings. My mom told me that." She added proudly.

The woman sighed. "Let me out here."

Rose slowed the car and heard the door slam before she'd even completely stopped.

"Bye!" Callie called from her window. "I like people from the olden days," she told Rose.

Rose looked in her rear-view mirror and got the shivers when she realized she couldn't see the woman. Probably went into the ditch or turned off, she told herself. Still, Rose felt her stomach roll like she'd missed the top step on the stairs.

The reserve gym was packed with people and their kids. Rose stood next to a box and handed out volleyballs to the kids lined up beside her. Callie was a foot away practicing spikes against the wall (missing most of them; Rose had been ducking her volleyball all evening).

Sarah was sitting on the stage with her friend Ronnie. Ronnie wore a spiked collar. Rose did not like the new Ronnie but understood that she was going through something since her dad's death. A ball went flying past Rose's head.

"For God's sake Callie — " Rose began, and then noticed that Callie was over by the water fountain.

"Sorry." Kaylee sauntered over and picked up the ball.

"No problem. Good turnout, hey?"

"You got that right. Can you make sure that I get on a team opposite my ex, Jason?"

"Jason Six?"

"That's my cousin. Jason Seven."

"Not a problem."

"I'm gonna spike this ball right into his stupid goatee."

"I look forward to seeing that."

"What kind of Native guy grows a goatee?" Kaylee asked. "A douchebag, that's who," she answered before Rose could offer up a reply.

Kaylee looked over Rose's shoulder. "Chief's here." Rose glanced behind her with a huge grin spread across her face — then as quickly as it had grown, it retracted back to a pouty moue. Taylor was there but Megan was, too. She wore a black tank top, sweats, and sneakers, but looked more chic than Rose would look in a cocktail dress.

"That's the Gambler girl, huh?" Kaylee said. "Nice cans."

"I hear they're fake."

Kaylee took a measuring glance. "I dunno, I used to play volleyball with a few Gambler girls and they're all stacked like that. Some bitches are just lucky."

Kaylee gave her own considerable rack a reassuring pat. Then she turned away to go scream at her boyfriend, who was searching through her purse.

Taylor spotted Rose and headed over. "Good job, Rose," he said. "I didn't expect so many people."

"We already ran out of toilet paper in the washrooms, so it's definitely a success," Rose replied.

"Hi, I'm Megan." Megan held her hand out to Rose.

"Hi," Rose said shyly. "I like your hair. It's so thick, like a medical textbook." She commanded herself to stop fan-girling.

"Oh it's a mess. I can't do anything with it with this hard water." She smiled at Taylor. "You need to work on that."

"Right, I'll make that my top priority before education, health care, and overcrowded housing," Taylor replied dryly.

"Do you guys want to play?" Rose asked.

"Absolutely," said Megan. "I love volleyball. I'm not very good, though, just played a little in high school and then in college. Can you make sure we're on the same team?"

"Uh . . . probably not . . . teams are sort of set in stone, " Rose said, pretending to study her clipboard.

Tayler shrugged. "Fit us in wherever."

"This is a nice gym," Megan said. "It reminds me of home."

"Where's that?" Rose asked.

"The Gambler reserve. You might know my dad — Edgar? He's the chief. My mother was a powwow princess. Sort of like the star quarterback and the homecoming queen." Megan made a face to downplay her bragging.

"Like you two," Rose said, as she imagined Megan would want her to.

"Oh no, we're not together. We're two friends working things out," Megan said. She brushed back her sultry bangs and Rose noted the flash of a very flashy ring on her right hand that looked suspiciously like an engagement ring.

Rose looked at Taylor. He was looking at the courts.

She fought the urge to throw her volleyball directly into Taylor's face.

"Yeah, my husband and I are doing the same thing — working on things," Rose pronounced loudly.

Taylor shot her a look.

"Oh, you're married! How long?"

Too damn long. "Uh . . . fourteen years, but we've been together for about seventeen."

"Wow, I don't know if I could walk away from a relationship that long. Like you've shared so much: memories, and hopes, and dreams. Why would you ever want to start over again?" Megan looked meaningfully at Taylor.

Rose and Gilbert had always had a separate-canoes-travelling-different-rivers-type of marriage, but Rose nodded her head anyway.

A group of gregarious teenage boys walked past and Taylor let them pull him away.

Chickenshit, thought Rose.

"Need any help?" Megan asked, glancing down at Rose's clipboard.

"There's not much to do. I mean, everyone knows how to play, we keep it sort of casual."

"You mean you haven't organized a warm-up or anything?"

"No."

"Aren't you worried about people hurting themselves?"

"I, uh . . . hadn't really thought about it . . . but you know the games don't really get that intense. It's for fun."

"Of course. I should go warm up." Megan bared her two rows of tiny, perfect teeth and grabbed the last ball from Rose's basket.

Around seven, the teams organized themselves onto the courts. There were three games going on at any time. Preteen girls volunteered to be the scorekeepers because it meant they could scope out the boys. There were no referees or line-keepers. People used the honour system, which meant that if you tried to cheat then a loudmouth like Kaylee would shout at you until your eyes teared up.

Rose hung out with the moms on the sidelines. Some of them were planning to play in a bit, others came by to be nosy. Annabelle had Mariah on her lap and joked around with two of her cousins, Casey and Nadine. They were discussing Taylor, of course.

"He makes me sweat. Like literally," said Annabelle. "Look at my pits."

Everyone looked and assured her that they were gross.

"Are we sure he's even a man? He looks like some different species, like a cheetah running among the wildebeests," said Nadine.

"Yum yum in my tum tum," echoed Casey.

Annabelle looked at Rose expectantly.

"We're very lucky to have such an athletic chief," said Rose. They laughed at her.

"Oh, c'mon, Miss Prim, you can do better than that," Annabelle said. "You don't have a man right now so you must be hornier than a three-headed goat."

"Even you're starting to look pretty good." Rose leered at Annabelle.

"Don't fall in love," Annabelle said, fluttering her eyelashes. "I'll break your heart."

"What's with the chick?" Nadine asked.

"He says they're not together, but she's wearing a big diamond on her ring finger. I think she wants them to be together," Rose said.

"Meow," said Annabelle. "Could be that they're together but he's not ready to admit it to himself. She's obviously staying with him. You think she's sleeping on the couch? Puleeze, you'd have to have shit for brains to believe that."

"Yeah," agreed Rose. She suddenly felt very stupid.

The four of them studied Megan. She stood at the serving line and measured the ball in front of her, threw it in the air, jumped at least a foot off the ground and hit the ball with the force of a jumbo jet. It slammed across the net. The players on the other team moved out of the way to watch it soar past them, hit the floor, and score a point.

"Scary," said Annabelle.

"Issues," said Casey.

"Don't mess with that bitch," said Nadine. "She'll spike your head into the floor."

"I would kill for a stomach like that," Rose said. "Looking at it makes me want to go slap my kids in the face."

"Whatever, give her a month on the rez and she'll fatten up like everyone else. She wasn't born that way. That's city food and gym living," explained Casey.

"I lived in the city, I got even fatter." Annabelle pinched her gut to demonstrate.

"That's cuz all you did was play bingo and take the bus everywhere."

"Did not, you cow."

The cousins continued fighting in the same good-natured way until one of them said it was time for a smoke break.

"You coming, Rose?" asked Annabelle.

"Nah, I'm trying to quit."

"For real?"

"Can't run and smoke. Too hard on the ol' bod." That morning she'd had a ten-minute coughing fit that woke up everyone in the house.

"All right, then. I was sick of you mooching smokes off me, anyway," Annabelle laughed. "Here, keep my kid." She handed Mariah to Rose.

Rose tucked Mariah into the mommy groove where her hip met her waist and walked around the perimeter of the gym. She stopped and picked up a few pieces of trash but for the most part she was proud of herself. Volleyball night was a big hit, so to speak.

She saw Kaylee's boyfriend set up Kaylee for a spike. Kaylee jumped higher than you would expect a big girl to jump and smashed a spike toward Tisha's face. At the last second, Tisha turned her face away and the ball glanced off the side of her head. There was much laughter at her expense.

Rose ducked with Mariah as a stray ball flew past her. "Dangerous for a baby here," she murmured into Mariah's ear.

Taylor played with a group of young guys. They would call out, "Chief, over here," and Taylor would send the ball right to them. They were hitting some powerful spikes and were clearly going to clean the floor with every team.

She saw Callie on Monty's team. Callie stood near the net and grinned. Anything that had her out with people (and not doing homework) made her gleeful.

She looked around for Sarah and found her serving the ball. Megan was gorgeous, but Sarah glowed. Rose smiled proudly as Sarah hit the ball hard enough to go over the net but no so hard that it intimidated the other players.

"I made that," Rose whispered into Mariah's hair.

Rose watched as Sarah bumped a ball to Lionel, who tipped it over the net. It scored a point and the entire team came together for a high five. As the cheering receded, Rose heard a moan. She turned behind her and saw Ronnie slightly hunched over, leaning against the stage.

"You okay Ronnie?"

"My stomach hurts," Ronnie said.

Rose shifted Mariah to her left and tilted Ronnie's face up. It was red and swollen.

"Are you allergic to anything?"

Ronnie shook her head. A ball went past Rose, barely missing Mariah. Rose glared at the offender. "C'mon, guys, baby here!"

Rose led Ronnie out of the gym into the principal's office.

"Sit there, I'll grab some Tums from the medical kit." Rose rummaged through the principal's desk with a familiarity that comes from being a part-time janitor.

"How bad does it hurt?"

"Morphine would be nice," grunted Ronnie.

Rose looked up from her search. The teenager seemed to be crumpling like a discarded Kleenex in front of her. Rose abandoned her search and reached for the phone. She dialled the number of the hospital; the line was busy.

Sarah entered the room at a run: "What's wrong?"

"Her stomach." Rose shifted the baby and the phone to her other arm and felt Ronnie's tummy. It was hard.

Ronnie yelped.

"Mom watch it!" Sarah said.

Rose tried the hospital again, the phone rang and rang in Rose's ear. "Is your mom home Ronnie?" Rose asked.

"Toronto," Ronnie whispered.

"I thought you said Ottawa," Sarah said.

Ronnie shook her head. "'nother conference."

The phone still rang. Rose hung it up. "Okay, okay, well, I'm gonna take you to the hospital," Rose said. "We'll call her from there."

Ronnie nodded.

"I'm coming," said Sarah.

"Let's go then."

"Mom!" Sarah pointed at the baby in Rose's arm. "You can't run off with someone's baby!"

"Oh, right. Give Mariah back to her mom." Rose pried the baby's hands off her neck and handed her to Sarah.

"And?" Sarah prompted.

"Thank her?"

"Callie."

"Yes! Tell your uncle to take Callie home." Callie would not be pleased about that but Rose didn't know how long they'd be at the hospital.

"My head hurts."

"We're going right away." Rose hooked her arm around Ronnie and pulled her to her feet. "Everything's gonna be okay."

Rose was limping towards the door with her charge when Sarah caught up with them. Rose inwardly groaned when she

saw Tisha close behind her, hands on her hips in the judge-
mental pose.

"What's going on here?" Tisha's tone suggested that she
was witnessing a drug deal go down.

"She's not feeling well, I'm taking her to the hospital."

"You're leaving? Who's going to lock up the gym?"

"Uh . . . right . . . Tisha would you mind locking up while I
take this girl to the hospital?"

Ronnie moaned under Rose's arm.

Tisha nodded stiffly and turned away, mumbling something
about unreliable employees under her breath.

"What a cow," Sarah said, loud enough for Tisha to hear.
Rose tried not to grin.

∽

The car flew across the unruly gravel roads. Rose was normally
a cautious driver but the sounds coming out of Ronnie's
mouth made her fearless. At first she called for her mom, then
her breathing got faster and shallower. Sarah chattered to her,
"We're almost there, it's about another five minutes, that's not
long, right? It's like the last five minutes of class, you feel like
it's never going to end and then it does and it's not so bad, you
just have to hold on."

Rose stopped the car in the emergency area and hesitated:
run inside screaming for help, or help the girl out of the
car? She decided on the latter. As the two big doors opened,
though, she let herself yell, "Help!" Nobody ran to their aid,
but the nurse behind the desk did hurry somewhat to call for
a wheelchair. Another nurse came from the back area and the
two of them took Ronnie from their hands. A wheelchair was
found and then Ronnie was wheeled behind the big doors.

Rose walked toward them but a nurse stopped her and
handed her a clipboard.

Rose wanted to protest, but she was pretty scared of hospitals to begin with so she shut her trap and sat down.

Sarah slumped into a chair next to her.

"Well?" Rose asked.

Sarah looked at the floor.

"Is she pregnant?"

Sarah shrugged. "I doubt it."

"Were you . . . was she doing drugs again?"

"No. I only did them that one time and you saw what happened."

"Yeah." Rose wished that she believed her daughter.

Rose got up and called Monty and gave him an update. She asked him to find Ronnie's mom's cellphone number. Then she asked him if he had stopped by Winter's.

"I went inside. It was a real mess, Rose. I feel like I should call someone." His voice was gravelly with worry.

"Like who?"

"The police. I know something's wrong. Cuz she would never do something like that to our house and where is she? What's happening out here? First Liz goes missing, then old Albert, now my wife — it's like we weren't even paying attention."

"Did you call her mom's?"

"They haven't heard from her, they didn't even know she was pregnant!"

"Whoa." Winter told her parents everything. They had a warm and loving relationship; Rose had always found that weird.

They said goodbye and Rose joined Sarah. She was sleeping in her seat, her legs stretched out in front of her and her arms folded over her chest like an old-time vampire.

Rose went up to the front desk. The nurse was working her way through a Sudoku puzzle.

"Did the doctor see Ronnie yet?"

"Ronnie?"

"The girl I brought in. Purple hair. Nose rings up the wazoo. Mohawk. I don't know how she could make herself more conspicuous."

"Doctor hasn't seen her. "

"Can I see her?"

The nurse looked her over. "You her mother?"

"Her aunt," Rose lied decisively.

"She's in room 214."

Rose headed down the hallway. It was a short trip. Ronnie was hooked up to an IV and sleeping. Her skin was so pale that her eyelids looked blue.

Dr. Sheila walked in. She was from South Africa and had a last name that made you sound racist every time you attempted it. So everyone called her by her first name. She'd been working in the Lowell hospital for a decade at least. She had married another doctor at the hospital — Dr. Lee — but had refused to take his last name.

Dr. Sheila said hi to Rose and then checked Ronnie's pulse.

"Is she okay?" Rose asked.

"I don't know." The doctor answered, her accent making it sound like a song.

"She was in a lot of pain so we put her to sleep but I'm not sure what's causing this swelling. And look at this on her arm." Dr. Sheila turned over Ronnie's arm. Rose could see the distinct imprint of teeth marks.

"That wasn't there when I brought her in." Rose hoped she didn't sound defensive.

"And then there's the x-rays."

"Is she . . . pregnant?"

"I don't know."

"How could you not know that?"

"Because her x-ray is . . . what's the word . . . blinded? You cannot see it clearly. There's too much in the way."

"Like fat?" Rose looked confused; Ronnie was a featherweight.

"Hair. Her stomach is filled with hair."

"Like she ate it?"

"I assume."

"Her own?"

The doctor shrugged.

I'd rather eat my own hair than someone else's, was Rose's first thought. "Would that be making her sick?"

The doctor shook her head. "No, there's something else afoot here." Dr. Sheila stared off into space. Then as if she had noticed Rose for the first time, she asked, "Are you on a diet?"

Rose blushed. "No, I've been running, training for a marathon."

"Good." She patted Rose on the shoulder. "I thought you were letting yourself go the last time I saw you."

An ambulance siren made both of them look up. Rose hurried toward the door and Dr. Sheila pushed past her. "Oh right, you go first," said Rose, and stepped aside.

Rose went back to the hospital bed and put her ear next to Ronnie's mouth to check her breathing (she wasn't sure why she did that) and then followed.

There was some commotion at the front doors. Rose could see Sarah across the room open her eyes and sit up.

Two paramedics were escorting a gurney into the building. Dr. Sheila met them halfway across the lobby. She asked them about heart rate and medical stuff that Rose remembered from watching *ER*.

She snooped over Dr. Sheila's shoulder to see who the patient was.

She recognized the stubborn set of the jaw and leaned over the gurney. "Winter?" The paramedic closest to her gave her a dirty look and elbowed her back.

Dr. Sheila was talking rapidly in medical lingo. Rose cocked her head, trying to make sense of it. Slow down, she wanted to say, or speak in English at least.

"She's pregnant!" Rose blurted out. "Almost three months!" Though of course these were Winter's coworkers and would know that too. Rose ran beside the gurney, keeping pace with everyone.

"Rose." Dr. Sheila pointed at the waiting area.

Rose stepped back and her feet met the wall.

"Where's she going?" she asked the nurses, but no one paid any attention to her.

Dr. Sheila followed the gurney as she talked to one of the medics. Rose called to her before she reached the big double doors. "Dr. Sheila!"

Before the doors closed in her face, Rose sent all of her hope flying through them.

Fifteen

SARAH WAS WALKING DOWN THE HALLWAY. She smelled cinnamon toast and her stomach rumbled. She followed the smell, bumping into the walls because she was always clumsy when she woke up. The smell ended at a doorway, but she paused before she went inside. Her surroundings told her that she was in a hospital, so that smell didn't seem like the right kind of smell. Sarah looked around for her mother. She wasn't there and neither was the nurse who sat at the front desk. Still, the smell beckoned her like one of those cartoon smells.

Sarah inched across the threshold of the door. Ronnie was lying in the hospital bed, looking shitty but smiling.

"Hey, you." Sarah took a step inside the room. Immediately she felt the temperature change, from warm to stingingly cold. Her body felt heavier and she felt her head turn, without her consent.

The Old Woman was there, so close Sarah could see her jagged teeth. She placed her hands on Sarah's shoulders and pulled her close. "Sarah." Her name was like a curse.

Sarah scrambled backward, felt her feet slip from beneath her and screamed, "Mom!"

She woke up in the car, her mom's eyes on her.

"Nightmare?"

"She knows my name."

Sarah didn't need to explain further. After seeing her aunt on the gurney, Sarah knew it was time to tell her mom everything she knew. Her mom probably didn't believe all of it, but she was willing to take her to see Gilbert.

Sarah looked in the back seat. Callie was wrapped in a star quilt, snoring softly.

"Where'd the kid come from?" Sarah asked.

"I went to the house and told Monty. He's on his way to the hospital."

They pulled up to the house. Michelle's car was gone, which Sarah was grateful for. She didn't want her mom and Michelle getting into it all over again.

Her mom looked at her. "Do you want me to come in?"

"Yeah."

They walked into the house after a quick knock. Gilbert was sitting on the couch in his gitch, eating cereal from a huge bowl. They had called him to let him know they were coming.

He put his bowl aside. "So?"

"Your daughter wants to talk to you."

Gilbert leaned forward, prepared for the worst.

Sarah looked at the TV, where a family was feuding against another family for glory and cash prizes. "I need someone to break a spell."

"You into witchcraft now?" Gilbert looked annoyed. "Damned Internet."

"We don't even have the Internet," Rose pointed out.

"Well whose fault is that, I wanted to get it — "

"So you could do your online gambling!"

"I'm allowed to invest my own money!"

Sarah spoke before they could start squabbling in earnest: "I was playing around with Ronnie . . . and I don't even know what we did. We went to this grave and we said some words and lit a candle and anyway now she's here."

Her dad leaned forward. "Whose grave was it?"

"Ronnie thinks it's this spirit they call the Old Woman or the Dream Woman."

Gilbert burped. He leaned back on the couch and stared at the TV. The topic was, "Things that have to be refrigerated."

"Milk," Gilbert said.

It was the top answer.

"Focus," Rose snapped.

"I'm thinking." Gilbert scratched his belly for a long time. Sarah watched as two flies mated on the edge of his cereal bowl.

"Well?" Rose said.

"I'm trying to remember what the hell I heard about this woman."

Hurry up, Sarah wanted to say, *Ronnie's sick, Winter's sick*. But she knew her dad. He got stressed out easily and when he did, he shut down completely. Her mom was shifting from side to side, looking like she was ready to punch him and Sarah shook her head at her.

During a commercial break, Gilbert finally spoke, "That old broad lived, like, back in the old days before this was even a reserve. Yeah. I remember my *mushum* saying she was a good woman. But then she went crazy and started doing all kinds of evil things to people."

"Like what?" Rose asked.

"People said she killed their horses. Others started getting sick. Some people even thought she poisoned the chief. A lot of bad luck stuff. So anyway, the chief and his Headmen decided to banish her. A bunch of guys went out to move her off and, I dunno, somehow she ended up dead."

"That's nice," Rose said.

"I didn't say it was a good idea but they didn't have any choice. People figured she'd start killing their kids next."

"What got her so pissed off?"

"When does a woman ever need a reason?" Gilbert chuckled.

"Don't be an idiot," Rose replied. "What else do you know?"

Gilbert dug through his chair and found a squashed pack of smokes. He looked up at Rose. "You have a light?"

Rose handed him her lighter wordlessly.

"The thing about this old woman is that she needs to feed all the time, otherwise she fades into the wind — like a memory or a fart."

"What does she eat?" Rose held out her hand for her lighter; Sarah could see that her dad was trying to palm it.

Gilbert shrugged. "That's all I know."

Sarah sat down on a wooden chair next to the couch. "What do we do make her go away?"

Gilbert shook his head. "My grandfather never taught me stuff like that. You might want to get a priest. They know all about exorcisms and stuff."

"Don't you know an elder or something?" Sarah asked. "You're always going to sweats."

"That was like over a hundred years ago, all the people that knew that kind of stuff are long gone."

"Can you think of anything else?" Rose was eager to wrap things up.

"Can you spot me twenty bucks?" He laughed again, then stopped, seeing their faces. "How's Winter?"

"She'll be okay," Rose said. Sarah knew her mom was lying from the way her hands were going white as they clutched the corner of the wall. "We should get back there."

Rose turned to go and Sarah got up to follow her.

"Rose," Gilbert said.

Rose looked at Sarah. "Go outside."

Sarah wanted to point out that the two of them had never censored themselves in front of her before and that she was in the middle of this whole thing and in fact she was the one who probably caused it all. But she had no energy to fight and the passenger seat seemed like the perfect place to rest her head. Rest, but do not sleep, she told herself. No more sleeping, period.

❧

Gilbert sat up straight in his chair. A cornflake was stuck to his belly.

"You probably know this already, but Michelle left me."

"I didn't."

"She said I wasn't what she thought I was."

"A man who could chew with his mouth shut?"

"She said I wasn't worth her time, then she made out with Bobby one night and the next morning she was gone."

"Classy." Rose looked at the door.

Gilbert stood up. His knees cracked and he stumbled a bit in her direction. Rose took a step backwards.

He took a deep breath. "I want you to know that I never stopped . . . y'know . . . "

"Screwing around?"

"No! I mean I've always . . . y'know . . . "

"Looked at other women?"

"Fuck, Rose, why are you being an asshole?" Gilbert tossed the remote across the room. They both watched as it hit the wall and the back cover came off and the batteries fell out.

"Is that what you wanted to tell me?"

"Rose . . . " His voice sounded small.

"Yeah?"

"Take care of her, okay?" He nodded his head toward the general direction of Sarah.

"I will."

"Also, can I borrow the car sometime?"

"We'll see." Rose headed out the door.

❧

Lloyd was working in his garden when they got there. His hands and jeans were black with dust. He watched as they pulled up, saw who it was, and then continued pulling weeds.

Rose hurried through the soil, making a dust cloud. She heard someone breathing hard behind her and saw Sarah labouring up the path.

Rose stopped a few feet from Lloyd.

"Dad, I need your help," Rose said.

"Yeah." His tone said, *why else would you be here?*

"There's a spirit-thing that Sarah sort of unleashed — by accident, of course — and I think it's doing bad stuff to Winter and this young girl Ronnie. They call it the Dream Woman."

"You don't say her name!" Lloyd's voice was rough with anger. And something else. If Rose didn't know any better, she'd say it was fear.

"You know her?"

Lloyd pursed his lips and shook his head.

"C'mon, Dad," Rose said.

Lloyd picked up his hoe and hit the dirt with it.

"Dad?"

Lloyd shook his head. "There's nothing I can do."

"I came here cuz I needed your help. I don't have anywhere else to go."

Lloyd hit the ground with the hoe. Rose reached for it. Lloyd tugged on it from his end. They played a silent game of tug of war until Rose finally let go.

"Jesus, Dad."

"You can't come in here and demand things. It's not done that way. No offerings, no respect, do you even know what you're asking for?"

"Who cares how it's done? Two people are very sick — isn't that more important than protocol?"

Lloyd grabbed his hoe from Rose. "Never should have been fooling around with that stuff in the first place."

"It's a little late for that. The demon's already out of the bag!" Rose took a deep breath. *Calm down Rose.* "C'mon, Dad. What are you afraid of?"

"I'm not!"

"Yes, you are. You've been preparing for something like this most of your life and now it's here. Do this and you'll get so much tobacco you'll have to buy another set of lungs to smoke it all."

Lloyd pointed at her. "This is why! The jokes! You have no respect!"

Rose glared at him. "I've been at the hospital with Ronnie and Winter. I know they're in trouble. You're the one who's not being respectful."

"I can't help you. Once the Old Woman is free — it's too late." Lloyd dropped his hoe and headed for the house. "The best thing for you to do is to take your girls and leave this reserve."

"Dad you can't walk away!" Rose yelled at his retreating back. He moved really fast through the dirt. Rose ran after him and tripped head first into the soft earth. "Oh fuck," she said through a mouthful of black.

"Asshole!" Sarah yelled. Rose looked up from the ground to see a clod of dirt go flying after Lloyd's head.

"Hey! Stop — " Rose had to stop to spit out more dirt. "What are you thinking? You don't throw stuff at your grandfather. You know better than that."

"He deserves to be punished."

Rose studied her daughter. Her eyes were flickering in and out of blankness.

"Men do cruel things and we must save ourselves."

Rose was startled to hear the Old Woman's gravelly tone underneath her daughter's normally lovely voice, not to mention that royal "we" that was seriously creepy. *Get moving, Rose,* she commanded herself, *your time is running out.*

Rose smiled like nothing was going on in her head and held her hand out to her daughter. Sarah pulled her to her feet. Rose reached out and touched Sarah's face.

"You're so white."

"Mom, you're getting dirt on me." Sarah rubbed her face with her sleeve.

"Sorry."

Rose headed toward the car.

"Where we going?"

"To the band office. You need coffee."

"I don't drink coffee."

"Mom?" Callie was standing beside the car. "How come we're not at home?"

∾

Winter woke up and felt like shit. Her hand went to her belly, as it did every morning, and she sighed happily. Then she put her hand down on cold ground and knew something was wrong.

She looked straight up and saw trees stretching up toward the sky. She sat up. "Why am I outside?" she asked no one. "Obviously I'm dreaming," she assured herself. Then she put her hand down on a sharp pebble. "Ow!" She looked at her palm and saw a dot of blood and suddenly it didn't seem like a dream so much anymore.

She got to her feet and dusted off her jeans.

A few feet away, a campfire was burning and Winter walked toward it. It was still spring enough that the sun didn't warm up the ground until the afternoon.

She saw an elderly woman sitting in front of the fire and Winter recognized her immediately. The woman showed her gnarled teeth to Winter in what was supposed to be a smile. Winter smiled back.

The woman pointed at some dried meat hanging over the fire. Winter grabbed a piece. It was tough, but Winter managed to get it down.

The woman nodded at her.

After she filled her belly, Winter wiped her mouth and looked expectantly at the woman.

She rose and beckoned Winter to follow.

The band office was more crowded than Rose had ever seen it. Cars were parked haphazardly around the parking lot. Probably every single car on the reserve was in that parking lot, even the tribal police car was outside.

"What the hell," Rose said.

"Yeah," agreed Sarah.

"Holy moly," Callie added.

There was a pile of people outside the front door and Rose had to push her way through to get inside.

She looked for Kaylee at the receptionist desk, but she wasn't there. She saw Annabelle and poked her in the arm. "What's going on?"

'Holy shit, Rose!" Annabelle said. "You're okay!"

"I guess so. I'm fucking tired but I'm okay. Winter's pretty sick though."

"Winter? What's wrong with her?"

"Gimme a sec and I'll explain."

Rose eased her way closer to the coffee machine and took a cup full of the dregs. The coffee looked thick enough to eat. She smothered it in whitener and handed it to Sarah.

"Nasty," Sarah said.

Rose gave her a look and Sarah took a tiny sip.

"Where's mine?" Callie asked.

Rose handed a cup to Callie and she took a sip and then spit it back into the cup.

Rose eased her way to back to Annabelle. She explained that Winter had been taken to the hospital the night before with the same symptoms as Ronnie.

"Well, fuck me," Annabelle said.

"Why's everyone here?"

"Seems like a lot of women been having these crazy dreams about a woman — or maybe they're not dreams, y'know? Anyway, everyone's here to talk to the chief. Also, I ran out of coffee at home."

"You have the dream?" Rose asked.

Annabelle nodded.

"Sarah's having them, too," Rose said.

Annabelle looked at Sarah, "Does she have bad teeth?"

Sarah nodded.

"Guess there's no dental plan in the spirit world," Annabelle said.

Taylor's door opened and he, the councillors and Nolan, the cop, poured out. The crowd rushed forward. "Taylor!" "Chief!" "Over here!"

Taylor jumped up on a chair. "We found an elder. He'll be here tomorrow. Everyone just has to calm down until then."

Questions flew through the air: "Why can't he come sooner?" "How come our own elders can't help us?" And variations on "What the fuck is going on?"

"I don't know," Taylor said. "I never heard of anything like this. I've talked with some of the older people and they said there was a story about this Dream Woman or the Old Woman."

The crowd moved restlessly.

"Now a woman and a young girl have been taken to the hospital. But there's no proof that she made them sick. That's just conjecture at this point," he added.

"Liar!" someone yelled from the back of the room.

The crowd broke into murmurs as people looked around for the offender. Rose was pretty sure it was one of the younger Jasons.

"Dumbass!" Rose was pretty sure that was Annie.

"There's no need for name-calling," Taylor said calmly.

A pop can flew at his head. He managed to dodge it. "Okay, c'mon, there's no need for that either."

"Go back to the city, apple!" This one was joined by a few other voices.

Rose stood on her tiptoes and yelled, "Shut up and let him talk!" Her face immediately turned red. She turned back and nodded at Taylor.

Taylor cleared his throat. "The hospital won't give us much information. The ladies are in stable condition, but that's all I know. I'm going to check in with the hospital and I'll give everyone another update then." Then he jumped off the chair and headed toward Rose.

As he closed the distance between them, Rose wished she'd had time to shower that morning.

"Hey," he said, "You doing okay?"

Rose shrugged.

"Let's go in my office and talk."

Taylor ducked into his office. Rose followed behind him, as did Annabelle, Kaylee and Sarah. Callie slipped in behind her sister.

"Oh," said Taylor, "I just meant Rose."

The door opened again and Megan squeezed through the women to stand by Taylor's side.

"Are we all here now?" Taylor asked dryly.

The door opened again and Tisha slipped inside. She pushed against Kaylee for more room and Kaylee moved aside grudgingly.

"It's like a goddamn clown car in here!" Annabelle said.

The door opened again and Nolan maneuvered inside, mostly because the women sidled away from him.

"What the hell?" Kaylee grunted.

"Official police business," he said, leering at her breasts.

Sarah plopped herself into a chair and leaned her head on her hand. Rose perched on the arm of Sarah's chair.

"Okay," Taylor said, and sat down in his own chair. "What's going on?

"It's a mass hallucination," proclaimed Tisha. "Textbook case."

"Oh, fuck off," Kaylee replied. "I've hallucinated before and this isn't the same."

"I think there's something wrong with the water," Megan said.

"Nobody asked you," said Kaylee.

"Why can't I have an opinion?" Megan shot back.

"Because you ain't a band member — you've only been here for two fucking seconds," Kaylee replied.

"Oh, whatever," Megan replied, but under her breath.

"What's going on?" Taylor reiterated. This time he looked directly at Rose.

"Bad stuff is happening because this Dream Woman woke up," she said. "I don't know why or how but she can make people really sick — Winter, Ronnie. The doctor doesn't even know what's wrong with them. And I'm afraid to let my daughter fall asleep."

"Has anyone else seen this woman?"

Sarah lifted her hand wearily and then her eyes drifted closed again.

"I saw her, too." Kaylee had lit a smoke and took a nervous drag of it. "She's a scary bitch. Crazy teeth, more wrinkled than a ball sack." Kaylee lowered her voice. "And she wants me to do things, like kill my ex-boyfriend and even my boyfriend and I'm not even mad at him."

Taylor looked stunned. He looked around. "Has anyone else seen her?"

All the women raised an arm.

"What are we gonna do!" Kaylee hit the top of Taylor's desk with her fist, careful not to bump any of her inch long acrylic nails.

Nolan stood up straight. "All I need to know is — can she be shot?"

"Oh, go on, the last person you shot was a cow!" Annabelle replied.

"It had rabies!"

"Nobody's shooting anyone, we need to know what we're dealing with here." Taylor sounded calm but Rose detected a note of hysteria in his voice.

She recognized the fearful look in Taylor's eyes; she'd seen it on Gilbert's face that time she asked him if he wanted to be in the delivery room for Sarah's birth.

Rose decided she should speak up.

"I saw her, too."

"Who do you want you to kill?" Taylor said in a tired voice.

"Gilbert." Four women said at once.

"Nobody. It wasn't in a dream. I gave her a ride . . . "

"You gave her a ride!" Tisha sputtered.

"I didn't know who she was!" Rose replied. "She was an elder who needed a ride."

"What did she say?" Taylor asked.

"She said she was visiting some people, but she didn't say who."

"So she's really here," Taylor said. "She's a real person?"

"Was she a zombie?" asked Annabelle.

"She's like a regular old lady. 'Cept really fit."

"Like fit?" Kaylee flexed her bicep muscle.

"Yeah. Stringy muscles."

"When did you see her?"

"Yesterday. Before the volleyball game, before Ronnie and Winter got sick." Rose stood up suddenly. "I have to check on them."

"No, you have tell us more about her!" Tisha said, grabbed at Rose's arm. Rose pulled away from her.

Kaylee piped up, "How did this happen anyway? Where they hell did she come from? Is there some kind of devil worship going on again?" Kaylee was referring to an incident a few a years before when some kids were accused of setting fires in the woods in the name of Satan. Upon further investigation, it turned out the kids were setting fires for the fun of it — a problem, to be sure — but not exactly as worrisome to the community as Satanism.

Thinking of the sleepy and somewhat guilty sixteen-year-old beside her, Rose jumped in: "Y'know, we don't need to start blaming people, that's not going to get us anywhere."

Tisha snarled, "You would say that."

Everyone turned in Tisha's direction, which made her puff up like a blowfish. "We all know it's your fault Rose Okanese."

"Just cuz I gave her a ride and maybe a CD does not mean that I'm in cahoots with her."

Tisha flared her nostrils: "That thing feeds off of energy — all kinds of energy — and who's been spending the most of it, running up and down these roads like the goddamn Energizer Bunny."

Rose actually laughed. "That's positive energy. That's me trying to do something good with my life."

"It's all the same to her. This is your fault. You woke her up, you made her strong."

Rose's face grew hot as she waited for someone to jump in and defend her. After a few moments she realized she'd likely go grey waiting for that to happen, so she stood up decisively. "I've got to check on Winter and Ronnie." Tisha grabbed her arm with her long bony fingers, "Make her go away." Her nose was particularly flared.

Rose looked annoyed, "And how the hell do you expect me to do that?"

Nolan stepped away from the wall. "Can I say something?" Everyone glared at him, expecting the worst.

"Look, I am only a phone call away. I'm here for your safety, your peace of mind, plus all of your... physical needs."

"Get lost, pig!" Kaylee called from the other side of the room.

"I was joking! You got it, right, Chief?"

Taylor stared at Nolan like he was a Model T car with a monkey driving it.

Rose shook off Tisha's arm and pushed her way out of the office. She was a little rough, although she did say excuse me and sorry to everyone.

Sixteen

WHEN ROSE WAS SIXTEEN YEARS OLD she got into a serious car accident. Winter had gotten her license the day before and wanted to show off her driving skills. They were driving down the curvy road into the valley when Winter lost control and drove over the side of the hill. They went down the hill, picking up speed and twisting wildly with every second. Rose remembered noticing that she felt no fear, only a calm acceptance: this is my new reality, dying.

She felt that same calm wash over her as she stared at Ronnie's hospital bed. She had a hand on Sarah's shoulder. Callie stood behind Rose. Rose could feel the exact distance.

Dr. Sheila explained how Ronnie's heart had failed, how her body had shut down and how she had slipped away in a matter of seconds. Rose heard this and nodded. Dr. Sheila's black eyes glistened.

"And Winter?"

"She is gone. Not dead!" Dr. Sheila added quickly. "She left the hospital."

"She was discharged?"

"Absolutely not. She was in her bed an hour ago and when the nurse went to check on her, she was gone."

Rose pulled Sarah behind her and rushed to the room across the hallway to Winter's room. She stood in the doorway, not sure what she was expecting to see. There was only an empty bed, stripped of linens, where her friend should be.

Rose took the girls down to the cafeteria and bought them something to eat. She ate nothing, staring across the table at them and wishing for a smoke.

She called home and reached Monty who had been driving around the entire day looking for Winter. She asked him to come to the hospital so she could make sure he was okay, but he said that he'd rather keep looking. There was silence on the phone as the two of them took uneven breaths and tried not to imagine the worst. Then Rose saw Jane appear at the end of the hallway.

"I have to go, Monty. Ronnie's mom is here."

Rose stood next to Jane as Dr. Sheila gave her the bad news. Jane nodded and then turned to Rose as if seeking a second explanation, maybe a good one this time.

"When I came back this afternoon, she was gone." Rose said.

"Did she say anything the night before?"

Rose shook her head.

Dr. Sheila offered some sedatives and Jane refused them. "It isn't traditional." Rose wanted to say something but Jane was notoriously stubborn. She didn't take anything after her husband's death, either. She retreated to the sweat lodge, cut off her hair, and asked everyone to stop speaking his name.

Rose walked over to the front desk and asked to use the phone. The nurse was busy watching Jane, and nodded absently.

One of Jane's cousins arrived and took her home.

Rose checked on the girls. They were half asleep in the waiting area chairs. They needed to go home. She was on her way to wake them up when the nurse called her name and held up the phone.

It was Michael, the latter of Cote and Son.

"You need to come down here." His tone was clipped. This was unusual for Michael, who was almost too affable for a guy who worked in a funeral home.

"I don't have time, Mike, I'm pretty busy. I'm just leaving the hospital."

"You need to come now. There's a problem with the body."

∼

Rose didn't want to bring the girls, but what choice did she have? Sarah was falling asleep every five seconds and Rose was afraid that she wouldn't be able to wake her up. Callie had designed a poking stick and was using it on her sister every time she got a chance. Sarah was too tired to complain. This worried Rose more than anything.

She parked the car and looked at the girls. "Stay in the car."

As she closed her car door, she heard theirs open behind her.

"Thanks for listening," Rose sighed.

Michael stood at the front of the room, wringing his hands. Rose didn't realize that people actually did that.

"So, what's the problem?"

"Come with me," he whispered.

"Where's your dad?" Rose whispered back.

"In the office. He's on the phone with the priest."

"Jane doesn't want a Catholic ceremony."

"Trust me, that's the least of your worries." Michael ushered her through the back door into the "lab" area.

Rose was taken aback by the smell. The prep place looked like the inside of a clinic, and just as clean. But there was a sharp chemical sting in the air and underneath it, lurking like a big-eyed ocean bottom dweller, was the "other" smell. That smell that every human recognized without knowing it. (And if you were a girl, you walked way around it and if you were a boy, you ran towards it to poke it with a stick.)

Michael led them to a small coffin. It was dark brown, nearly red. It had a delicate carving on the front and it could be called pretty if it wasn't a box for a human being. Michael stopped beside the coffin and put his hand on the front of it. Rose's feet had stopped.

Michael gave her an encouraging look, and Rose took the last steps.

Her palms started to sweat. Her babbling mechanism kicked into overdrive: "I'm not scared. It's weird. Y'know, I've seen bodies before but not a young person. And this is not any person, this is someone I know. I mean, I know everyone around here, everybody knows everybody, right? The whole place is like an episode of *Cheers*. But this young person, she probably never even watched that show."

"Are you ready?" Michael looked at the girls questioningly, and Rose nodded at him. Whatever it was, they would bug her until she told them anyway.

He opened the coffin. Rose looked inside. She looked at Michael.

"Where's the body?"

Michael nodded. "In there." He pointed and Rose saw white things in the coffin. She looked closer.

"Bones?"

"Bones."

"Bones!" Callie rushed forward. Bones were not scary to her.

Michael looked at the door. "The body was here earlier. I know because I put it in this coffin. Then I came in this morning and this is all that was left."

Rose nodded. "Did someone take the body and leave these instead? I mean are they hers?"

Michael shrugged. "I'm not an expert but — " He glanced at the girls. "They're about the right size."

Sarah and Callie took a step backwards.

"So what do we do? Call the police? Report a body theft?" Rose asked.

Michael sighed. "My dad . . . he's not good with things like this . . . "

"What do you mean?"

"I mean he's ready to call down an exorcism. He wants the body out of here — like yesterday."

Rose nodded. "Do you have a bag?"

Michael opened a cupboard. He held out a plastic bag then with the disgusted look on Rose's face went back to the cupboard. He pulled out a duffel bag. It read, "Cote's Curling Crew" on the side of it.

He handed it to Rose.

It took a long time. At least fifteen minutes. Rose did it by herself for the most part. After watching in open-mouthed horror for a few minutes, Callie eventually joined in and grabbed a few. Sarah stood behind them and stared at a mark on the wall. When Callie dropped a bone on the floor, Sarah hissed at her to be more careful.

Rose zipped up the bag and nodded at Michael. He held the door open for her as she hefted the bag over her shoulder. The bones were heavy, but she didn't want to complain.

Rose slipped into the car after putting the bag into the trunk. She looked at the girls.

"Well," she began.

"We don't need to talk about it." Sarah's voice was resolute.

"Okay," Rose said. She looked at Callie, who shrugged.

Rose was too tired to feel guilty. In fact, she felt a bit giddy. The Chinese curse — well, she thought it might be Chinese — floated into her mind: "May you live in interesting times." Maybe this would be a growing experience for her daughters, like the Great Depression. But not such a harrowing experience that they would spend their life recovering from it. *If they lived* . . . the phrase floated into her mind and she pushed it out and slammed the door. Everything would be fine. Everything. Would. Be. Fine.

Rose poked Sarah, who gave her a dirty look. "Just checking," Rose mumbled.

∾

Jane decided to hold the funeral in the reserve's original graveyard. Mostly old people were buried out there these days; elders who'd been converted to Christianity as residential school students and then who had returned to the old ways in their later years. Jane's family had never gone to residential school. When the police had come for their children, Jane's grandfather had taken his family deep into the woods.

Not that Jane had a choice about where her daughter could be buried. She told Rose that the priest had left a lengthy message on her machine about how he'd heard about the evil "de-fleshing" and cited some Bible verses before the machine cut him off. Apparently the elder Cote had been running his mouth. What a snitch, Rose thought.

There was a giant fir tree in the middle of the graveyard. It was a coveted location but nobody complained when Jane decided to put Ronnie under its boughs.

Rose took the black bag out of the trunk and walked over to where Taylor stood. Jane had asked him to attend, and he'd agreed, although somewhat reluctantly. He didn't want to leave the band office because someone had broken in the night before. They'd stolen food, the curtains, and other odds and ends. They'd also spray-painted a nasty message to the chief on the wall. Rose hoped she'd have time to check it out after the funeral because Taylor hadn't felt like talking about it over the phone. She was planning on examining it, convinced that she could identify the culprit through choice of word and spelling mistakes. And then they'd be on the business end of one of Rose's glares, that's for damned sure.

Rose grunted her way up the soft incline.

Taylor rushed toward her like she was water after a couple of hours in the sweatlodge. "What took you so long?"

He took the bag from her shoulder.

"I had to feed my girls. How's the flock doing?"

"They are hungry, angry, and to be honest, a little scary. I think Kaylee threw a hubcap at my head when I stopped in to check on them. It was like she had it on her, waiting for me to show up."

The night before, fifty women had bedded down in the band hall. Rose had driven up with her girls, thinking that there might be safety in numbers, but she could hear the arguing from outside the hall and had decided to head home. Monty and Rose had taken turns staying up with Sarah. She'd still managed to slip into a deep sleep two times, and Rose had to shake her pretty hard to wake her up. Rose glanced at the car. The girls were leaning against it, both of their faces white and chalky.

"My kids look like the night of the living dead," Rose said. "What time is the elder coming?"

"He's not." Taylor said. "He called me his morning, said he had a sweat. And he decided it's not something he can handle. He said he doesn't want to endanger his reserve. He thinks she can spread."

"We should run away," she blurted out.

Taylor smiled sadly. "She's from our band. She's our problem."

He grabbed Rose's hand and helped her up the hill. His fingers were long and slim, yet strong, and they reminded Rose of her mother's hands. That probably wasn't a comparison he wanted to hear.

"I'm open to other ideas." Taylor added. "I got a hall full of women, a bunch of frightened men, and now this . . . this girl. Where's the body, anyway?"

Rose pointed at the duffel bag on his shoulder. "That's her."

Taylor shuddered, but quickly regained his composure under Rose's gaze. He took the bag from her shoulder and laid it on the ground.

"Did you tell Jane?"

"Tell me what?" Jane looked pale and shaky, but her voice was strong. She was leaning pretty hard on Monty. Monty looked like hell as well. His usually bulbous belly was deflating.

"About the bones," Rose said.

Jane nodded. "This is her, then?"

Rose nodded.

"You got all of them?"

"Yeah. Me and my girls."

Jane zipped open the duffel bag. There was a chalky smell.

"Who did this?" Taylor asked.

"*How* would be my first question," Monty commented.

Jane zipped it closed. "The old lady. She was a flesh eater." Her voice was casual, as if they were discussing the weather. "Before they stopped her, she'd killed a man. They only found his bones."

"That is some Hannibal Lector shit," Rose replied. Then she guiltily glanced toward the car and made sure her girls were out of earshot.

"What else do you know about her?" Taylor asked.

"I know how to kill her," Jane said.

Rose had an urge to high-five Jane, but felt a graveyard was the wrong venue. So she made a fist with her hand and punched the air with it.

Monty gave her a look that suggested she was mentally impaired.

"How long will it take?" Taylor was all business.

"Two nights and a day." Jane's voice fell to a whisper as her knees sunk to the ground. She knelt beside the bones and bent her head low, her arms wrapping around the duffel bag in an awkward embrace that only a mother would attempt.

Rose and the others stepped away from the tree and stared in the direction of the horizon, trying not to hear the weeping behind them.

∾

As Taylor performed the ceremony, Rose could hear his voice in the background, but her thoughts were louder. If only she'd stayed at the hospital or gotten there sooner or worked harder to reach Jane. Rose held Callie's and Sarah's hands tightly, feeling greedy for them. She was in her own world so didn't notice when everyone was suddenly staring at her. "Jane wants you to say a few words," Sarah explained.

Rose opened her mouth and nothing came out. For a long time. Then she remembered. "I was about Ronnie's age when my mom passed away. From cancer. Wasn't fast like with your husband, Jane. It was slow. She came near to beating it and everyone congratulated us like we'd won the lottery. And we did. For awhile there. Then one evening I saw her and my dad standing in the back yard together . . . and I knew. It was back and it felt like when you think winter is over and you throw off your coat and start walking around in short sleeves and you think you're safe. Then when the cold wind hits you — it's worse somehow. I had a small family like Ronnie, just me and my mom and dad. And when my mom died, we broke apart and never really fixed that. We should've." Rose took a good hard bite on her lip to get to the next part. "I have a lot of regrets in my life but that's gonna be a big one. That I never sat that little girl down and told her that she wasn't alone. You get old and you get busy and you forget what it feels like to be young and scared and to miss someone so bad you wish you could die." She stopped on that word and didn't look at anyone. Callie gave her hand an extra squeeze.

When the words were done, they dropped handfuls of tobacco over Ronnie's meager pile of bones.

Seventeen

ROSE STOOD ON HER FRONT STEPS looking at the moody sky. Nightfall was coming on and she was dreading it. She wasn't a particularly sensitive person. She once slept through a tornado. But she could feel this. A dark humidity, spreading through the reserve, clogging the air and making it hard to take full breaths, like in the summertime when a wildfire was raging — which happened about once a week every July and August. (People kept burning their garbage even when the band office warned them not to.)

Rose went back inside. The girls were watching Monty make dinner. He was taking his time with the lasagna. Rose had never noticed before that he was as methodical as Winter and twice as slow.

He rambled as he cooked. "When she comes back, I think we'll go to Costa Rica. They have good hospitals there and she can give birth and relax. It'll be the two of us. I'll have to make sure to bring a bunch of mysteries for her. She liked the beaches down there. Said they weren't too touristy. And they have good restaurants, she'd never be happy anywhere without good food."

Rose nodded. Monty sliced French bread into one-inch sections.

They gathered around the table and ate listlessly. When dinner was done, they sat there, unwilling to speak but scared to leave the company of others.

Rose announced, "I'm going for a run."

Everyone looked at her.

∾

Once outside, Rose's legs were giddy with unspent energy and her walk quickly transitioned into a run. In a matter of minutes, she was full out, arms pumping, her lungs stretching to keep up with her. Her heart was pounding in her chest like a drum.

Rose wanted to stop, but didn't. The frantic effort stilled her mosquito swarm of thoughts. A few more steps and her thoughts were reduced to breathe in, breathe out.

It was then that she saw her mother standing on the edge of the road, wearing that old green and white housecoat that she used to putter around in all day long. Rose called out to her, but Callista turned away and headed into the ditch toward the bush.

Rose veered in behind her. She reached out for her mother but she was always one step ahead. She was walking but moving faster than Rose was at a full-out run. "Not good for the ol' ego," Rose thought.

Rose hit the woods at breakneck speed, which would still appear to be a light jog for most people. She followed as her mom wove in and out of the trees. Rose felt her arms being scratched by twigs and leaves. One grazed her face near her eye and she finally slowed down. "Mom!" she called, but her mom kept moving.

Rose could smell a campfire: light, fresh, and warm. She squinted but couldn't see the glow through the branches. She kept running, jumping over low shrubs and feeling the long grass brush against her thighs. She wondered how many wood ticks she'd be picking off later.

She saw a clearing and slowed down. There was a person sitting by the fire. She had her back to Rose, but Rose recognized her in an instant. Even sitting on a log, Winter had perfect posture.

"We've been looking for you everywhere!" Rose proclaimed.

Winter looked dazed. "Where's Monty?"

"He's safe. He misses you. How's the baby?"

Winter put her hand over her stomach as if she had forgotten the most important thing in her life until Rose reminded her.

"Has something happened to the baby?" Rose squatted in front of her friend, trying to make eye contact with Winter's wandering eyes.

"Can you keep him safe?"

"Who? Monty?"

Winter nodded.

Rose glanced around the camp. "Come with me," she said. "This is not a healthy place for a pregnant woman. For one thing, you shouldn't be inhaling this smoke." She noted the sharpened sticks, two evil looking blades, and what appeared to be a machete lying by the fire. "And I've heard that doctors recommend less than two knives a day. Any more is just overkill."

"Go." Winter pushed her away.

"No way, José. Get off your fat butt and come with me." Rose pulled on Winter's arm while Winter pulled back.

Rose heard a stick snap and glanced across the fire. The old lady was there, a knowing smile creeping across her ancient face.

Rose didn't think. She ran.

∾

They slept in the living room that night, the four of them crowded around the television. They took turns shaking Sarah awake. She protested and slapped at their hands.

It was shortly after midnight — between episodes of *Two and a Half Men* — Rose met Sarah's eyes over a snoring Callie. "What's the point? I can't stay awake forever, Mom."

"But it's not forever — it's only one more day and one more night. That may seem like a lot to you but trust me when you get to my age, that's barely a blip." This was a lie. Rose's head was pounding from lack of sleep and had been for the past five hours.

"It's harder for me though. You don't hear her."

Rose reminded Sarah of the fire in the bush, of Winter, of the sticks, of the Old Woman's grating laugh, of Ronnie. Sarah sat up straighter. They switched to movies, staying away from their usual horror movie fare and moving toward romantic comedies. They were halfway through *Pretty Woman* when the phone rang.

Rose jolted to sitting. "Fire?"

"It's the phone, Mom," Sarah replied.

"Where is it?" Rose patted through the blankets. She grabbed Callie's ankle by mistake and Callie woke up.

"I don't want to go to school," she whined.

"Where is it?" Rose was getting panicky as the phone hit its fourth ring.

"I saw it in the kitchen," Monty mumbled from the big chair.

The kitchen surfaces were dotted with dirty pots, dishes, and pans. Apparently no one thought doing dishes was important during a crisis. The phone rang again, angry at being ignored, and Rose pushed dishes out of her way. Still no phone.

Rose went through the cupboards, opening and closing them with anxious loudness.

Then she stopped and listened. The phone rang and it was coming from down low.

Rose squatted and opened the cupboard under the sink and there it was. She picked it up.

"Hello?"

"Who is it?" Callie stood in the kitchen door.

"They hung up."

"Well that was rude."

"Why was the phone under the sink?"

"I didn't want to get it wet."

Rose star-sixty-nined the phone. "It's the band office." She redialled.

The phone rang on the other end. It went to voicemail. Rose dialled again and reached voicemail again. "They're not answering."

Monty put his jacket on. "I'll check it out."

"They can wait until the morning. We're not the police."

"I'll check it out." Monty headed out the door.

Rose followed him out into the baby-blue light before dawn. She shivered on the front steps. "Don't do this, Monty."

"Someone has to go."

"Not really." Rose's brain was struggling. It was taking every neuron she owned to produce an explanation for why he shouldn't go. "It was probably a wrong number. And if you go there, they'll feel dumb, you'll feel like you overreacted. It'll be awkward for everyone."

"Stay inside." Monty climbed into his truck.

Rose watched as he backed out of the driveway and then as his headlights turned down the road.

She had a bad feeling. In horror movies, it was always a terrible idea to split up, especially if you were a minority. Rose went back inside. She put the deadbolt on. It hung off the wall on one screw, so she added a butter knife to the doorjamb.

"That should keep out a dinner bun," Sarah observed.

Rose gave her an exasperated look. "Let me know if you have any better ideas."

Rose headed back into the dark kitchen and bumped into Callie standing in the middle of the floor. Rose shrieked. "Don't do that." Rose switched on the light.

"You shouldn't have let him go." Callie's look was accusing.

"I tried to stop him! Besides, he'll be fine, Monty is a strong guy and he's smart. If anything is wrong, he'll come straight home and then we'll call the police."

"What if there are no police?"

Rose stared at her daughter, unable to fish an answer out of her mind.

∾

Rose felt like she had stared at the clock the entire night. At a little after five, she dialled the number of the band office and got a busy signal, which could mean anything from someone was using it or it had been pulled out of the wall. Rose was willing to bet on the latter.

She made a pot of coffee and told Sarah over and over that she shouldn't have let Monty go. Sarah stared at her with glazed eyes and chewed absently on her gum. It was slightly louder than Callie's snoring and Rose felt like snatching it out of her mouth.

Was this what the end of the world was like? Not like *Mad Max* at all but rather like regular life except a thousand times more annoying.

Rose made herself sit down. She was getting sleepy when Sarah asked her if she would still love her if she killed Gilbert.

"I'd make sure it was painless," she assured Rose.

Rose was alert after that.

After the sun came up, Rose cleaned her kitchen from top to bottom. She fried some eggs and bacon for the girls and made them eat everything on their plate. She cleaned up their makeshift beds in the living room and swept the floors. Then she threw a load of laundry in the washer. It was almost nine by the time she acknowledged that she would have to leave the house. She picked up the phone; it was dead.

"Get your jackets," Rose told the girls. Then she went to her bedroom to grab the aluminum bat that she once used to kick Gilbert out of the house. What was that fight about again? Oh right, that was when he wanted to have a threesome with Rose and one of his backup singers.

"Just once to get it out of my system," he'd assured her.

It was one of the last times Rose had lost her temper with him, hating the way her voice became so shrill and the fear in Callie's eyes when she swung at him with the bat.

Sarah shrugged on her jacket. Callie ran into her bedroom, yelling, "I need to get something!" over her shoulder.

Callie ran out to the car with her volcano science project.

"What are you doing with that?"

"I don't want to leave it at home."

"We're coming back, Callie." But even as Rose said it, she heard a frisson of doubt creeping into her voice.

When Rose was a little girl, she used to get a tummy ache before something bad happened. Like when she was seven years old, the night before the motor in her parents' old car caught fire in the McDonald's parking lot, her stomach had rumbled. She also had tummy pain the morning their car blew a tire on the highway, sending them fishtailing across a couple of lanes. Her stomach had even ached the entire day that the car's brakes failed as they were pulling into the yard. Lloyd, unable to stop, drove right through the chicken coop. As Rose looked back, she realized that her parents should have gotten rid of that car a lot sooner.

Her mom said that Rose's tummy was better than the weatherman at forecasting. Lloyd had grunted something about how knowing bad news never helped anyone or got chicken feathers out of his radiator.

As she drove toward the band office, Rose's belly was aching, but she didn't even need that to know that trouble had settled on the reserve like a determined band of Jehovah's Witnesses. There was smoke pouring into the sky and it was coming from a location directly in front of the car.

"Smells smoky." Callie stuck her head over the seats. "Think they're having a barbecue today?"

Rose shook her head.

"I don't want to go there," Sarah mumbled. Sarah's head was bobbing on her neck as she struggled to hold it upright.

"We have to get Monty." Rose stepped on the gas.

The cars were the first sign of trouble. They were facing all four directions at different angles, like blindfolded drunks had parked them.

Then there was the hall; it was a smoking ruin, three walls gone, one wall black and halfheartedly standing up. A determined six-year-old could kick it down.

"Oh, for fuck sakes," Rose said. "They burned down the bingo hall."

"Holy shit," Callie said, with extra emphasis on the "shit," confident that she wouldn't be called out for swearing.

"She's . . . in the band office," Sarah said with a yawn.

Rose parked on the edge of the cars closest to the band office. She turned and faced the girls.

"This is more than I expected. Maybe we should drive away and go get the police."

"They're already here." Callie pointed at the police cruiser caught in the car rodeo.

Rose's gut tightened.

"All right then. You two stay in the car."

"No," said Callie. "I'm not staying here if you're not here."

"Well grab something in case you need to protect yourself." Rose reached for her trusty bat, it had seen her through many tense situations. (And yet, had never once been used to play baseball.)

Callie rummaged around in the back seat and then popped up. "Can I use this?"

Rose half turned in her seat. Callie had a machete in her hand.

"What the hell?" Rose slammed the back of her head on the window. "Ow! Where did you get that?"

"It's always been back here. I rest my feet on it."

Only Gilbert would have a super sharp knife in the back of his car. Idiot. Also what was with all the machetes on this reserve? It was Saskatchewan, for God's sake, not the rainforest.

As Rose considered these questions, she stared blankly at the machete held in the hands of her elementary-school-aged daughter.

"Mom?" Sarah waved her hand in front of Rose's face. "You stroke out or something?"

"I don't think we should do this. Like maybe we should think about it a little more, there must be something else who can handle this, if not the police then the army, what about . . . there must be some kind of special forces for evil things!"

Sarah sighed and opened her car door. She let it slam shut behind her.

Callie put her hand on her mom's shoulder. "It'll be okay."

∽

Rose marched toward the band office. Now that she was out of the car, she felt curiosity overtake her. Behind her, the girls were arguing over who got to hold the bat. (The machete was safely locked in the trunk.)

Rose hissed at them to be quiet and stopped for them to catch up to her.

The path to the band office was strewn with clothes and garbage. There was a desk wedged in the doorway. Rose squatted down and looked through the desk legs into the band office. There was a group of women standing in a circle, armed with bats, broomsticks, and floor hockey sticks raided from the sports equipment room. "Oh great," she muttered, "I probably won't get those back."

Rose saw Kaylee among the women. Kaylee looked to be chewing out one of the others.

Rose was contemplating throwing a rock at Kaylee's big broad forehead — on one hand, it might shock her out of the zombie-state but on the other hand, she might then beat the shit out of Rose — when she heard someone behind her.

She turned and saw Monty gesturing at her from a bush. Callie scurried in his direction. "Uncle!"

Monty furiously waved at her to keep her voice down.

Rose pushed Callie out of the way. She saw Monty and Taylor huddled together. They only had their underwear on. Rose tried not to stare at Taylor's body and glued her eyes to his forehead.

"Oh hi there. It's good to see you, Taylor…I mean, Chief. You look great…I mean, well," Rose twittered nervously.

"Cut the flirting, Giggles. Where's the car?" Monty asked.

Rose pointed with her lips. Taylor and Monty headed up the path. Rose pushed Callie in front of her. "C'mon," she whispered to Sarah who was focused on the band office behind them. Rose shook her arm, "Sarah, c'mon, we're going." Sarah nodded and followed her mom.

They were slipping into the car when Rose noticed that she wasn't with them.

"Where's Sarah?"

"Oh no!" Callie's eyes went big. Then she took off back down the path, her short legs pumping.

Rose ran after her.

Sarah was back at the front door of the band office, pushing the desk out of the way.

"Sarah!" Callie yelled. "What the hell!"

Sarah's face turned and stared at them; her expression was blank. Rose recognized the look from her meeting in the woods with Winter.

"She's a zombie!" Callie pulled on her mom's arm.

"No she's not," Rose whispered back. Even though that was exactly what Rose thought she looked like, too.

Rose heard women's voices approaching so she sprinted toward Sarah. There was no time for finesse: she grabbed the sixteen-year-old from behind, put her hand over her mouth, and dragged her back down the path. Callie followed, attempting to grab her sister's kicking legs.

"She's so kicky!"

Monty took over once they got closer to the car. Sarah managed to squeeze out a scream when Rose passed her over to her uncle. Rose glanced at the band office door. A woman was standing there. Despite the distance, Rose recognized those flaring nostrils: Tisha. The councillor smirked and turned toward the open door and yelled: "I found them!"

Rose started up the car and backed up so quickly that gravel flew.

◞◞

They were a few miles down the road when Monty told her to slow down. "They aren't driving," he said. "One of the first things they did was disable all the cars."

"Why?"

"She doesn't like anything man-made."

"So you saw her."

Rose saw Monty nod in the rear-view mirror. She looked at Taylor sitting beside him. He looked deep in thought but he nodded as well.

"Sarah fell asleep," Callie tattled.

Sarah looked so weak lying in her uncle's arms that Rose didn't have the heart to wake her up. "Let her sleep for a minute." Rose adjusted the mirror to see Taylor better. "You okay?"

Taylor looked up. His eyes were wide and he looked about twelve years old. "That was surreal."

"How come you're only wearing your gitch?" Callie asked, hanging over the front seat backwards.

"They took our clothes." Monty explained. "That was the first thing they did — after cutting the power and the phone lines, that is. Old Gladys climbed a telephone pole, can you believe that? "

"What were they doing?"

"They're taking over. After they took our clothes, they tied up all the men."

"How'd you guys get free?"

"This guy has small hands," Monty pointed at Taylor. "He slipped out of the ropes and then he helped me."

"Really? Like the same size as mine?" Callie held up her palm.

"They're average sized," Taylor replied and kept his hands at his side.

Rose turned left at the four-way stop. "Where we going?" Callie asked.

"Jane's."

"We have to go back." Taylor said.

Rose turned her head and the car skidded. She slowed down. "Why would we do that?"

"There's a lot of guys back there and" — he threw a quick look at Callie — "they're t-o-r-t-u-r-i-n-g them."

"Torting?" Callie asked. "Whazzat?"

Rose slowed to a stop. She kept her eyes in front of her. "How many guys?"

"At least thirty."

So many? Rose sighed.

"Lionel, Jimmy, Roach, Beaver, the three Edgars, all the Jasons . . . and, they have Gilbert and your dad," Taylor said.

"They have my dad?" Callie said. She pushed her mom's shoulder, suddenly frantic. "Mom they have my dad!"

Rose nodded. She was replaying the last argument she'd had with her dad in her head, her angry words slamming around from side to side.

"A bus," she murmured. "We need a bus." She backed up the car and turned around.

∾

The front door of Jimmy's house was open, the door waving in the wind, lonely for its people to return. Rose knocked once before entering but Monty pushed past her, explaining that Jimmy's wife, Jenny, had brought him in at knifepoint.

"Why would she do that? He's such a sweetie," Rose said.

"Big porn collection," Taylor replied.

"Oh." Rose had a disappointed tone in her voice.

Taylor and Monty headed into the bedroom to borrow Jimmy's clothes. Their movements were in sync; their shared night of terror had bonded them.

Rose made sandwiches for her and Callie, and they ate them in the kitchen. Callie kept trying to get Rose to tell her what "torting" was, and Rose kept changing the subject. Sarah sat across from them, her long eyelashes resting on her cheeks, much like they had when Rose used to rock her to sleep on the front steps of the house (Sarah liked to fall asleep to the sound of crickets).

The men came out of the bedroom in their Jimmy uniforms. The clothes were loose on Taylor and fitted on Monty.

Rose found a bus, gassed up, parked in the driveway. All the mirrors on the vehicle were gleaming. "Jimmy, you are such a peach."

Rose ran a hand over the dust-free dashboard. There was an impatient knock on the door. Rose hefted the big handle and pulled on it. The door curled open. Callie clambered on first. "Cool . . ."

"I'll drive," Monty said as he helped a slumping Sarah onto the first seat — the way her head flopped around, Rose was reminded of Raggedy Anne.

"No, if one of them sees a man driving, they'll probably start shooting. This way we at least have a chance." Besides, Rose had always wanted to drive a big bus.

Monty sat next to Callie. Taylor plopped down directly behind the driver's seat. Rose could almost feel his breath on her neck. Rose shifted the bus into gear too quickly and the entire bus jerked.

"Mom, what happens to the little boys?" Callie asked.

"They don't mind them so they're with the other kids," Monty explained.

"But when does a boy become a man?"

"I been asking that question my whole life," Rose joked, wishing she had Winter to high-five. Sarah snickered. She was half-awake at least.

"Probably when he can shave," Monty replied, ignoring Rose. "They put all the men into one of the offices, then they made them give up all their stuff, then they started picking and choosing which ones got special treatment."

"Who'd they choose first?"

"Kaylee's ex-boyfriend, one of the Jasons. They started off by holding him down and shaved off his goatee. No shaving cream or nothing!"

Rose turned at the four-way stop. "He did steal her car and emptied out her bank account — and he hasn't paid child support since her daughter was born."

"Then they picked on Evan. Apparently he got two girls pregnant last year and didn't claim either of them. Plus, he stole his *kokum*'s old age pension."

"Guess he had it coming," Rose commented.

"Who next?" asked Callie, clearly liking this game.

"Lionel."

"Lionel!" Rose glanced up in the big mirror at Monty.

"Apparently he called his sister-in-law a b — a bad name one time."

"She is a bad name." Rose swerved to miss a particularly big pothole. "One time she drove right past me when I had a flat tire. Cold day, too."

"It's not exactly a court of law. They can say whatever they want and then do whatever they want. No one deserves that," Monty said.

"It's like they were more animal than woman." Taylor shuddered.

"So much for the gentler sex," Monty nodded sagely.

Rose did a giant eye-roll that would have made Sarah proud if she'd seen it.

"So what's the plan?" Taylor asked.

"Rose?" Monty had an expectant look on his face.

Rose looked in the big mirror at them. "I had the bus idea!"

Taylor rested his chin on the back of Rose's seat. "We can't pretend to be your prisoners because they already know you aren't one of them. But Sarah . . . "

Rose shook her head. "Won't work. You get her near a weapon and she'll take you down like you tagged her in an ugly Facebook pic. She stays with me."

Taylor nodded. "We can give ourselves up again. They take us prisoner and you go and get the rest of the guys. Then you come back and rescue us or we break free again."

"I don't like that plan," Monty protested. "My wife is leading the crew, in case you didn't notice. I'm next on the kick-to-the-gonads list."

"So you're saying you won't sacrifice yourself for Gilbert, then?" Rose was all wide-eyed innocence.

Monty snorted.

"I thought you might say that." Taylor pulled something out of a plastic bag and handed it to Monty.

Monty unfolded a dress. It wasn't Jenny's best. Likely she'd only worn it during maternity. "Are you crazy?"

"It's the best disguise. This way we go in, and Rose waits for us."

Monty made a face, but started putting on the dress.

"Uncle Monty is putting on a dress? Can you see this, Mom? He's putting on a dress!" Callie was incredulous. Transvestites were not a local sight in their part of the world. Rose made a mental note to take her to the city more often.

"What about your hair?" Rose asked.

Monty tucked it behind his ears. It did look a tiny bit like a pixie cut but his big mannish face was still peeking out under it.

"I hope that's not the best you can do."

"You got lipstick?"

Rose handed him her purse.

"Park in the back," Taylor said. "The men are in the classroom nearest to the back of the office."

"Am I gonna be able to get back out again?"

"It's dry and this bus is higher than the ruts."

Rose heard Callie laugh as Monty explained that lipstick could also be used as blush according to an Oprah show he once watched.

"Nobody on the roads, huh?" Taylor leaned on Rose's seat. Her blood pressure rose in direct correlation with his proximity.

"Phones are out, too," she rasped.

"Like an end-of-the-world movie. I always thought I had the ability to survive anything — "

"Why?" interjected Rose.

"Because . . . I work out? I dunno. Human nature I guess. But you don't expect people to turn on you so fast. Like one minute Kaylee was asking me if the Starblankets could have the west side of the gym and then the next, she had a knife at my throat. I couldn't say a thing to her. It was like she didn't know who I was. I was this thing that she wanted to hurt."

Rose glanced at his throat and saw a red scratch there.

"Then the Old Woman came in. You could feel the hush. All their eyes followed her. I could feel myself being pulled in. Then when she looked at me, all I saw was pure hate. You ever see that before?"

Rose shook her head. "Not even when I rear-ended Tisha's car by accident."

"Why aren't you like the rest of them?" Taylor asked.

Rose's eyes swept the sides of the road, hoping to see a green and white housecoat. "Maybe it's crazy but I think it has something to do with my mom."

Rose turned off half a kilometre from the band office. There was a back road that the water truck used for deliveries. The bus climbed over the ruts confidently. Rose parked the bus off to the side. She opened the big door and the men climbed down the stairs. Rose stared at the back of the building, knowing that a hundred bad things could be happening inside.

"Change of plans. I'm going. You girls stay here."

"Hey!" both girls protested. Though Sarah's was more like a softly sighed "hey" and then she fell back asleep.

Rose jumped down the stairs and caught up with the guys.

"You were supposed to stay put," Taylor said.

"You two don't know how to fight women," Rose said in her bossy voice.

"I agree with you there," Monty admitted. "But then can someone explain to me why I've got more make up on than a Dolly Parton impersonator?"

Rose looked at Monty. He had expertly applied lipstick to his lips, a bit of eye shadow to his upper lids, and added a dab of colour to the apples of his cheeks.

"Honestly, I think it's pretty subtle," she commented.

He grunted.

They padded through the woods. There was a slight clearing before the band office where there was an old set of swings and a barbecue that was used for family fun days every summer. The barbeque was chained down; not everyone on the reserve shared the belief in communal property.

Rose crouched down and looked at the windows. "Which one are they in?" she asked.

"Third from the door," Monty said.

Then both of the men looked at her. Rose figured they expected her to morph into Hannibal from *The A-Team* and start laying out a plan for them. Then they'd start building guns out of twine and an old rubber tire, all while exchanging wisecracks. But she had no plans, *A*, *B*, or otherwise. What she wanted to do most at this moment — and felt most confident of doing well — was peeing. But she could never do that anywhere remotely near Taylor.

After a minute of the three of them looking at one another, Taylor cleared his throat. "We might as well walk in. We have surprise on our side."

"That sounds good," Rose agreed.

"Simple is always best."

"If it works for cooking, it should work for everything."

"Shut up!" Monty hissed. "God, the two of you sound like a couple of lovesick teens."

Rose blushed and punched Monty's arm.

"What the hell was that for?" he asked.

As they crept towards the school, Rose heard a chanting coming from the band office's lounge area. She opened the back door and the chanting rose considerably in volume. Rose guessed the old lady was riling them up for something big.

Rose and the men headed the opposite way from the lounge area. There was a hallway that led to the councillors' offices and the nursing station. Seated directly in front of the doorways was Tisha, with a rifle in her hand.

Who would let Tisha have a gun? Rose wanted to know. Her personality was weapon enough.

Still, Rose made her face in the shape of a warm smile and Tisha smiled back automatically, until she recognized Rose.

Then Tisha swiftly brought the rifle to her shoulder. Rose knocked the rifle upwards. In a move she remembered from Tae Kwon Do classes as a kid, Rose stepped in and stuck her elbow right in the middle of Tisha's bony chest. The blow knocked Tisha on her ass. Rose wrested the gun from her as she hit the ground.

Then Rose saw Tisha's chest rise as she took a deep breath intended for a scream loud enough to bring the building down. Rose dropped on top of her and clamped her left hand over her mouth.

Monty pulled the rifle from between them.

"Some help here?" Rose had Tisha in a headlock on the floor. Tisha was kicking her legs and hitting Rose's shins with alarming accuracy.

"You're doing fine."

Tisha bit her hand. Rose swallowed a yelp. She hissed at Monty, "give me something to gag her with!" *There's something I never expected to say,* Rose said to herself wonderingly.

Monty pulled the sash off his dress. Then he pulled Rose's shoe off and she felt him tugging her sock off.

"Oh, you're not gonna like this," Rose whispered into Tisha's ear. She meant in a nice way but, of course, Tisha took it the wrong way and delivered a hard elbow to Rose's ribs.

"Gahh," Rose grunted.

"Shush!" Monty said as he leaned close to stuff Rose's sock in Tisha's mouth and tie it in place with the sash.

"Sorry, Tish," Rose whispered. "I didn't have time to change my socks this week."

Tisha made a gagging sound. Monty helped Rose up.

"Take her," Rose said.

"I need to keep my hands free," Monty said. "In case more stuff goes down."

"You lazy sack of shit, you." Rose was just warming up, but Taylor shushed her.

He pushed open the door to the office. Men leaned against the wall in their underwear looking like shorn lambs. Others were playing cards. Rose saw that tighty-whites were the choice of the majority. Only a few opted for the blessed modesty of boxers. Nolan sat in the corner with his legs crossed, clearly regretting his skimpy cheetah-print number. Rose hadn't realized that they made panties for men — but then again, why not? And of course, there were the mangled undies, more holes than cloth, more punchline than setup. Rose kept her eyes studiously away from the men who had made the regrettable decision to go commando.

Rose saw Gilbert way in the corner sitting on the floor wearing that familiar pair of ragged Budweiser shorts. His eyes met hers and he scurried backwards.

Jimmy pushed his way to the front and looked at Taylor. "Is that my shirt?" He looked at Monty. "Is that my wife's dress?"

Monty waved the men up. "Get off your asses, we're going now."

The men wandered over, giving Rose and her prisoner nervous looks. Tisha stamped her feet and flared her nostrils and many of them flinched away from her. "Oh go on, now," said Rose, "You all know that Tisha's bark is worse than her bite." As if on cue, Tisha snapped her teeth at Rose's arm.

Taylor was peeking out the door. He stuck his head back in. "Coast is clear." The men formed the semblance of a line.

Once out the door, a few men ran off into the field like scared rabbits. Rose tried to call them back, but she was still struggling with Tisha in her arms. (She wasn't sure why she got stuck with her.) Other men stood in the back and looked aimless. Monty ushered them toward the bus hidden in the trees.

Rose handed Tisha to Taylor. He pushed her onto the bus and reached back for Rose. Rose shook her head.

"My dad's not here."

"We don't have time Rose," Taylor said. "We'll come back for him."

Rose didn't bother answering, she started running back toward the office.

"Wait!" Taylor called after her, but Rose was already halfway to the door.

The back door of the band office opened and women poured out. Rose was no gun expert but she saw what was, at best, a pellet gun and, at worst, a rifle. She stopped and addressed them: "Hi, I'm a woman like you." For good measure, she cupped her breasts. Then she saw the gun cock and she dropped her boobs. Rose turned on her heel and ran.

"Go!" she yelled at Jimmy, who had reclaimed the driver's seat. Rose leapt onto the bus and leaned on the door closing the lever with her tummy. Jimmy put the bus into reverse and hit the gas. The bus ploughed through a willow bush as the first gunshot rang out.

One of the windows shattered and everyone hit the floor with an efficiency that would have made Navy Seals envious.

Another shot rang out, then another and another. One of the women sure was gun happy, Rose observed.

She could hear someone weeping. Rose recognized the voice and crawled toward Callie. She put her hands over Callie's ears. By the time the bus hit the main road (still travelling backwards, Rose marveled) the gunshots had stopped.

Taylor told them to head to Jane's house. "It's on the north side, near the old water works station."

You don't have to tell Jimmy that, Rose thought to herself, he's the goddamned bus driver. But she kept her mouth shut, happy that someone else was willing to take the lead.

It was a quiet ride. The men kept their eyes down and wrapped themselves in their arms.

Rose wondered if being attacked by a group of women was going to have lifelong consequences for them. She caught herself wondering if it meant the band could then apply for a grant to deal with post-traumatic stress disorder — and realized that she was becoming quite the little bureaucrat.

"What if they do something bad to grandpa?" Callie fretted. "Would they hurt an old person?"

"Course not," Rose lied.

Eighteen

JANE MUST HAVE HEARD THE BUS coming because she was standing on her front porch, a mean-looking hunting knife in her hand, when they pulled up. Jimmy hit the brakes a tad hard and heads flew forward.

Rose jumped up from her seat, "S'okay, she's with us." The bus moved forward.

As soon as Jane saw the men on the bus, she stuck her knife in her apron and went back inside the house.

Rose and her girls, Taylor, and Monty piled off the bus. A few men followed, tentatively, but most of the men stayed put. Nolan stuck his head out the door and in a voice as soft as lamb's wool, asked for some food, "If that wouldn't be too much trouble, ma'am. Please and thank you." Rose arched an eyebrow — now that was a change — then smiled and nodded.

Rose pushed Sarah in front of her. Callie had one thumb on her mother's belt loop and the other one in her mouth. She looked around her nervously. Rose wished she had the strength to carry her on her hip. She looked back at the bus, half-expecting Gilbert to be following her. But he was sitting in his seat, his eyes on the seat in front of him, seemingly unaware of his family. It didn't seem possible after the prior 3,456 times he'd failed to show concern for them, but Rose felt the sting of disappointment again.

Monty picked up Callie. Callie protested at first but then settled her arms around his neck.

Rose could hear Taylor behind her. He was talking to the shell-shocked guys, offering up the kind of platitudes and gentle teasing that came naturally to personable and popular people. She was never able to muster up anything herself. At funerals, the best she could come up with was, "I brought some sandwiches — where should I put them?"

Jimmy and another guy escorted a kicking and punching Tisha to the base of Jane's veranda and secured her to one of the poles. Her hands were tied behind her back.

Rose knew that they had removed her gag when she heard Tisha calling out, "You fucking bitch!" and other colourful profanities.

"Why is that woman calling you names, Mom?" Callie asked.

"Why did you assume it was me?"

Callie grinned back. "Sorry, Mom. I shouldn't have assumed."

The house was humid with the smoke. Rose smelled mint, lavender, and something else she didn't recognize. It was sweet and cloying and slightly burnt her nostrils. Jane sat at her table, a rolled smoke in one hand and her hunting knife in the other. Her ashtray was overflowing onto the red and green tablecloth. Rose noted the poinsettia design.

"I gotta start my Christmas shopping!" Rose blurted out.

Sarah turned her head and performed the slowest, most tired eye roll Rose had ever witnessed.

"I always get so behind and then I'm running from store to store on Christmas Eve," Rose babbled on. "I keep wanting to try online shopping but then I'd have to get the Internet and I'm not even sure they have it down my road. Also, what happens if what you buy is the wrong size — do you send it back? And who pays for that? What if it's something big like a fridge? I mean, I couldn't afford to mail a fridge."

Everyone stared at her.

"How about focusing on the end of the world right now?" Monty suggested.

Rose mouthed sorry to him. She glanced around the kitchen. It looked like a machine gun had shot at it with dirt bullets. Rose never would have figured Jane for a bad house-keeper, but then, these weren't exactly normal circumstances.

"So . . . how did it go?" Rose wasn't really sure what "it" was. A spell? A ceremony? A medicine?

"You take her men away?" Jane asked.

"Except for my dad."

Jane grunted. She stabbed at her tablecloth with her hunting knife. "That hurt her for sure."

"Can we stop her?" Taylor asked.

Jane shrugged. "My grandmother taught me a few things but she's very strong this time — "

"This time?"

"*Kokum* said she knew of at least two times they had to fight her off. She's been here longer than anyone. She came with the land. That's what *Kokum* used to say . . . she's never had this much control over the women before . . . "

Tisha screamed from outside, it was a screeching sound like someone was holding hot coals to her feet.

Rose rushed to the window. Tisha squirmed against the bungee cords holding her to the pole. There was a group of men cowering in their tighty-whities about thirty feet away from her, their hands crossed protectively over their personal areas. Clearly, being possessed had not increased Tisha's chances of winning Miss Congeniality.

"But we can do it? Right?" Monty asked. "And then we can get Winter back?"

Jane nodded. "We'll wait for morning."

"But my dad . . . " Rose grabbed Jane's arm. It was wet with sweat. She quickly let go.

"She gets stronger at night. She could turn any of us, she could turn me. And then what? I'm a slave to the thing that took my daughter? Not a fucking chance."

Taylor put his hand on Jane's shoulder. It was tentative, as though he worried that she would slap or elbow him. But she let him keep it there. Long enough for Rose to get jealous again. She inwardly slapped her face. Jesus, if this was love, Rose was willing to let Brad Pitt and Angelina Jolie keep it all for themselves.

Rose turned her attention to the pot boiling on the stove. "What goes in it?"

Jane smiled crookedly. "I started off with a mixture that fixes broken hearts. The Old Woman had a family once, y'know. She was happy and loved before she grew cruel."

"Who made her sad?" Callie asked.

"I don't know." Jane went to the pot and stirred it with her knife. "Then I added the roots that kill. They never get it wrong. And the last ingredient — Saskatoon berries to make death taste sweet so hopefully she'll take the hint, and stay dead this time."

∾

Rose was sitting in the shade with her girls when Jane and Monty walked out of the house carrying two big boxes. To Rose's dismay, Monty had changed out of his dress into a pair of sweats and a T-shirt.

The men lined up as Jane pulled clothes out of the boxes. "Gary wasn't a big man but he owned a lot of sweats. I also got a pile of maternity clothes that could fit a wood buffalo." The men thanked her shyly as they picked up a shirt and pants from the Gary pile.

The pile of men's jeans was nearly at the bottom when Jimmy reached the front of the line. He reached for a pair of stretched out yoga pants and a red maternity smock: "That's always been my colour." Rose thought not for the last time that his wife was the smartest and luckiest woman in the world, even if she had forgotten that for the moment.

Dinner was rabbit stew. The men snared a few rabbits and skinned them. Monty and Rose then cooked them up in a big pot.

The men were nervous as they walked up to fill their bowls. They trusted Jane and Rose a little, but wouldn't go near Tisha and Sarah.

After Rose caught Sarah glaring at Gilbert, she took him aside and told him to stay clear of his eldest. He looked confused, as usual.

"Why's she mad at me?" he asked. "Never done anything to her. I've been good to her. Made sure she had school clothes and food to eat. Didn't I teach her how to ride a bike?"

"No, Monty did that. And not to get too technical but the amount of money that you give me could only feed and clothe a doll-sized version of her."

"I help," he retorted, his bottom lip sticking out stubbornly. "Plus, I took them to the fair that one time."

"Well there you go, father of the year."

Then the unthinkable happened. Gilbert started to cry.

At first, Rose thought she heard the sound wrong. Like maybe he was coughing or something. She leaned close. He was definitely crying. She shifted from foot to foot, kept her eyes on anything else and stifled the desire to smile.

"What's wrong?" Rose asked, thinking maybe he'd stubbed his toe or was really tired or had a stroke.

"She-she-she doesn't lo-love me?" he hiccupped.

This was why Rose hated talking about feelings. Especially with Gilbert, who lived in his own world where grown-up emotions were locked behind a double thick door of weed and rye.

"She does," Rose began, "but not right now. She'll come around."

"Is it the old lady's bad medicine?"

"Yes." And your shitty behaviour, Rose wanted to add. But Gilbert was alone now and there was nobody (i.e., Maryjane or Jack Daniels) to protect him. Rose handed him a piece of bannock and patted him on the shoulder.

He stayed away from them after that. He sat on the other side of the fire as evening wore on. But Rose noted that his eyes kept turning toward them.

Callie fell asleep with her head on her mom's lap, and Sarah was stretched out behind her. Taylor came over with a blanket he'd gotten from Jane's clothesline. Rose saw Gilbert's eyes narrow at that move; she turned to hide her smile.

Taylor sat down next to her. They stared at the fire and thought about all the people left in the band office. Rose said a thousand silent prayers to every saint she knew, forgetting for a while that she didn't believe in anything. She looked for Monty and saw him standing on Jane's steps, his eyes on the moon, peeking out from a thick grey cloud. Rose felt a cold breeze on her bare arms and shivered. It had been a long time since she remembered feeling the sun.

Someone started singing. Low at first but then the song caught and more voices were added. Rose had heard her dad sing it years ago, when he was first going back to the old ways. She had gone to a Horse Dance ceremony with him. Halfway through he came up to her with a crooked smile on his face and told her that he had sung one of his grandfather's songs.

"I remembered it. After all these years, can you believe that?" His eyes were shining. Rose left shortly after that because the ceremony required that women wear skirts and by late afternoon, the mosquitoes were feasting on her shins. Looking back, she realized it was one of the only times that the two of them had talked about how he was doing.

She heard Taylor's voice join the chorus and was jolted back to the present. He was clearly tone-deaf but it was adorable. She held her teeth tight to keep from giggling.

After the song ended, old Frank cleared his throat. His voice was rich with forty years worth of rolled smokes and strong coffee. "My old lady woke me up in the middle of the night and said, 'Someone's here.' I got up thinking it was teenagers. Sometimes they need help with their cars . . . I swung out of bed, starting putting my pants on, and then I saw the glint of something in the light. I turned around and she was standing on the other side of the bed with a knife in her hand. Her eyes were dead like a sleepwalker's . . . "

Lionel sat next to Old Frank. "My cousin Lauren and my oldest niece, Alliyah, she's seventeen, they walked into the living room. I was watching soccer with the sound turned down so as not to wake the kids. They both had bats. I could have taken them, but what if I hurt one of them? So I walked out the door with them. I knew something was wrong when I asked about the kids still sleeping and my cousin said nothing. That woman wouldn't leave her kids alone with no one in the house. She's always worried that they'll eat up all the fruit." He chuckled softly. "She's right, they're like starving dogs for apples and oranges."

Another man took up the thread after him and another man after him. Their stories had similar beginnings and the same ending. The women took them to the band office, by force if necessary. Only one man, Orny, fought back — his ex-wife woke him up by kneeing him in the back. "It's never a good thing to see that woman in your room at 3 AM!" he chuckled.

Once at the band hall, they were forced to take off their clothes and shoes.

"I saw Jason Ten there with the women," Lionel said. Jason Ten was the only openly gay guy on the reserve. "I asked him what was happening, but he only stared at me. So I asked him again and he punched me in the kidneys."

"That's when we should have escaped, before they took our pants," said another man. Rose nodded, that was sage advice; always leave before your pants get taken away.

"I thought it was an initiation for something," Jimmy spoke up. "Jenny would never hurt a fly, so I thought whatever this is, it couldn't be bad."

Then the Old Woman entered the room. The men had heard of her, some from old stories, others recognized her from the dreams the women had described.

Old Frank spit out some chewing tobacco. "I knew we were in deep shit. I know a spirit when I see one. I told the boys next to me, hunker down and suck it up 'til we can make a run for it."

There was a gauntlet. The women stood in two long rows armed with bats, brooms, and hockey sticks. The Old Woman stood at the top of the row and beckoned to the men.

Lionel shook his head, "I couldn't figure out if it was worse to be first or last. Cuz if you went first they were strong and full of energy — "

"And piss and vinegar!" chimed in another guy.

"But if you went last," Lionel continued, "then you had to listen to all the other guys getting it, feeling that fear twist in your gut."

"First was worst." Evan moved into the firelight. He had his arm in a makeshift sling, his lip was cut, and his nose looked like it had moved an inch to the left.

Once everyone was through, the Old Woman let the woman select the first men to be singled out for more.

"I thought I was a pretty good guy."

"Never did a damn mean thing to any woman in my life. Intentionally."

"I didn't know women got mad about so many things."

"It's funny though," said Jason Six, his eyes on the flames, "I never even knew how much Annabelle cared about me until she was taking a hockey stick to my package."

Rose and Taylor shared an amused look.

Charley Big Guns was the most confused. "I'm the goddamn bingo caller, for God's sake! I can't control which numbers I call!" From the bruises down the side of his face, you could see the old ladies had gone after him with vicious delight.

"I never knew she was angry." This from Taylor. "I knew Megan was unhappy and I knew she was confused. She was always confused. Never knew what she wanted — first, she wanted to be married, then she wanted to be single, then married again — but it turns out that all this time she was pissed. 'Why did I leave her in the city? Why did I want to run home like a big baby?' She couldn't have told me this before?"

She probably did try to tell you, Rose thought.

"Yeah, that pretty girl sure gave it to you." Lionel agreed. "Felt bad for you when Tisha and Kaylee joined in."

"Everyone always wants a piece of the chief," Taylor shook his head ruefully. All the men laughed.

ॐ

Rose woke up with her head on Taylor's shoulder. His head was leaning forward. Her neck was strained so she stretched it out a bit. As she half turned, she saw that Sarah was gone. Rose eased Callie's head off her lap and crawled into the darkness, hoping that Sarah had only rolled a few feet back. But Rose's heart already knew.

Rose shook Taylor awake. "She's gone," she whispered. He got to his feet, though he was still half-asleep.

"Should we wake up the others?" he asked, as they hurried to the bus.

"No point."

The bus was filled with sleeping bodies, Rose saw with a sigh. Waking them would make enough noise to warn Sarah and God knows who else that they were coming.

Taylor nodded at Jane's stable. "She has a horse, doesn't she?"

Rose nodded. She'd warned Sarah enough times to stay away from the horse, as Ronnie didn't know how to ride but liked to dare other kids to try.

Rose tugged on Taylor's shirt. "But the horse doesn't like people."

Taylor shrugged. "I don't think any do, really."

Taylor grabbed a handful of grass and opened the stable door. He came out a minute later, leading a horse. "She was skittish but I calmed her down." Taylor patted the horse's shoulder. "I have a little experience with horses, used to go to a camp with horses, played some polo, y'know. She's a good horse as far as rez horses go." He sounded rather proud of himself so Rose didn't bother to point out that the horse was clearly a male.

Taylor helped Rose on the horse and then she helped him on. Riding double on a horse would have been romantic except for the huge horse spine cutting into her butt. Still, Rose would have been happy riding a camel with Taylor.

Unless this old lady could give her minions the power of flight, Sarah was on foot. And Rose knew the speed of her lazy teenager, having waited for her to saunter out of the house a few thousand times, only to have her go back in because she forgot something. There was no way Sarah could have gotten more than a few miles. Taylor moved the horse to a trot. Rose felt like her intestines were being juggled.

"Is this the only speed?" she muttered.

"There's a faster one but you're not gonna like it." Taylor hit the horse's sides with his heels and they began to move at a gallop so fast Rose could feel her hair fanning out behind her.

Rose forced thoughts of crashing to the ground and learning to speak with her eyelids out of her mind. She focused on figuring out where they were.

It was still dark enough that she had trouble identifying landmarks until she spotted a small farm with outbuildings.

"That's the old Adams' place. I recognize their chicken coop. We better watch out for their — "

A loud barking jolted the horse. It shot forward a metre and Rose grabbed Taylor's waist tighter.

"What kind of dog?"

"Doberman. But he's really dumb."

"It's not his intelligence I'm worried about right now."

The horse ran into a gulley. As it leapt across the stream, Rose stifled a scream into Taylor's back. Taylor held onto the horse's mane and let out a long paragraph of swear words. Rose was a little impressed.

The horse hit a freshly ploughed field and picked up speed. Taylor and Rose clung to their handholds. The dog's bark faded into the background.

Rose heard Taylor hiss a yes and he patted the horse's neck. He half-turned to Rose, "So where — "

A whole new cacophony of barking broke in. "What's that?" he asked.

"Rez dogs."

"You're fucking kidding me." Taylor kicked the horse in the side and he took off again. But the barking was coming from all around them.

"How many are there?" he asked.

"Dozens," Rose said desolately. "There's a dog shooting day next month."

"Until this moment, I *was* thinking of getting rid of that. You can say goodbye to that, mutts."

The horse slowed down, his ears moving back and forth trying to figure out the safest direction. Taylor slapped him on the butt with the end of the reins, but the horse only gave an angry shake of his head in response.

Rose could make out the pack of dogs to the right of her. "Over there," she pointed. Taylor turned the horse in the opposite direction and the horse leapt forward. More dogs popped up, their heads sticking out of the long grass.

The horse reared. The dogs ran forward, barking loudly. The horse kicked at them.

"We should jump off," Rose suggested.

They fell off instead. Rose landed in a squat and managed to keep her balance. Taylor fell on his butt and knocked her down with one of his flailing arms. The horse was kicking wildly at the dogs, so Rose and Taylor crab-walked away from its wild kicks.

The horse hit a dog in the face and then, satisfied with the dog's whine, took off back in the direction of Jane's farm. The dogs followed him.

Taylor and Rose ran in the other direction.

"Do you know where we're going?'

"Yeah," Rose puffed.

"Sure?"

"Yeah!" Rose looked up at the bush in front of her. They were close to the band office. Down Rabbit Hill, up to the back road that teenagers liked to race on, past the slough and then a short cut through the bush and then the band office. She moved from their frantic run to a slower, even pace.

"You're fast." Taylor huffed beside her.

Rose slowed a bit and he caught up to her. Then he started running one step ahead. Men. Annoyed at his competitiveness, Rose sped up.

They were both struggling to breathe when they reached the slough. It was wide and shallow, the reserve kids tried it out as a swimming hole every spring. They'd wade in and find the mushy mess at the bottom. The water never got deeper than their thighs and only the most determined among them would swim in it. The rest of them would walk home smelling of murky water.

"Go around?" Taylor asked.

"It's about half a kilometre in each direction." Rose took a step in before she could think about it too much. The water filled her shoe and snaked up her legs. She took another step in. It was cold and gross. She took another step and the slough let go of her foot with a reluctant slurp.

She heard Taylor wade in behind her. "Oh, this is disgusting," he muttered.

"Don't think of pea soup," Rose offered. *And definitely don't think about the raw sewage that has probably leaked into this thing.* Rose had never trusted this particular slough, as it was so close to the band office, the hall, and the school. She'd never seen a plumber maintain any one of those buildings.

"Where do you think she is?" Taylor's voice broke the uneven sound of their slogging.

"I think she's there already. We would have seen her if she was still on her way. She must have left as soon as I fell asleep."

"Wouldn't she be okay? I mean, she's one of them."

"Ronnie wasn't okay." Rose was grateful that it was dark and he couldn't see her wipe at a stray tear. *Can't crack now,* she reminded herself, still have to rescue the kid, the old man, and the friend. Maybe Kaylee, too. She was always good for a laugh. And of course Annabelle and the old ladies, Gladys, Odie, Annie. Well, everyone, actually. She had to rescue every single person and then she could sit down and have a good cry. And a bag of chips.

Behind her Taylor tripped forward and fell into the water. Rose heard his head go under with a glug. She stopped and turned her head back, "Taylor?"

Taylor's beautiful face emerged a second later covered in a dark phlegmy liquid. He spit some of the water out of his mouth. Rose inwardly gagged for him.

Rose held out a hand which he gratefully grasped. She pulled him to his feet.

"You okay?"

Taylor brushed droplets of water and some plant life off his face.

"Why did I leave the city again?"

Rose wiped his face with the edge of her sleeve.

"I never could figure that out."

"I had a good life. A nice house, with a yard. One of the neighbourhood kids would cut it. I used to go to barbecues at my friend's houses. I never met anyone on welfare, nobody tried to borrow money off me, nobody accused me of stealing money from the band — "

"Somebody said that?"

"That Evan kid after I caught him trying to siphon gas out of my car. It's a BMW, for God's sake. Did he really think he'd be able to do it?"

"Sometimes the challenge is worth the risk." What the hell was Taylor thinking anyway, driving a BMW on the punishing rez roads?

"I came here to make a difference."

"You have." Rose drew out the second word so that he knew there were a lot of things she could have followed that with but there wasn't any time to elaborate. She kept trudging.

Rose saw the bank in front of her. The floor of the slough grew harder as she climbed. She turned and looked at Taylor and noticed an uneven gait. "Where's your shoe?" His foot was black with mud.

"Back there." He said with a mouthful of disgust that suggested he did not want to elaborate either.

They trudged up the bank and into the woods. The ground was littered with shrubs, rocks, and sticks; Rose kept stumbling and swearing. Then she remembered Taylor's bare foot and cringed for him. But he didn't make a sound of complaint.

The band office was visible through the trees. They stopped short. Taylor leaned up against Rose. "Pretty close, huh?" he whispered into the back of her neck and Rose's vagina jumped and said, "Yippee!" It was good that vaginas spoke a language that nobody could hear.

The back door opened and a woman exited.

Rose crouched down quickly and Taylor followed.

The woman threw out a pail of something and turned on the outdoor tap.

"How's the foot?" Rose whispered.

"It's no big deal. Our ancestors didn't have shoes." He picked up his foot and pulled a small sliver sticking out of his instep. There was a trickle of blood.

"They had moccasins."

"I'm sure they didn't wear them all the time. Their feet were tougher than ours."

"Like hobbits?"

Taylor snickered, and Rose covered his mouth with her hand as the woman looked around.

Rose held her breath until the woman went back inside with the pail.

"Now we split up." Taylor stood, and pulled her up at the same time.

"Split up? I don't like that."

Taylor stepped ahead of her. "You have a better idea?"

"I thought we could run in and grab them and run out again — element of surprise?"

"I'm going around the front. When they come after me, you go for your dad and Sarah." Taylor's words were clipped, like an army commander speaking to his troops.

"Whatever you say, bossman." Rose never wanted to be a soldier. Except maybe like Bill Murray in *Stripes* who was sarcastic and laid back — that was the kind of soldier she'd be.

Taylor grabbed her shoulders and looked at her. He had a complicated look on his face, like he was angry and also sort of constipated.

"I was kidding — " Rose began. Then he kissed her. Rose went from shivering cold to supernova sweating in three seconds.

"All right then." Taylor stepped back and tripped over a tree root. Rose steadied him with her hand. He squeezed it, then he was gone. She watched him run — he was a lot faster than she was. She realized that he had been holding back earlier because he didn't want her to struggle. *Men*, she thought, *always doing nice stuff like that just to make you feel guilty*.

Rose squared her shoulders like a soldier and got her mean face on. *Okay, old lady*, she thought, *I don't care how strong and weirdly ripped your muscles are, you are going down*.

Rose tore a branch off a tree (it was already half dead so it wasn't that hard). Then she scurried the distance from bush to band office.

As her hand reached the door handle, she paused for a brief second and looked up at the sky. "Some help would be nice."

～

The door banged shut behind her but Rose hardly noticed. Women were running past her into the main room so she joined in the group. They were frothing at the mouth with excitement, so Rose figured someone had spotted Taylor. Rose reached the community room/lounge/café bar/poker room/ torture area, and saw the women streaming out the front door. Rose spotted her dad in a chair. There were ropes around him and his face was bloody.

"Dad!" she whispered.

"Rosie?" Lloyd glanced at her over his shoulder. "Where the hell did you come from? You smell like a sewer."

"Thanks, Dad. Good to see you too." Rose worked her fingers through the ropes, they were crazy-tight with complicated knots. Rose had no proof but she blamed Megan — she seemed like the kind of asshole who would know sailor's knots. "You able to run?"

He pointed with his lips at his knee. Rose cringed when she saw the bone sticking out of it. She'd taken the Pesakestew band office first aid training, six times in a row (you got paid for the whole weekend and there were good snacks provided). so Rose knew what a compound fracture meant, how the open wound could result in infection and, most importantly, that she should not move him.

Rose took a deep breath and looked for something sharp. Her fingers were getting nowhere with the thick ropes.

Then, helpfully, a knife appeared in front of her. Less helpfully, the knife moved to the base of her throat. Rose's eyes lit up when she saw the sharpness of the blade and grabbed it from her attacker's hand.

"Thanks," she said and began sawing at the ropes. Rose's attacker — it was Gladys — took a step backwards, confused by Rose's casual manner.

Rose wasn't laid back so much as aware that she had no more time. It was like the time she baked that cake for Sarah's eighth birthday party when she realized that Gilbert had taken off with the money she'd given him to buy a cake for a party weekend. Her guests had been pulling up in the yard as she started icing her homemade cake. Sarah had stood beside her in her yellow birthday dress, her eyes on the door, the cake, the door, the cake . . .

As the ropes fell to the ground, Gladys came at Rose with a bat. Rose grabbed the bat and threw it across the hall. Gladys clawed at her, Rose gave her a shove and Gladys fell back on her bum. "Sorry there, Gladys."

Gladys was still struggling to get up when Rose turned back to her dad.

She bent to look at his knee and knew there was no way he could walk. She picked up the knife and put it in his hand.

"For protection," she said.

He was supremely irritated. "And who am I gonna use this on?"

Rose replaced it with her big stick. "Better? You can poke people with it."

There was a flat dolly in the caretaker closet. Rose had seen it when she was sweeping up the week before. She took it out and returned to her dad. She was helping him onto it when someone punched the back of her head. "What the hell!" Rose turned. It was Sarah.

Rose grabbed the long slim limb already in the air for a second swipe. "I don't think so!" Rose twisted her daughter's arm behind her back.

"Owww . . . " Sarah whined.

"Hey, hey, she's just a girl," Lloyd warned from behind her.

"Do you see what I'm dealing with here?" Rose exclaimed. She looked at the doorway; women were heading back inside.

Rose leaned close to her daughter's ear. "You smarten up right now, Sarah. This Old Woman may be scary but I can be a hundred times worse. You got it?"

Rose pushed her forward. Sarah turned around slowly. Her almond eyes were half awake. Rose looked back at her, also wary.

"Are you Sarah?"

Sarah grabbed the stick from Lloyd's hand and took a swing at Rose. Rose caught it right in the gut. "Oh for fuck sakes!" Rose ducked another one aimed at her head.

"Don't hurt her!" Lloyd called.

"We don't have time for this!" Rose put a table between Sarah and herself.

Sarah lunged across the table and took Rose down. Rose hit the ground with a grunt as Sarah fell on top of her. When she caught her breath, Rose commented, "Wow, you're fast." She'd never pegged her oldest for an athlete, but it looked like she'd underestimated her. Sarah reached for her throat.

Rose threw her daughter on the floor with a flick of her hips. Sarah may have been faster and younger but she was no match for her mother's pig farm muscles. Rose sat on top of her and held her arms down.

"C'mon now, Sarah, wake up. If you won't do it for me then do it for your grandpa, your little sister, your dad — well forget him. Do it for Ronnie."

Sarah's arms went slack and she blinked. "Mom? Mom!"

Rose ducked at the warning sound in Sarah's voice and missed the edge of a bat grazing her head. She rolled off of Sarah and onto her back. Michelle stood over her, the bat behind her head as she prepared to sledgehammer Rose. Rose moved slightly and the bat missed. Michelle struck again and hit Rose's thigh. "Jesus, Mary, and Joseph!" Rose screamed. Smiling, Michelle took another swing, this one connected with her tummy. Rose made a grunting sound.

Rose kicked at Michelle's knee and caught the edge of it. Michelle staggered, then caught her balance — her big city Pilates training kicking in. Michelle raised her bat up again and then dropped it as Sarah brandished a stick against her back.

Rose got onto her knees and pried the bat out of Michelle's hands. "Hello, cunt," she said.

Michelle fell down before Rose could strike and rolled onto her back, her limbs in the vulnerable puppy position.

"Cuz?" Michelle's eyes were teary.

Rose sighed; she had been looking forward to punching Michelle into consciousness. Rose stepped over her cowering cousin but couldn't resist a kick in the general vicinity of Michelle's rear end.

Rose saw Sarah pushing her grandpa toward the back door and turned around to look for a weapon and instead, found a fist in the face. It hit her square in the right cheekbone. The little sharp knuckles of her attacker stung and propelled her backwards onto her rear end. She looked up and saw a halo of brown hair. "Oh shit, not you!" Rose heard herself say.

"Where's Taylor?" Megan growled.

"Like I'd tell you!" Rose scooted backwards, looking to the right and left for a weapon as Megan stalked toward her.

Rose spotted a coffee cup upturned and threw it at Megan. She easily ducked it. But Rose used her precious won second to scramble to her feet. She ran for the receptionist counter, hoping to launch a defense from there or maybe just hide and have a long cry — she was open to a lot of things. But she had taken only one step when Megan did a forward flip then a roundhouse and then landed square in front of her.

"Holy crap." Rose nearly clapped her hands. "My body would literally fall apart if I tried something like that."

Megan grabbed her by the shirt and pulled her close. "Where is he?"

Rose noted a few silver fillings in the back of Megan's mouth. Aha, so she wasn't perfect after all!

Megan shook her and Rose's already sore body rattled painfully. There was a lot of strength in those cheerleading arms. Rose figured her only defense would be that Megan would get tired of manhandling her. "I d-d-don't kn-know where he is."

"Don't lie." Megan slapped her. Rose felt like she was looking through a kaleidoscope. She kicked Megan's shin; the power of her kick couldn't have broken through a paper bag and Megan didn't even notice.

Megan dragged her toward the coffee area where Rose noticed a broken glass coffeepot. She tried to put the brakes on but her feet couldn't decide on a direction.

"Megan!" Megan and Rose looked at the front door. Taylor stood there, silhouetted in the doorway as sunlight streamed in behind him. The man did know how to make an entrance.

Megan dropped Rose like she was a bag of fattening Doritos. Rose embraced the floor like an old friend.

Megan marched toward Taylor like a soldier confident of her mission. Taylor held his body square, ready for the worst. Then as Megan pulled back her fist, Taylor made a run for it. Rose figured she should do the same.

Rose ran to the back door. Sarah had the cart with her grandfather half in and half out.

"It's about time," Sarah snapped.

Rose glared at her, too breathless and scared to give her shit.

Rose added her shaky arm strength to the cart and forced it out the door. Lloyd gave a loud grunt as it jolted over the threshold.

"Sorry," Rose and Sarah said simultaneously.

Once they were all through, Rose blocked the door with a chair, knowing it would only give them, at most, half a minute.

Sarah looked at the darkness. "There's no car. Why didn't you bring a car?"

"There was a horse," Rose offered.

"Why don't you ever make plans?"

"You were missing, I wasn't exactly thinking straight."

Rose started pushing the cart and Sarah joined her. The ground was rough and muddy.

"Once we get to the bush, we'll dump you off and you can hide in there."

"You're leaving me in the woods?" Lloyd's eyes were incredulous.

"It's not a freakin' ice flow. Look — it's almost morning. Jane and the rest will be here soon."

Lloyd didn't look impressed by the idea, but he didn't complain when they helped him off his cart.

"And Sarah, you stay here and watch your grandpa."

Sarah's expression reflected a distinct lack of confidence in her mom's idea as well. "You mean hide."

"Yes."

"You're not."

"I have to lead them away."

"No." Sarah crossed her arms, a move that Rose had seen before — it meant that lead was entering her sixteen-year-old veins.

"Look you say I never plan anything — well, this is me making a plan. Now sit down and shut up."

Sarah plopped down beside her grandfather, her eyes wide with shock.

Rose heard the band office door squeak open and took off with the cart. She pushed it up the hill with a strength she didn't know she had. She lingered at the top of the hill so that she would be seen, and was rewarded with the sound of footsteps behind her. Rose pushed the cart toward the slough and let it go. She heard a splash as she doubled backed through the willow trees. She watched as a group of women ran past her.

The harpies stayed on the other side of the hill, arguing about something. Rose recognized Kaylee's voice, bossy and loud. Their personalities were peeking out from under the old lady's influence. It seemed the further away from her they got, the better chance they had of breaking free altogether.

Rose crept along the bush. The group was headed back into the band office.

Someone touched Rose's arm and she yelled. A hand clamped over her mouth.

"It's me."

Rose didn't recognize the voice and used her peripheral vision to spot some brown hair streaked with light gold. She recognized the fancy highlights because she'd helped paint them on only a couple of months ago.

"Winter?"

Winter nodded.

"You're you?"

"Are you, you?

"I've always been me!"

"Let's go." Winter headed back toward the road.

"We can't go, we have to wait. For Jane."

"Jane?"

"She knows how to bring down the Dream Woman."

"And she's on her way?"

Rose nodded. She stared into Winter's eyes; Winter looked so tired. "How is the baby?"

Winter looked sad. "I don't know Rose."

"We can go to a hospital right away. There's a car coming and — "

The smell of rancid meat wafted over to Rose. She turned and the Old Woman was standing behind her, her thin lips pulled back in a mockery of a smile, her teeth dotted with drops of blood.

"Winter!" Rose turned to run and grabbed her friend's arms. As soon as her eyes met Winter's, she knew. "I trusted you!"

A wave of Sunday night loneliness washed over Rose as the mask slipped back over her friend's features. Hands came from everywhere and locked around Rose's arms. She struggled and felt the hands tighten.

"Sarah," croaked the Old Woman.

Rose spit in her wizened face.

The Old Woman's expression of amusement did not change. She reached for Rose's arm and pulled it toward her mouth.

Like Callie at the doctor's office on inoculation day, Rose started screaming well before the Old Woman's sharp teeth touched her. Then they bit down and she had no breath left to scream.

"Rose." Rose's eyes focused on Winter, who was smiling down at her. "This is a good thing. You are helping her grow strong."

"Don't want to," Rose bit out.

"The Dream Woman helped everyone when she was alive. She grew powerful and her husband became jealous."

"Help me, Winter," Rose urged. Her friend had to be in there somewhere.

The Old Woman bit down again and Rose screamed. Winter continued to speak: "He took her daughters and hid them. And when she went to the chief to ask for help, he turned her away. When she returned home, her children were dead and so was her husband. By his hand. You see, Rose, men do evil things."

"Make her stop!" Rose pleaded.

The teeth descended again. The pain carried her up to a terrible height and dropped her into an abyss. She felt the sharp teeth hit her bone and Rose's body sagged. Still, they held her up — so many hands, Rose had no idea whose was whose, like a creepy, angry mosh pit.

A motor roared from the front of the building. Then someone leaned long and hard on the horn. The Dream Woman was distracted and the women dropped their hands.

Rose fell to the ground. Dazed, she glanced at her arm. Blood was flowing, though not as fast as she would have imagined. *I'm missing a chunk of my arm,* she thought.

The women ran past her. She crawled to the side trying to avoid their legs. Then as soon as she was clear, she scrambled toward the trees. She stopped suddenly, remembering she had important things stored there, though she couldn't remember what. "What am I doing?" she asked herself. "What am I thinking of?" She heard an angry scream, a yell, the sounds of hard things hitting soft things and lots of footsteps coming from the front of the building.

"Go there." She commanded her feet and they listened.

In front of the band office, she dodged a few slow-moving women. They were wandering with blinking eyes, as though waking from long naps.

Rose saw a truck and the school bus. Men were piling out of both. Most of them wore a version of hockey equipment, from helmets to shoulder pads. Hockey sticks seemed to be the weapon of choice. Only one person carried a lacrosse stick. *The sport really hasn't caught on in our parts,* Rose thought.

Rose saw Jane emerge from the bus and headed straight toward her. She waved her forearm at Jane helplessly.

Jane looked down: "She found you, then?" She grabbed Rose's arm and looked at the wound closely. "She has some real chompers on her, doesn't she?"

"The size of her teeth wasn't my first concern. What are you going to do?" Rose's teeth were chattering.

"She needs to drink this." Jane held up a small bottle.

"Can't we just throw it at her?"

"She's not a fire." Jane tore off a strip of her T-shirt and began to wind it around Rose's arm. Rose tried to be stoic but her feet did the "owie" dance.

Rose looked back at the band office. There was a group of women in the front struggling with the men. The Dream

Woman stepped forward, held out one of her hands and the men fell backward, as if struck by a huge wind.

"I thought she was supposed to be weak in the morning."

Jane looked pointedly at Rose's arm. "She just fed."

"We're not going to get near her," Rose said, her voice sounding pitiful, like a kid with ten cents too little in a candy store.

The Old Woman walked through the crowd, knocking men aside. Her eyes were locked on a point in front of her.

"She's coming for me, isn't she?" Rose's tummy had become a champion gymnast.

"Apparently she likes the way you taste."

"Shit."

"She's going to feed on you and then she's going to kill you."

"I assumed that."

"But before she does, can you get her far away from here?"

Rose held out her hand for the bottle.

Jane handed it over. "I'll make sure you get a good burial."

"You should write for Hallmark." Rose tucked the bottle in her bra. Then she checked her sneakers; they were tightly laced. She paused to stretch out her hip flexors, they'd been giving her trouble lately.

"Go! She's coming quick."

"All those cars are in her way, I got time."

The wrinkled demon kicked a car and sent it careening into another one.

"Holy shit."

Jane wasn't kidding about her gaining in strength. Apparently forearm meat was like a kind of spinach.

Jane jumped backwards into the bus and closed the big door. "Run!" she yelled at Rose through the glass.

Rose didn't even pause to look behind her.

She began with a slow jog. A fast start only resulted in injury, her dad told her once. When it came to long-distance running, patience was key. She glanced behind her; the Old Woman was closing the distance between them.

Still, sometimes you had to boot it, her dad had also said. Rose kicked it up to her top speed. She turned onto the main gravel road, her body at an angle.

Her dad had always told her to stay off gravel because it ruined your joints. Like concrete, it was hard on the body. Grass was better. But Rose figured that advice didn't matter when you are being chased by a cannibalistic demon. Then gravel was awesome because you could hear the creature's footsteps behind you.

Rose risked a glance. It was only the two of them now. The Dream Woman had left her followers behind. She wasn't running; she moved with long strides.

Running is mostly mental, her dad used to tell her. Keep your mind strong and your body will follow.

Rose ran past Kaylee's house. She noted the pretty garden in the front that Kaylee had planted with her boyfriend and daughters.

Next to Kaylee's house was Gladys' tiny bungalow. The elders lived in one-bedroom houses tailored for the modest needs of elders. Great idea in theory, but, in reality, Gladys lived there with three of her grandchildren. Their parents lived in the city and worked two jobs to keep the family off welfare. Gladys picked up the slack and the kids got fresh air. Not the best solution, not the worst.

Rose passed a road that led to the garbage dump. It was growing all the time and the band hadn't figured out a good solution to deal with it. They were lucky they had enough land that nobody had to live near it.

Next was a row of housing for pregnant and single mothers and fathers. So far only one single father lived there, Marcel and his twin boys. Their mother was a Swedish girl he met while at a soccer tournament; she left him for an Apache guy from the States (apparently, she had quite the Native American Indian-man fetish). So Marcel was raising his little half-Swedes with the help of the six single mothers who lived in the complex. Rose figured it was only a matter of time before one of the helpful moms snared him for her own.

Rose passed the dugout. She had no cramps but that wasn't surprising to her. She hadn't had anything to eat or drink for at least twelve hours. Fasting made the mind clear, people told her, and she could understand what they meant. Right leg, left leg, repeat.

She didn't have to turn around to know that the old lady was almost an arm's length behind her. She could feel the energy crackling from her.

Rose asked her body for another gear and found it. She was rewarded by hearing a guttural grunt. Rose smiled through gritted teeth.

Rose ran past a slough that was three-quarters full after the melt. Ducks had settled on it with their ducklings. Rose thought she could hear their heads dipping into the water.

She felt the hand on her collar; it was icy cold. Then she felt her feet leave the ground as she was ripped backwards.

Rose hit the ground with a dull thud. Breathless, deaf, she knew she had a second before the whoosh of pain; she reached into her shirt for the bottle. Then the pain and breathlessness hit and tears came to her eyes.

The Old Woman kicked her in the ribs and the bottle fell out of Rose's hand. The pain was layered on top of her other injuries. Rose reached out blindly for the bottle and inwardly crowed when she felt it. Pain radiated through her body but she focused on her fingertips rolling the bottle closer, a millimetre at a time. She heard the Old Woman's leg move backwards and knew the next kick was coming.

This one really hurt. Rose closed her eyes and drifted into unconsciousness. She wanted to stay there in the darkness but knew there was something she had to do. What was it again?

Rose opened her eyes. The Old Woman's hands were reaching for her neck. Rose slapped at her with her good arm. Her fingers wound around Rose's throat and burned her skin with their cold. Rose shifted her body from side to side helplessly. Can't buck this one off, she thought. She figured she was dying when she saw the flash of light behind the Old Woman. Then the light took shape — dark hair, determined face — the next thing Rose knew, the angry demon was flying over her head. Rose saw Callista standing there, looking satisfied at the kick to the ass she'd delivered.

Rose reached for her mother but Callista shook her head. Rose turned her attention back to the bottle. She grasped it with her hand and opened it as the Old Woman's cold fingers reached for her. Rose took a mouthful of the liquid and held it.

The Old Woman jumped back onto Rose and her skinny claw-like hands gripped Rose's throat. Again. But this time, Rose pulled her head off the ground and kissed her: full on the mouth, tongue and everything. Rose had never Frenched a woman before and figured this wouldn't count. For one thing, she wasn't the least bit attracted to the woman and two, the woman in this situation was most definitely a dead thing — her breath alone made that clear.

The liquid flowed from Rose's mouth into the demon's. The Dream Woman felt it hit her throat and screamed. She rolled off Rose and tried to cough up the liquid.

Rose scrambled backwards, wiping her mouth free of demon cooties.

The Old Woman glared at Rose and crawled towards her. Her eyes blazed with rage. Rose stared her down. "You have to go," she said.

The Old Woman howled at the sky and the wind picked up — it was howling with her. Rose's hair swished around her head and she pushed it out of her face, afraid to take her eyes off the woman.

The Old Woman began to sink into the clay ground. She flailed with her powerful arms and gravel and dirt flew in all directions. She was trying to push herself away but Rose could see that she was losing. It seemed like there were a thousand tiny hands pulling her down, reclaiming her into the earth. She screamed again, her terror so keen it cut through Rose. Rose covered her ears but she could feel the sound reverberating through her body and settling into her bones. Even her fillings hurt.

The demon's eyes met Rose's. They were a woman's eyes now and Rose saw fear in them. "Let go," Rose urged. "It's the only way you can be with your girls again."

The Old Woman took one last breath and wailed so loud that the trees shuddered. The she closed her eyes and the strong muscle and bones melted into the ground, until only the black outline of her body remained.

Rose sat back, flat on her butt, too drained and too shocked to move. She remained still even as rain began to fall in fat drops on her face. She watched as the rain washed the road clean of the Old Woman's memory.

When they found Rose, she was sitting on the road, giving her hamstrings a really good stretch.

Nineteen

Sarah borrowed the car at night. Well, not really borrowed, she took it while her mom was dead to the world. Her mom slept hard every night because she trained like a beast during the day. And when she wasn't training she was busy at work. Sarah would have complained except she liked seeing her mom's eyes sparkling.

Sarah parked near the fence and climbed through the barbed wire fence. The ground was always dry these days. People said that meant it was going to be a long, hot summer; Sarah couldn't be happier.

She climbed up the hill. Her eyes danced over the tiny mounds, some marked with only a stick. One of these days, someone would have to take inventory. Maybe it could become a project for school, taking stock of all the people who'd been buried in this tiny cemetery and why. Warriors, her grandfather said, every single one of them.

Sarah was only interested in one grave tonight. Under a tree, the mound still fresh, it was higher than all of the other ones. She sat down next to it and stuck her finger in the still black earth.

"You changed your hair." The voice came from the tree.

Sarah looked up, Ronnie had her legs stretched out on a branch.

"Well, you look comfortable," Sarah replied.

"I told you bangs would work on your face."

"I look like my little sister."

"You're crazy."

Ronnie jumped out of the tree and sat on the ground next to Sarah.

"Did your mom visit this week?" Sarah asked.

"Yeah, she looked good. Her and your grandpa are planning a sweat and then a feast."

Sarah wondered if she should go. She'd probably run into her dad there. "My dad keeps looking at me like he has something to say."

"How long are you gonna torture him?"

Sarah nibbled the end of her fingernail. "Auntie Winter says forgiveness gives you pretty babies." Not that Sarah wanted one of those.

"How long are you going to torture me?"

"Oh sorry! Forgot." Sarah pulled a baggie out of her pocket. Ronnie took it eagerly.

"Thank God, I was dying."

Sarah cringed. "Really, do you have to use that word?"

"It's just a word." Ronnie handed her a blue whale. They were Ronnie's favourite.

"So I think Taylor and my mom are doing it," Sarah blurted out. It didn't sound so bad when she said it out loud.

"He's hot."

"He's old."

"For you. Speaking of?"

"Nothing on the horizon."

"Someday there will be."

"You don't know."

"I know things." Ronnie said it with a solemn air.

Sarah swatted her arm. "You do not."

"I do!" Ronnie pushed Sarah and she lost her balance, falling flat on her back under the tree.

Ronnie fell beside her and the two of them looked up at the sky. The leaves on the branches were thick enough to obscure their view of the stars.

∽

The runners wore ear buds and jangled their limbs to the beat. Only Dahlia and Rose did not have them. Dahlia preferred the purity of the wind to pop music. Rose didn't have any because Sarah refused to lend hers that morning.

People were intimidated by Dahlia and stayed far away from her. But Rose went to stand next to her.

God she's tall, Rose thought, and tried not to feel stumpy.

"I'm Rose," she said to Dahlia's flat chest.

"Dahlia."

"I know your dad."

"He's over there," Dahlia pointed. Rose waved at Mr. Ingram. He didn't notice her; he was too busy watching Tyler Horton.

Just then, Callie demanded her mom's attention. She would have kept asking Rose questions until the race started but Winter and Monty led her away. No doubt, to fill her to the brim with sugar, Rose figured. Well, she'd get her chance to return the favour soon enough.

The marathon runner and the nervous amateur stretched together until Dahlia noticed Rose's scar and asked about it. Rose had taken a deep breath in preparation of the entire tale when the gun went off.

The two of them started the race sideways.

Dahlia recovered easily and straightened herself out. Her pace was graceful and faster than Rose could have ever expected. Her running looked as easy as breathing. Dahlia disappeared over a hill and Rose put her head down and focused on her own race. She found her pace after a few steps and was surprised to see the other runners fall back behind her. She figured they were saving themselves and kept going.

Rose was passing the fifteen-kilometre mark when she saw Dahlia's slim shape in front of her. Rose kept expecting her to move out of her sight but she didn't. She actually seemed to be slowing down.

Rose kept up her pace until she caught Dahlia. She matched her step for step until they were running in sync. Rose wasn't sure why Dahlia was letting this happen.

Was it because she felt sorry for Rose, the mom wearing boy's shorts with a taped arm and bruised legs? Or was it because Dahlia ran a marathon a week before and wasn't feeling 100 per cent? Or was it because she felt like running with someone who looked like she had a story to tell?

Whatever the answer, Rose was grateful. A marathon is a long time to run without company, especially when every deep ditch and every turn in the road kept her eyes twitching.

Dawn Dumont is the author of *Nobody Cries at Bingo* (Thistledown Press, 2011) which was shortlisted for the City of Edmonton Award and the Alberta Reader's Choice. She writes and performs comedy across Canada. You can also catch her on the APTN reality comedy series, *Fish Out of Water* which she co-hosts with comedian Don Kelly. (She's the one screaming and falling out of canoes.) She is also the afternoon drive DJ for *Voices Radio*, broadcast across Canada. She writes a monthly column for the *Eaglefeather News* called, "That's What She Said." Dumont divides her time between Saskatoon, Edmonton, and the rest of Canada.